I0763489

"What a wonderful experience. Robert has created a story where the thrills, chills, and unexpected happenings will keep you glued to the pages. He's a fantastic storyteller!"

—**Dennis Caplicki,** former White House attorney

SECESSION

The Tragic Fragmentation

Robert Miranda

Secession: The Tragic Fragmentation

ISBN: 978-1-7356567-3-1 (paperback),
978-1-7356567-4-8 (hardback),
978-1-7356567-6-2 (hardback with dust jacket)

This is a work of fiction. Names, characters, businesses, places, events, and incidents are either the products of the author's imagination or used in a fictitious manner. Any resemblance to actual persons, living or dead, or actual events is purely coincidental. The only thing real is the late, loving and faithful dog, Micah. This is the author's way of giving him immortality.

Warnings

There are a few short periods of graphic violence, both involving humans and animals. Those sensitive to this should be aware.

This fictional story takes place at a future time. The political landscape, while important, is the background for this adventure. The reader should understand that the author is neither supporting nor criticizing any political ideology.

DEDICATION

This book is dedicated
to my late wife,

Anna Laurel.

Since her childhood, she was the sole caregiver for
numerous people who were helpless.
This extended throughout her lifetime.
She had no vices.
The pain shall never leave.

Acknowledgment

The author would like to acknowledge the close friends who read the author's prior book, *Eternal Infinity*, and gave valuable feedback.

While *Eternal Infinity* and *Secession* can each be read as stand-alone books, readers have recommended that *Eternal Infinity* be read first, as it will facilitate an enhanced understanding of the characters and prior situations germane to this follow-up.

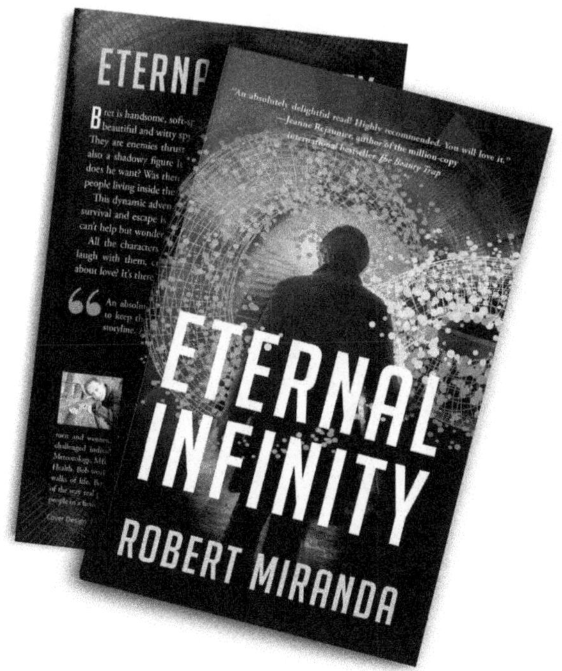

Prologue

Bret's idealistic view of the world encouraged him to build a secret operation located inside a mountain. He collected a group of colleagues from various countries to maintain worldwide contacts. They were mainly engineers and doctors.

Much of their work was devoted to treating disease through new uses of natural substances and patenting new drugs. As time went on, he acquired some weapons of mass destruction. He thought it would be a way of keeping world peace.

When government intelligence accidentally discovered this, they sent Ani to spy on his work. They gradually fell in love. They both knew the operation wouldn't be allowed to continue. The danger to Bret and his friends was clear.

Ani's superior, Jim, was dispatched to negotiate an end to everything. It had to include a safe evacuation for those living inside the mountain. The government agreed to new identities in exchange for the dismantling of the weapons.

With limited choices, Bret decided to trust the deal that was made. He felt his friends were in no danger. It wasn't the same for his safety. He correctly surmised the promise made to him personally wasn't sincere.

Ani felt the same way. She also sensed a lethal danger.

Bret devised a complicated plan for escape. Although it was designed for just one person, Ani demanded she go along. Even though Bret didn't understand the danger to Ani, their love was too strong, and he agreed.

They made their escape and took up residence on a South Sea island owned by his longtime friend Niz. Niz was older, fabulously wealthy, and eventually married Bret's mother, Essi.

Entering the beginning of our story, Bret and Ani now have a child. They named her Lisa after Ani's late childhood friend who lived in the same orphanage as Ani but eventually died from abuse.

Lisa was a rare child. She was beyond genius. She went to a hybrid school that divided classroom training with homeschooling. This was only open to both wealthy and genius-level children spanning the globe.

By the time she was eight, she finished the equivalent of high school. At ten, the same was true for two college degrees. Now, as a young teen, all was complete for two PhDs.

There was one problem. Before being conferred any formal recognition, the school required a trip to a foreign land and to keep a journal of one's choosing. So Lisa decided to concentrate on museums and national parks.

That led to other problems. Every corner of the world was in the most hazardous situation since the prior world wars. Lisa had to sit and review all the possibilities with her parents and grandparents, especially Niz.

Niz made his fortune by finding the rarest of items for the wealthiest people in the world. He also had a side profession of being a secret advisor to US presidents of both parties. He was an expert on the history of great nations along with the causes of their rise and fall, with no politically ideological axe to grind.

Although upper-level math and physics were easy for Lisa, her special interest was a nonpolitical study of this history. She spent many hours discussing events that weren't found in the media or any of her history books. Historical revisionism was rampant. Niz felt the most accurate accounts were from the obscure writings of the people who actually lived during the times of the events.

List of Characters

In addition to Bret, Ani, and Niz, the following is a list of characters who appeared in *Eternal Infinity* and are here once again:

Alex and Lana — Ex-Soviet married couple who were Bret's closest friends during the mountain-living time.

Bags — An organized crime figure who developed a friendship with Ani after she supplied vending machines for his buildings.

Carlos — South American friend and mountain resident.

Earl, a.k.a Chengua — Southwestern tribal chief whose help was invaluable in organizing and managing the economic cooperative.

Essi — Bret's mom, married to Niz.

George Finectus — Northeastern Native American chief who organized nationwide tribes to become an economic power. He became the first president of NASA, the Native American States of America.

Hans — German friend and mountain resident.

Jim — Ani's superior at the intelligence agency.

Micah — Bret's loving and faithful German Shepherd dog.

Nkuma — African friend and mountain resident.

Pramesh — Friend from India and mountain resident.

Red Hawk — Midwestern tribal chief whose reservation hosted the mountain people.

Sam — George's attorney who always accompanies him for major meetings.

Steve — Niz's son who now runs Niz's business now that Niz has retired.

Vera — Bret's friend from France whom he met when she was a child and who helped him in one of his endeavors when she was an adult.

Wang — Chinese friend and mountain resident.

Chapter 1

The thick morning dew was dripping off the leaves as two identical black vans rolled through a rural area of northern Virginia. The van was extended, designed to seat more people. The seats were all taken.

The two vans turned onto a semiprivate road leading to several estates. The trees were so old, the branches had grown together, creating an image of a tunnel or extended garden pergola. Even though the sun was out, the thickly grouped leaves were dripping so much dew, wipers were necessary.

The vans pulled up to a large gate and were met by two men wearing sunglasses with black suits and ties. They reminded the occupants more of funeral home workers rather than gate guards.

The guards directed the vans to the main house. As the group drove ahead on the grounds, they passed several guest cottages and then saw an enormous southern colonial complete with three-story columns. One of the drivers remarked they probably have enough bedrooms for all of them.

The vans stopped halfway around the semicircular drive by the twin front doors. Just as with the gates, there was a black-suited, sunglass-wearing escort waiting for them. He showed no emotion when the passengers exited the vans.

The average person would've been shocked to see every person was wearing a surgical mask, dark glasses, and a baseball cap. It was next to impossible to identify anyone. It was almost as if they were cloned. The only obvious differences were that different races and genders were present.

Once inside the house, it was immediately noticeable that the foyer was as large as a typical-sized living room. There were too many people to stay in the foyer, so they were led to what appeared to be an oversized conference room. Several remarked they had never seen a conference room table so long. The escort directed the occupants of one van to sit on a single side of the table and the others to sit facing them on the other side. In front of each person sat a folder with multiple pages.

Through a different door walked another man. He was similarly disguised like the van passengers. However, it was evident he was older and spoke with a slight Eastern European accent.

"Some of you know me from other meetings at other locations. Some don't. For those of you who don't, I am your facilitator. You can just call me F1. By the way, this is not my residence. It was rented to me by an unknown person."

The attendees started browsing through the folders. They contained vital information about the future.

"Here is a summary of our meetings up to date," the host said. "The agreements have expanded, and disagreements have dwindled. The differences, which are only pertinent to your states, have been eliminated."

Several people decided to interrupt with questions. F1 held up his hand with his palm facing out and waving back and forth.

"This will be our last gathering. Time is short. I made it clear last time there will be one person speaking for each side, that being S1 for the Socialists and C1 for the Constitutionalists. You can prepare a list of comments during the breaks."

Today's meeting would be the most important meeting in

the USA since the founding fathers' gatherings. The people present were special envoys of those who were most powerful in their states. They wanted a workable plan. Some were sent by governors, congressional reps, businesses, or a combination.

"I hope we can work the rest out today. Otherwise, all is lost," C1 said.

"Let's face it. We'll never be friends. I just don't see how we can be stopped after we present our ultimatum to the president," S1 said.

"If it's presented right, things will fall into place. As I've said several times, I am against this secession. I believed it then as I believe now, very bad things will come about in the future," F1 said.

"Then why are you working with us?" S1 asked.

F1 walked around the room. He was sighing and taking deep breaths, trying to frame his words correctly. "Skirmishes have already broken out between states. This is reminiscent of prior battles and wars between Georgia and Florida, as well as Kansas and Missouri. Another all-out war would make the union and confederacy battles look like a walk in the park. The human carnage would be unthinkable."

"Nobody wants that," C1 replied.

"Go ahead and carve up this country," F1 said. "Sooner rather than later, you will experience Armageddon."

"That book is meaningless to me," S1 said.

"Whatever. Please stay on topic," F1 said.

Both groups went back to their papers. There were some surprises, but they first reviewed what they agreed on. Partitioning of the military was relatively easy. There were nuclear weapons in every state. There were air bases in every state. The deep-water ports were in areas that both parties felt would secede to them. The navy would be easily divided.

The gold and oil reserves would be equally separated. The currency would initially be prorated. Each country would do what they want—be it a money reform, scrapping the dollar, or status quo. The biggest problem was going to be the USA wanting to keep the Federal Reserve while the present parties wanted it dismantled. Part of the ultimatum would be that about two-thirds of the states would stop paying income taxes.

The internet would have their separate controls just like China and Russia. This would control the social systems. Both sides agreed areas such as entitlement programs were strictly internal and no other nation's concern.

One area of contention was interstate commerce. C1 wanted open borders for businesses. S1 balked. S1 finally relented, as he knew they always had the option of closing the borders later.

They all wanted to discuss how the map would look later. The only way this could work with the public was with an election. It was necessary to compare polls. They all wanted to get a feel as to how the public would vote. Both sides were in agreement that the states that seceded from the USA could roughly be divided among the two participants and the USA.

F1 also said it looked that way, but with an important caveat. "The USA may just be able to squeak through if the election goes to a runoff. I'm not sure either one of you could win any state by eliminating either one. I think any runoff would hurt both of us and let the USA win most of the states."

"Our polls indicate you're correct. There is an easy solution. Part of the ultimatum will insist on a plurality," S1 said.

C1 said, "That's true. If you include the splinter parties, we can both win our desired states by around thirty percent."

"What if the president refuses this?" F1 said.

"He's already been made aware the Secret Service will no longer protect him. If he refuses anything in the ultimatum, the shooting could start," S1 said.

F1 said, "The president has been informed of people starting a secession for years. My sources tell me he thinks it's just talk by lunatics. I don't think he's aware of any alliance between both of you."

F1 had a surprise for both sides. They had no idea he knew about their negotiations with foreign countries outside the hemisphere. That was also a massive problem for the USA. There were at least fifty countries willing to recognize and begin diplomatic relations with these new spin-off nations from the division of the USA. Some were even going as far as offering to open an embassy immediately following an approval vote. This was the biggest quandary for the president. Many were considered neutral at best and unfriendly at worst.

F1 asked if they wanted to share their secrets in that regard. He felt transparency was essential for this temporary alliance to succeed.

C1 was surprisingly candid. He gave details about the inquiries. "We have commitments from the UK, the Netherlands, Denmark, and the Baltic countries in Europe. In the Middle East, we have Israel. In Asia, Japan and Pakistan. Here in the Americas, we have Costa Rica and Canada. Most others haven't refused. They're taking a wait-and-see attitude."

"We have some big guns on our side, namely North Korea, China, and Russia. Most of South America and Africa will give us embassies," S1 said.

"With the dissolution of the UN, EU, and NATO, I'm not sure anything can stop this process except a massive election loss," F1 said.

S1 said, "Let us worry about that."

The statement shocked F1. He thought it seemed to be an indication that ballot tampering was imminent. The rest of the meeting was spent smoothing out petty differences in nation building.

"What about some of these splinter groups? They might unexpectedly win a few states," C1 said.

"They're small potatoes. We can swallow them up later. Let's just worry about our presentation to the president," S1 said.

Calls were made to their powers-that-be. The negotiations at this meeting were mainly between the Socialists and Constitutionalists, and the USA was hung out to try. No sooner were these calls made than the most powerful political bosses in several states called the president and demanded an emergency meeting.

With all the advanced intelligence methods and technology, it was hardly believable the president was perplexed by such a demand. Every advisor he spoke to said the same thing: They weren't exactly sure what was going on. The only way was to grant a meeting and find out.

The speed at which this next meeting was arranged was incredible. The president made a hasty arrangement for a locale outside DC in a rural area. Even reporters weren't privy and couldn't follow him.

Everyone was flown in the same evening to start business early the next morning. They were all transported to an army base in the middle of nowhere. When everyone gathered in the same room, one could cut the tension with a knife.

The president was accompanied by several advisors. Every one of them had a dumbfounded look on their face. Some phony pleasantries were exchanged.

It was time to get down to business. "I just heard you people go by a letter followed by a number. Why not just call me P1 then?" The president's sarcasm was thick. "I've been a little lax about these meetings, but that's what I suspect this is all about. I don't recognize a couple of you."

"You can just call him C1 and me S1."

The president and each of his people were handed the hastily prepared document. There were copies for each of his people. His mouth was agape. He kept shaking his head as he read.

"Is this a joke?" the president said, looking up at them. "I mean, are you folks insane? Do you understand the implications of this?"

He was told this was no joke. The tension in the room escalated.

The president was red-faced and moving nervously. "I can have all of you arrested right now and tried for treason."

C1 said, "I wouldn't advise that. Your rank as commander in chief no longer holds. We have commitments from many of the generals and admirals. We're quite sane and quite serious."

"I'm not sure you're playing with a full deck, but I'll bite. What do you plan to do if you're seized now?" the president said.

"Don't try my patience. I have an air force general on standby. He's agreed to order a wing attack on one of your bases. Once the shooting starts, history will compare you to the largest mass-murdering despots the world has ever known," S1 said.

"You can't be serious. You can't win. Even our allies will back us up," the president said.

C1 said, "I didn't realize you were so beloved by other countries. You do know there are other countries in the world who would love to take a crack at the USA? Most of the world would love to see this once great nation carved up."

"Leave us," the president said to the room. "I want to speak to my advisors."

One congressperson reminded the president not to take too long. The wheels had already started. As the secessionists waited in another room, the president had a serious conversation with his allies.

His first question was whether to take this group seriously or just have them all arrested, calling it a coup attempt or at least an insurrection. Every advisor told him he needed to take it seriously.

"And what if I don't?" the president said.

Once again, the unanimous warning was that it was serious and at least look at what could happen. Even the president agreed a shooting war between the states was out of the question.

They began to examine the ramifications, because there was only one demand: to hold plurality elections for the purpose of secession. Each state would determine their own destiny. It was clear that there was no option to keep the USA intact.

The president wanted to know what bad things could happen if he chose to ignore the ultimatum without any shooting. He borrowed the idea of calling the advisors by letter and number. He would address them this way.

A1 said, "Adding the Constitutionalists and the Socialists, they have a majority in Congress. They'll immediately impeach you. Even your handpicked judges in the Supreme Court will run for cover."

A2 said, "Assuming they have the wherewithal to do without the tax money, you'll have to print so much that the dollar will be used for toilet paper. The country will go bankrupt in a very short time."

"Is there any chance the military won't follow my orders?" the president said.

A1 said, "Many states have been building up their state guard for years. Even without USA army defections, they're quite formidable. My guess is you would eventually win a nonnuclear civil war. Even so, the civilian casualties would likely be in the millions."

A2 said, "I agree. There will be little left to build on."

P1 said, "I don't know what to do. What are your thoughts?"

A1 said, "I suppose a piece of a country is better than none at all. Who knows? Maybe you will win a peace prize for avoiding the most devastating war this century. Even with a smaller country, it would almost guarantee your reelection."

A2 said, "Based on prior voting, you can probably keep at least a third of the country."

"And?" the president said.

A1 said, "Close your eyes, bite your tongue, and go make that deal."

Chapter 2

Some years later, it was time for Lisa to fulfill one of the requirements for one of her multiple degrees. This was a decision as to which nation or continent to visit and write a dissertation about her experience.

Lisa was more than precocious. Even though she was a young teen, speaking with her was much like speaking to an adult. Her parents, Bret and Ani, gave her a lot of leeway in making her choices in life. But they would still have the final say.

It was necessary to sit with her most trusted advisors. This included her parents and grandparents. Also present was Niz's son, Steve. When Niz retired, Steve took over their rarity procurement business, and from childhood, Lisa was very close to Steve.

Modern times in the world had become extremely unstable. The choices for this tour would hinge on both Lisa's interest and whether the political and social circumstances would direct her to a safe location.

Having had a dual role as a successful business owner and a secret advisor to presidents and prime ministers on both the right and left, Niz was uniquely capable of giving practical advice. His knowledge of the present conditions of each geographic area of the world was unmatched.

Much of the behind-the-scenes political cause and effect dominating the world had largely been expunged from books and the internet. In prior talks, Niz would impart as much as he could to Lisa. At present, he decided the best way to help her decision-making process was to review each geographic area she had expressed interest in.

Lisa wanted to concentrate on national parks and museums. That would help eliminate some of the areas.

"Let's start with sub-Saharan Africa," Niz said as they all sat together. He thought this would not be a viable area for several reasons. While she was interested in just about everything, archaeology, paleontology, and anthropology would be the sum and substance of her trip. And the available natural history of those nations was spotty. Lisa's interest was more in how nations rose and fell, as well as what happened in short periods of time.

There were also military problems. It was similar to the 1960s when Marxist dictatorships grabbed hold of many of the countries. As the rulers plundered the resources and money, wars broke out within the countries and with their neighbors.

Lisa didn't need to be convinced her choices were better elsewhere. Bret and Ani voiced a sigh of relief.

Niz said, "Let's look at the eastern part of Asia next."

Since the middle part of Asia didn't hold enough interest for Lisa, Niz concentrated on what was formerly called the Orient and the island nations of the Pacific. Being a history buff, Lisa had great interest in the various Chinese and Japanese dynasties. However, Niz had some serious reservations.

With Russia sitting things out, China was aggressively trying to expand its territory. Their government made clear their isolationist policies of the past millennia had been a mistake, and they were currently building islands and making serious inroads in western South America. The larger nations in the Pacific had also become alarmed when a defecting diplomat revealed an internal memo where party members had their sights on Australia, which put in motion a major change.

China also was already in a precarious position due to a western disputed area with India. They had already fought two wars for that area. As a result, they had an unwritten agreement to avoid having heavy weaponry in that area. However, China decided to ignore that and temporarily grabbed the area.

It was a severe problem. India had almost the same size army as China and was a nuclear country. India had a trick up their sleeve. They also had one of the largest and most modern navies in the world. So they sent a force into the Pacific Theater.

Since India had modern ship-to-ship missiles that China had no answer for, many experts believed the Chinese navy would be decimated. China temporarily retreated.

What shocked the world was the news that a secret mutual defense treaty was soon to be signed. The countries included India, Japan, South Korea, the Philippines, Australia, and even China's old enemy, Vietnam. Their ally, North Korea, was a non-factor since the USA provided nuclear weapons to South Korea.

China made a hasty treaty with Pakistan, but Asia was a powder keg. It was easy to see why Russia decided to sit this one out and concentrate on Eastern Europe.

Considering everything, Niz recommended thinking long and hard about this region as a consideration. Bret and Ani became antsy.

Fortunately, Lisa was true to her maturity. "Let's move on," she said.

"Okay. Let's discuss the Middle East," Niz said.

Lisa and her grandfather talked about this area constantly. She was intrigued by the various civilizations that existed for so many millennia. The ancient writings of the region painted a clear picture of the history. Lisa had always wanted to visit Israel, the former Mesopotamia, and the surrounding Arab countries. She was fascinated with Egypt, which was nearby even though technically part of northern Africa.

Of course, there was a similar case to Asia, only worse. The Arab-Israeli wars were constant. Now that Iran had a nuclear bomb, some Arab nations thought they could win a war with Israel. Even with saber-rattling from the USA, there was no end in sight.

Ani stepped in. "You're not going to that region."

"But, Mom—"

"Forget it," Ani said.

"I agree with Mom," Bret said. "There's so much you can learn in other parts of the world. Wait for peace, or at least a truce. You're young enough."

Niz said, "So let's look at perhaps the most complex area of the world, Europe."

In recent years, the state of affairs in Europe had caused a distancing of many nations in the past decade. Niz noted the euro was plummeting and countries were forced to go back to their old currencies. Since ending the EU, NATO, and the euro, turmoil abounded.

Since the USA withdrew from NATO, that had effectively ended the alliances as member nations could make their own defense treaties. The UK immediately followed the USA and formed their own alliance with some European and Asian nations. Noticeably absent from these alliances were two other powers: France and Germany.

France immediately made a treaty with Russia. Joining them were some countries whose Socialists merged with the Communists and won elections. They included Italy, Greece, and Spain. Hungary made a separate deal with Russia.

The UK persuaded the Netherlands and Denmark, along with most of the old Eastern Bloc nations. Interestingly, Germany sat on the fence.

This wasn't a recipe for peaceful coexistence. Battles broke out between the Balkan nations and quickly spread to the other nations of Eastern Europe.

Niz said, "The problems have severe roots. There's religious zealots and various forms of violent nationalism. Even with that, I suppose you can consider this as a possibility . . . depending on how many countries you want to visit and which ones. The violent crime rate in the USA hasn't grown since the secession."

Bret said, "Maybe she can just go to England. It's relatively safe, and there's so much history."

Ani said, "Haven't you heard about the riots going on in London? It's the first time the London Bobbies are now carrying guns. Also, the IRA has recommenced activity inside England. They resurfaced years ago."

Lisa said, "Let me think about it."

Niz said, "I almost forgot to mention South America. Although they have a rich history with civilizations such as the Incas, I don't see a lot there that you would be interested in, Lisa."

If that weren't enough, Niz started talking about some of the regimes there. He characterized this continent as the most unstable on earth. There was an expression, which involved the speed of old vinyl records. The same was used to describe South America: RPMs, which were revolutions per minute.

One by one, countries copied the old Soviet elections, which had one candidate and the public just voted yes or no. A lot of convincing wasn't necessary.

Lisa said, "We can scratch that off the list."

Niz said, "That leaves North America. How about we concentrate on the former USA. So much to address, but I'll try to abridge it."

He spoke about how the USA had become the most politically polarized nation in the world. A parliamentary form of government was out of the question. Under the present system, maintaining control and order was out of the question. The only way was to change the rules.

Prior to the secession several years ago, the Democrats were controlling the House and Senate. They had used the living constitution argument to erase the Electoral College. With the high population in urban areas, as little as nine states elected the president by popular vote.

At the same time, New York City, Puerto Rico, and Washington, DC were admitted as states using the same maneuvering. The extra six senators and multiple house members assured control of the executive and legislative branches.

The Supreme Court had the largest change. Not only was it expanded, but one justice died mysteriously, two retired or resigned, and two new appointees said they would not follow the constitution after confirmation.

While all this was happening, Canada was having its own problems. For many years, the Quebecois had been trying to seize power of the province and secede. They finally got a majority elected and not only seceded but joined France as part of New France.

Feeling isolated, the four Atlantic Canada provinces had threatened to secede and apply for statehood in the USA if Quebec had gone through with their own secession.

Noting that those provinces identified more closely with Republicans, the Democrats blocked their attempt to become part of the USA. The conservative faction of the party said enough was enough. They called the moderate Republicans "Democrat lights" and left the party to join other conservative parties to form a constitutional party. This was another propellant for the idea of secession.

Now the Republicans lost a large part of Congress, and it turned them into an ineffective party that had no power whatsoever. To prevent a perceived anarchy, some moderate Republicans joined the Democrats.

Lisa said, "The Democrats had all three branches of government going into the foreseeable future. What went wrong?"

Niz said, "There's an old saying, 'Anything that can go wrong will go wrong.'"

For years prior to the secession, an increasing number of Democrats gravitated toward the socialist ideology. Now they felt they had enough votes to change the party. They first wanted to change the name of the party to the Socialist Democrats. The party heads refused. Feeling they had the support of the voters, they made increasingly powerful demands, including scrapping the constitution. They said it was written by old White men for old White men.

The lines had been drawn, including threats to leave the government. The Democrats felt, with Republican support, they could hold on. Although conservatives spoke about secession for years, it was the Socialists who made the initial moves.

The USA president never envisioned an alliance between the Socialists and the Constitutionalists. They began having secret meetings on how to force the government's hand. They had their own allies in the military and banking sectors. The president was blindsided. He didn't even understand the degree of recognition coming from foreign nations. The birth of diplomatic relations between other countries and the seceding states had begun.

Niz said, "It's all a lot more complicated than my explanation here, but this was basically the end of the fifty states of the USA."

Lisa said, "As I understand it, the Constitutionalists wanted the constitution strictly interpreted as the founding fathers had written, the Democrats and other moderates wanted it to be a living constitution with an ability to interpret as they saw fit, and the Socialists wanted it scrapped in favor of one that emphasized equality of the masses."

"That's about right. Even with all the negativity, I'd still probably go with this geographical area of the world since it has a combination of relative safety and appeals to all your interests," Niz said.

Lisa said, "How come there were so many different nations created? Some of the votes were surprising."

"There were a lot of unexpected results, especially because plurality voting was involved," Niz said.

In New Mexico, a large portion of the state had been conducting business in Spanish. Many people there considered Mexico more stable and voted to join that country.

In Vermont, the northern half were mainly French Canadians and were happy to join France.

With the exodus of European descendants to other states, Michigan and Minnesota became a majority Muslim population and their own country. Before the election, the polls worried Wisconsin. People in Wisconsin perceived being surrounded by an unfriendly nation. The media advertising noted their best chance for protection would come from Illinois to the south. Illinois was definitely going socialist. It wasn't surprising since Milwaukee once elected a communist mayor.

California was the one state that had an agreement to having two votes for possibly splitting their state. The Socialists worried they could lose all of California to Mexico because of the demographics. The southern third easily went to Mexico, and the Socialists held the top two-thirds of the state.

Going against the objections of the chief of the Indian Alliance, who built unity among the reservations, they used the term Native American. The chief preferred the term Indian. Now the Indians/Native Americans had a country of their own.

Roughly, most of the USA was carved up between the new and current USA, Constitutionalists, and Socialists. The other new nations were free to cut their own military and economic deals.

Niz handed Lisa a chart of the election results. Everyone was quietly waiting for Lisa's response. It was a grueling day, and everyone was getting tired.

Ani said, "And the verdict is?"

Lisa said, "It's a no-brainer for me. I want to go to the land where my parents were born."

USA (United States of America)	**PRSSA (People's Re-public of the Socialist States of America)**	**CSA (Constitutional States of America)**	**ISA (Islamic States of America)**
Arkansas	Northern California	Alabama	Michigan
Colorado	Connecticut	Alaska	Minnesota
Florida	Delaware	Arizona	
Hawaii	Illinois	Georgia	
Iowa	Maryland	Idaho	
Kansas	Massachusetts	Indiana	
Maine	New Jersey	Kentucky	
Missouri	New York State	Louisiana	
Nebraska	Oregon	Mississippi	
Nevada	Rhode Island	Montana	
New Hampshire	Washington	North Dakota	
North Carolina	Wisconsin	Oklahoma	
Ohio	State of New Africa (formerly Washington DC)	South Carolina	
Pennsylvania	State of Colorgratia (formerly NYC)	Tennessee	
South Dakota	Puerto Rico	Texas	
Virginia		Utah	
West Virginia		Wyoming	

Seceded to join the Province of New France (formerly Quebec)	**Seceded to join Mexico**	**NASA (Native American States of America)**	**Seceded from Canada and consolidated to one CSA state**
Vermont	New Mexico	Native American Reservations	New Brunswick
	Southern California		Newfoundland
			Prince Edward Island
			Nova Scotia

Chapter 3

On the first leg of their journey, Bret, Ani, Lisa, and Steve arrived in Florida. Steve had taken over his father's business. Niz was happy to give it to his only child. He had procured almost impossible to find rarities and had many clients around the globe. Steve could help keep an eye on Lisa and meet with some of his many clients.

Bret decided they would start their trip with some theme parks because Lisa had been working so hard. A little vacation would be relaxing for all. Unfortunately, not all the news was good. Florida stayed with the USA.

Unlike California being able to partition the state before elections, the competing parties could not get an agreement in Florida. This caused a lot of resentment on all sides. The Democrats and Socialists could not agree on the southeast area and the Constitutionalists wanted the entire west coast. The other parties, including the small minority of Republicans, fought that.

The real desire was tied to the strategic location. There were so many ports as well as the nation's air force to easily access the Southern Hemisphere and Western Europe. The USA won the state by the slimmest of margins. Other groups challenged the voting, but the agreement was clear . . . results were final.

The family enjoyed the theme parks for a couple of days even though there were mass protests in the area. The corporate owners did their best to keep a calm atmosphere inside the parks. The park owner's headquarters were located in Northern California, which was part of the People's Republic of the Socialist States of America. The PRSSA offered to send troops to guard the theme parks, but the USA nixed that idea.

After a few days, the family woke to see their rental car vandalized. Bret gathered everyone together. It was early in the trip, but some decisions had to be made. The media was reporting that the protests were turning into rioting and vandalism.

Bret said, "My apologies to everyone, but this is not working. I think we should go on."

Lisa said, "It's okay, Dad. I had a lot of fun."

Ani said, "Why don't we head up to Washington, DC or whatever they call it now? It's a new state but still the capital. The media thinks there's relative stability there."

The name Washington, DC was indeed changed in order to reflect the demographics. It was now the State of New Africa. Even though Ani received her intelligence training there, so many changes had occurred since then. Much of what Niz had told them had already become history.

They decided to continue by driving to the former Washington, DC. As they approached the beltway outside of the former DC, there were severe traffic jams. This was common years ago, but now it was worse as portions had been closed by the government. The only vehicles in the closed lanes were continuous streams of large trucks heading north. The trucks had no advertising and were painted dark gray.

Traffic had come to a stop. Bret saw some motorists exiting their cars and having a conversation. So he got out and went over to ask one of them what was going on.

"What's this all about?" Bret said, pointing to the trucks.

"Man, have you been living on Mars? Those trucks have been rolling for a couple of months now."

"Where are they going?"

"They're taking all the records, furniture, and anything else they can salvage from the former DC to the new capital of the USA."

"Where's that?"

"Philadelphia, you dolt."

Now that DC was part of the PRSSA, a new USA capital was needed. It was decided to move the USA capital back to its first home since Pennsylvania had voted to stay with the USA. The government feeling was strange in that it was so close to a seceding capital. Nevertheless, the USA was hopeful for good relations with the PRSSA. The CSA was a nonfactor because there were no direct borders in that area. The former DC was bordered by Maryland, Delaware, and Virginia—none of which were CSA states.

Ani was right about the relative calm. When they finally arrived in the city and headed to the mall area, they expected the same long pathway with museums and memorials. But it looked different from the old pictures and her memory.

Some of the museums were closed. There was a large sign saying the Washington Monument had been renamed. The Jefferson Memorial was in the process of being dismantled.

The family was informed by a policeman that many downtown buildings were now closed to the public. Ani remembered getting a tour of buildings such as the FBI and the Bureau of Printing and Engraving. She loved watching the currency being printed. Alas, Lisa would have to miss many of the fun historical places in the former capital they had been planning on seeing.

They had some difficulty finding their way around because the names of streets were changed. Gone were any streets with a CSA state name. Also gone was anything related to the founding fathers. Anything that had to do with European heritage was slowly being removed, especially statues.

Having a keen interest in art, the family decided to stop at the National Art Gallery. When they arrived, they observed covered-up paintings being removed from the gallery. Even with this, Ani felt it was safe for Lisa to wander the gallery by herself.

On her own, Lisa headed straight for the Renaissance section. Much of the art in the first room was done by Italian and French artists. She walked up to a painting and stood beside another teen about her own age. The teen was an African American girl, and she seemed to be mimicking the brush strokes of the artist. The teen got as close as was allowed and used a magnifier. She was obviously a serious observer.

Lisa didn't think anything of it. She moved on to another room. Then they accidentally met by another painting in a different room.

The girl looked at Lisa and smiled. "Do you like it?"

"I do, but I don't think I can appreciate it like you. Are you an art student?" Lisa said.

"I am. You got that right. You look like a tourist. I'm Showmeena. You can call me Mina."

"That's a nice name. I've never heard that name before. Does it have a significance?"

"It really means nothing. My mom said the common biblical names are too plain. She wanted something fancy for her baby and made this up."

Mina lamented that so many of these artworks would be

gone in the coming months. They were being moved to Philly.

Since they hit it off so well, they decided to ask their parents at the museum to meet each day at a different attraction. They became inseparable.

The Smithsonian aviation portion had been moved to Virginia years ago. Now the rest would be moved there. Since Mina was local, she asked her parents if she could accompany Lisa's family to Virginia. Her parents were elated she had a new friend and would leave them so they could partake in what Ani called girl talk. Little did they know the young teens would be speaking about serious topics.

Mina seemed somewhat melancholic. She spoke about her father being an attorney for the new government. She felt all these conversions about the secession were unnecessary. Lisa agreed.

"I don't know about this president. His thoughts seem to be more of a dreamer than reality. He may be Black, but he's drifting from his message," Mina said.

"You said your dad works for him."

"That's part of the problem. All those years of schooling and we may end up dirt poor."

"Aren't lawyers good earners?"

"This president has a dislike for all people of means. He especially calls doctors and lawyers bloodsuckers."

Mina was referring to the president and his allies following the old Soviet model of putting all doctors and lawyers on a smaller salary. He was going by the labor theory of value where the value of goods and services are worth the amount of labor that goes into them, not the market.

Lisa said, "Does he have a choice?"

Mina said, “I’m not supposed to tell anyone, but I like you. He won’t tell me where yet, but we’re moving to a USA state. If that doesn’t work, there’s always the CSA.”

Lisa was perplexed why it was such a secret. Mina hugged her.

“You don’t understand things here. Any resignation, and my dad’s life would be in danger.”

“You could always move to where I live.”

“Where are you?”

“An island in the South Sea.”

“Please text me. I may someday ask for your help.”

Lisa was so happy she made a new friend. When she told her family however, Bret had a different reaction. He felt nobody should be invited who was hardly known.

“You know Grandpa Niz has complete say over who can come to our special paradise.”

Lisa had been taught invitations were carefully screened by Niz. For now, they wanted to enjoy the present and experience places the average person could no longer enjoy. The skyscrapers and museums were outstanding.

“Wait until you see New York City. It’s a city like no other in the world,” Bret said.

Lisa and Mina met on Lisa’s last day in the area. They promised to stay in contact.

Chapter 4

When they arrived in the former New York City, Lisa was awed by the Manhattan skyline. She was still wondering why the name change.

Since the city achieved statehood, the mayor now had the dual role of mayor and governor. He felt it was time to stop celebrating the old Duke of York and rename the city in a way that was more reflective of the current population.

Since the flight of people from Staten Island, the vast majority of residents were minorities in other parts of New York City. He termed people of color and undocumented immigrants the backbone of his great domain and so renamed the area the State of Colorgratia.

The family had planned to spend two weeks in Manhattan because of the wealth of attractions. But transportation was a problem. It was near impossible to get a taxi, and the crime problem in the subway system had intensified more than they'd known. The bus routes only ran to smaller areas. This wasted a lot of time.

Steve temporarily left the others to go to the jewelry exchange on 47th Street. The widow of one of his late clients loaned him a diamond ring. She wanted it weighed and examined. While the stores on 47th Street had many retail kiosks, Steve went to the second floor of one of the buildings on 47th Street, where there was a lone office, protected by metal bars, of an importer who also wholesaled on that street. He was a close friend of Niz's. The man was over ninety years old and was a Hasidic Jew.

Steve didn't want to scratch the jewel with a diamond pen, even if it was fake. The importer shook his head, removed the diamond from its setting, and put it on a scale. He pointed to the weight reading. He knew something was wrong.

"I knew that was fake. It's a zircon. Zircons are heavier than diamonds. I'll give you a certification so she doesn't think you pulled a switch," the jeweler said.

Steve knew the widow would be distraught. What could he do? She trusted him. All he could do was rejoin the touring family.

Ani's idea was to use the tour buses. They ran every ten minutes and covered most of the areas they wanted to see. Their list included the South Street Seaport, Chinatown, Little Italy, the Statue of Liberty, the Empire State Building, the former and now vacant UN, the Metropolitan Museum of Art, the Museum of Natural History, the Lincoln Center, Broadway, Central Park . . . the list went on. They had to pare down the list to seven days.

While the outer boroughs were somewhat in disarray due to crime and violent protests, Manhattan seemed okay.

After several wonderful days, Steve approached the rest of the family at breakfast and said he needed to borrow Bret for the day. One of his clients had specifically requested Bret's presence. It sounded strange because the clients shouldn't have even known of Bret's existence.

Concerned about street crime and his family's safety, Bret balked at the idea. Steve mentioned it sounded very important.

Ani said, "Oh, don't be a baby. Lisa and I will be fine. We

won't go out at night until you get back."

The traffic was snarled on the roads and bridges, but the two of them made it past the congestion and headed upstate. Steve handed Bret written directions to a location about an hour's drive north of the city.

Bret said, "Why not the GPS?"

Steve said, "The address is filtered out. We know this guy is rich, but he must be on a different level."

Bret said, "Don't you know him?"

Steve said, "Neither my father nor I ever met him in person. We always had a go-between, and his name was anonymous. I do know he purchased the single most expensive item my father ever dealt with."

They kept driving north in what was a countrified setting, but their route kept them close to the Hudson River. They knew it was an area of old money and dotted with grand estates.

When they reached the apparent location, there was a meager sign reading PRIVATE PROPERTY, NO ADMITTANCE. They turned and started driving down a dirt and gravel road heading toward the river.

When the main road was out of sight, they approached a large double gate. Two men were standing outside. Unlike most uniformed guards, these had black suits and black ties. After Steve and Bret gave their names, one of the guards made a call. A few seconds later, the gates opened, and they were waved on.

They saw a mansion up ahead. It gave a new meaning to what they'd seen before. It was six stories high with an observation tower at the top. On a clear day, the Manhattan skyline could be seen.

An older man let them in. He seemed to be a butler.

He said, “Please wait here. I’ll inform the master.”

They waited in a huge semicircular foyer. The perimeter was lined with paintings and sculptures.

Bret said, “Look at these signatures on all of the paintings. Are they copies or real?”

Steve said, “You can bet all the tea in China they’re originals. I can’t imagine the massive value in this foyer alone.”

The butler returned and said, “The master will see you now.”

He led the pair to a door and let them inside.

It was a library, two stories high with a catwalk for the second story. There wasn’t a wall without books. It was larger than many public libraries. There was a single executive desk with an oversized chair and two chairs facing the desk.

Eyes wide, they looked at each other in shock.

There was an elderly man on the second floor with his back to them, apparently looking at a book.

“Sit down, gentlemen.”

The elderly man walked over to a small elevator and came to their floor. He walked over to the desk holding something. As he sat, he saw them staring and pointed at them. Their eyes opened wide in surprise as he approached them.

“Do you know me?”

“I’ve seen your picture many times in the media. You’re known as one of the richest men in the world and politically active,” Steve said.

The man pressed one of the buttons on the desk. The butler entered.

“My guests and I will have a brandy, and they will join me for lunch,” he said. He looked at the two men, “Many people like brandy afterward. I like it before."

He then put the object he was holding on the table. It was strange. It was the size of a book and a few inches thick. But unlike a book, it was shaped like an hourglass, except the edges were sharp, not sloping.

"Any idea what this is?"

The men shook their heads no.

"I want to show you something." He opened a drawer and pulled out a hammer, a pair of scissors, and a cigarette lighter. He then proceeded to try to cut, burn, and pound the object. Not a mark was made. "It won't cut, burn, or dent. It's actually a book with the spine dead center."

"I'm flabbergasted. Where did it come from?" Steve said.

"It was excavated, and it's very old. The symbols have no rhyme or reason. It's basically undecipherable."

Steve said, "How old is it?"

"Using every technique we know of, the best guess is over two million years. It's my second greatest possession."

"I don't want to be intrusive, but what is the first?" Steve said.

"I'll tell you later."

"I've kept quiet, but please tell us what we're doing here," Bret said.

"You'll see after lunch."

The butler came back into the room and informed the trio that lunch was being served.

The host led the way to a dining hall. The table was so long that the host sat at the head and requested Steve and Bret sit on either side of him.

As the men expected, it was a sumptuous meal. They discussed benign topics as they ate.

After dessert, the host changed the topic with no warning. "Okay, now let's get down to brass tacks," he said, with a stern look on his face.

The host reached into his left breast pocket of the sport jacket he was wearing and pulled out an envelope. He took a letter out of the envelope and showed it to the two men. The heading showed it was from New York State, which was now part of the PRSSA but had not changed its name.

"I'll skip the long drivel and tell you the pertinent part. It basically says my personal wealth runs contrary to what the PRSSA is trying to accomplish through redistribution. I am being informed my real property, finances, and personal articles will be seized next week and given to the people."

"I always thought you were sympathetic to their cause," Steve said.

The host said, "Even billionaires make mistakes."

"What will you do?" Steve said.

"After our lunch has ended, I will be leaving immediately. I have spies just like them. They're not only taking everything, they'll also be arresting me. It won't be next week; it will be tomorrow."

Both Steve and Bret felt sorry. They asked about mediation or some other resolution.

The host sighed. "Both of you are so worldly, yet so naive. These are the worst of times. Now, a few people make things happen, a few others watch things happen, but most ask what happened. There is no middle of the road when it comes to surviving."

Bret said, "What can we do if it's like that everywhere?"

"You can survive just like you did when you fled the

mountain for Nizland. I know all about both of you. Wealth has its perks."

The host reached into his other breast pocket, took out a folded piece of paper, unfolded it, and showed it to the men.

They were shocked.

"Look at the one on the left. He's the typical incompetent survivalist. He has an unusable gun designed to drop an elephant. He'll barricade himself along with loads of placebos, like gold coins and freeze-dried food. He expects the government and neighbors to wither gracefully as he consumes his stores. The truth is he's cold meat.

"Now look at the one on the right. He's a thinking paranoid. He's well-armed, well-supplied, and mobile. When the government and starving masses hit his home, he won't be there to go down with it. I'm the latter of the two."

The men were both amused and saddened by the caricatures. There was no time for further theory. They had to get moving.

The host led them back to the library, and they all got onto the elevator.

"Sub," he said into the elevator speaker.

There was no such floor written on the panel. There was just numbers and *B* for basement.

The elevator started to descend. According to the panel, the basement was on the lowest floor. But when they got to the basement level, the elevator kept descending lower. When it stopped, the doors opened to a small room. They exited the elevator. The man pressed a button on the wall, and part of the wall slid open. It was easy enough for an unauthorized person to open, but what was behind it wasn't.

There was a heavy metal, bank vault–looking door behind it. The man started punching in a combination of codes and using voice activation. After a moment, the door opened, and he led them inside into a small apartment.

"This is my shelter in case of a nuclear attack. Alas, it's almost useless in the present situation."

He showed them around. There was a sitting room and kitchenette in front, a bath and storage in the middle, and a bedroom and office in the back. He led Steve and Bret to the office where there was a desk, a chair, and a structure that looked like an easel with a cover over it.

The host looked at Bret and removed the cover.

"Now you see why I requested your presence? You got this for me through nefarious means. I made Niz richer on this one item than most millionaires have in their lifetimes. I keep it here and look at it from time to time."

Bret's heart was pounding. He prided himself with doing the right thing. Throughout his entire life, he never had stolen anything else. Although obtained by underground means and Niz sold it, it was still the only painting ever sold for ten figures. It was arguably the most famous painting in the world.

"Here's the crux of the matter. I can't take it with me. Being a righteous guy, I'll allow you the opportunity to return it to the museum."

"And if I refuse?" Bret said.

"Upon your leaving here, I will personally burn it to ashes."

"Please don't. I'll agree."

Steve said, "I can have a jet here tomorrow at—"

"That won't do. That won't do at all. This leaves North America tonight, or the deal is off," the man said.

Steve said, "Your terms are impossible."

"Not really. I've taken the liberty of hiring two pilots and their aircraft. They're waiting upstate at a small airfield. I'll give you directions."

"Are they trustworthy?"

"I don't know them personally. It's short notice. All I know is they're certified for overseas flights with thousands of flying hours. Their fee is already taken care of."

The host pulled a cell phone from his pocket and told Bret to use it upstairs to make arrangements. He could then leave it, and it would be destroyed.

"It's a special phone. Even if the government tries to ID it, the calling and receiving numbers will be garbled. While you're making your calls, I'll have the painting crated."

As they left the vault, Bret was last and thought he saw a flash behind him. It was almost like an expressionless person nodding. It was less than a second, and he felt it was just a hallucination. It didn't matter that he saw the same thing in his dreams over the years.

Bret contacted Vera in France. Being the curator, she was ecstatic. She said she would call him right back with instructions. Bret had given her food when she was a child in poverty. She had since worked her way up to being the curator of one of the most famous museums in the world. Bret had promised to return the painting someday.

Bret called Ani and told her he wouldn't be back for a couple of days. He wanted to know how she was doing.

Ani said, "The government decided to start expropriating all apartment buildings. The landlords are rioting and burning random buildings all over the city. It's really getting hot around here."

Bret said, "Get out now. Head to Philly. Steve will meet you there."

Steve wrinkled his forehead. He wasn't happy.

"I thought we would go together," Steve said.

Bret said, "You're the only one I trust my family with. Besides, I'd rather do this on my own. Just drop me off upstate."

It didn't take long for Vera to call Bret back. She gave him the location where the pilots should fly to. Bret was surprised at the speed of her return call. She told him preparations for this event had been planned for years. It was just a matter of approval from the highest levels in the ministry.

A small crate containing the painting was sitting in the backseat. The man had one of his workers crate the painting and leave it in Bret's car, and the two men sped off. The drive would take several hours. As they chatted, Steve felt an itch and started scratching his nose—an ominous sign of impending trouble Steve had had since childhood. Bret disregarded it as he thought it was just Steve's insecurity.

They finally reached the airfield. It was small, and other than a few prop planes, there was only one jet. The pilots were waiting. No names were exchanged.

"Just call us Pilot 1 and Pilot 2."

Bret boarded with his cargo. Steve watched the takeoff with a despondent look on his face. His nose was itching like crazy now. It was a bad sign.

Chapter 5

They flew through the night. Early the next morning, the jet was passing into French air space. Both their military and ground control were informed to let it pass without questions.

A short time later, they entered wine country. Even at their altitude, the lush green vines were all that could be seen. As they neared their destination, the pilots used the older technology VOR to home in on the exact location.

The landing strip came into view. The small tower had no controller. Instead Vera was giving ground info like wind direction and speed. The local wineries thought nothing of the visitor. This was a government-only field, and they were used to the government bringing VIPs for wine tours.

After landing was complete, Bret deplaned with his precious cargo. There was a small one-story building next to the control tower. Vera was standing in front and vigorously waving with a broad smile. She was still gorgeous.

The pilots walked out and started checking the jet. At the same time, a tanker truck pulled up, and one person topped off the tanks with fuel. The pilots took this opportunity to stretch their legs and walk around.

Bret and Vera embraced, and her grip was especially tight. Bret thought this episode about returning the priceless painting would be ending soon.

"Come inside. There are some changes," Vera said.

Inside, she motioned for him to sit down at a table and

gave him some coffee. Telling him to relax, she left for a few minutes to put the crate in her car. When she returned, Vera was carrying a briefcase.

Vera said, "There's money in here. I have to speak with the pilots. I'll explain later."

Vera took the case and approached the pilots near the jet. She said she had another job for them.

Pilot 1 said, "What's in it for us?"

"A slice of the pie," Vera said.

Pilot 2 said, "How big a slice?"

Vera dialed the number lock on the case and opened it, showing them a lot of currency. Then she closed it while dialing the lock to a specific number.

Vera said, "This is only part of the whole slice. You will need to return your passenger to the airport you departed from and transport those three boxes you see by the building to a place you'll be informed of when you make your first stop. They contain ancient rarities and are priceless and have a seal. If you break it, the next party will know. You will receive the rest of your money upon delivery."

Vera told them they had ten minutes to decide. Otherwise the deal was off. She left carrying the case.

Pilot 2 said, "What do you think?"

Pilot 1 said, "I say yes. I think I know what to do."

Pilot 2 said, "And our passenger?"

Pilot 1 said, "We'll take care of him and dump him over the ocean. Then we turn south and head to the Trading Post. We have plenty of fuel."

The Trading Post was a small Caribbean island where people traded ill-gotten goods. Fences were there all the time and dealt in precious metals, drugs, and anything else that brought in money.

Vera reappeared, and both pilots gave her a thumbs-up sign. She went over to the boxes. They were on a luggage cart, and she put the case on top while rolling it to the jet.

After they loaded everything onto the plane, Vera put her hand up. She had a stern look on her face.

Vera said, "There's another change. I have to detain your passenger. The government is coming to arrest him. If you don't want to end up in the Bastille, you better take off, and I mean immediately."

She didn't have to repeat herself. The pilots hopped in their jet and were gone. Vera went inside. Bret was pointing out the window.

Bret said, "They left without me."

Vera said, "That's right. Come on. We have to get out of here."

They left the building and started driving in Vera's car. Bret needed to know what she was doing.

"Okay. Now tell me what's going on," he said.

"Many things. The first is I got a message from your friend Steve. Those pilots are drug dealers and killers. You wouldn't have made it across the pond."

"I can handle myself."

She put her hand on Bret's hand. Vera said, "Remember the ministry guy who covered up the heist? He's a full minister now. I spoke with him, and he quickly arranged this. He said something I didn't like."

"What."

"He said he's finally closing the book on this. That means he was going to kill you to protect himself."

"The pilots want to kill me, and the government wants to kill me. I'm a popular guy."

"The money was counterfeit, and the boxes had booby-trapped worthless trinkets."

"What about the fueling guy?"

"Too dangerous. The pilots might have seen him. He has no knowledge of what's happening. Let him leave. There's a bomb in the boxes I gave them. The big guy is leaving no stone unturned. If the bomb doesn't go off, the navy or air force will shoot the jet down over the ocean. After that, my superior will only have one other witness to rid himself of."

"Who?"

"Me, you fool."

Bret saw a tear rolling down her cheek. He knew she was worried. After all she did, he was determined to help if he could.

"I'm just worried for my daughter. Let's talk about something else. We can pick it up after dinner," Vera said.

They were driving through the endless back roads lining the wine country. Vera needed to go to a place where Bret would be temporarily safe. She knew exactly where they could go.

Vera turned into a modest entrance. The sign in front gave it away; they were the most expensive winery in the world. For each vintage, the wines were completely sold out, even before the harvest.

"You know these people? I'm impressed. The estate is so big," Bret said.

"I brought you here because they generally don't allow visitors and never wine tours. I guess I have an open pass because I'm pretty high profile among oenophiles."

Vera told Bret to wait in the car because the servants didn't speak English. He observed a butler and maid come outside, both hugging and kissing Vera. They seemed to be in agreement with everything Vera was saying. Vera was smiling when she returned.

"The owners are away, but they'll give us two bedrooms for the night. I told them you were a big VIP traveling incognito."

Bret was blushing. He grabbed Vera's hand. "I don't know how to thank you."

With a sly smile, she said, "I'll think of something. They insist on giving you a tour. We can go clean up a bit and take the tour. They'll serve us dinner on the veranda."

Bret was looking forward to the tour because he was a wine lover himself. When he got to his room, he was dazzled by his bedroom. It was large for a guest room. The furniture was handcarved and looked centuries old. After washing up, Bret and Vera met the guide downstairs for the tour.

The tour started outside. The guide explained the differences in the soil and weather and how it affected the grapes. The casks in the cellars were very unassuming. The ultimate enjoyment was the blind tasting. They were given both a horizontal (different wines from the same vintage) and a vertical (the same wine from different years).

Vera couldn't believe it when Bret could identify the best vintages. Quite a few ounces of wine on empty stomachs made them a bit tipsy. Thankfully it was time for dinner.

They arrived at the veranda where dinner was being served. The stone veranda overlooked beautiful gardens. Even with the reputation of fine French cuisine, the chef outdid himself with dinner. If the situation wasn't so serious, it would have felt like a dream vacation.

As they were waiting for their coffee after they finished eating, Bret said, "You wanted to finish dinner and now you've had your dinner. Let's talk."

Vera said, "Your wife . . . do you love her?"

Bret said, "Very much. I sense some problems in your marriage?"

"You're very perceptive. I'm afraid my husband's married to the bottle. He's been abusive to me and my daughter too."

"How about taking your money and leaving?"

"What money? That sot pissed away our money. We live paycheck to paycheck. Do you know how difficult it is to get a divorce in France, especially in my position?"

"What can you do, especially with this closing the book business? Your boss wants to tie up loose ends?"

"I accept my fate. I'm just worried about my daughter."

Bret was concerned there was no end in sight. Then the tears started again. Only this time, she covered her face.

"Bret, . . . I don't want to die."

"Let me think. Maybe I can help you."

"Remember when I was a child, and you gave me that sandwich because my mom and I were starving? I can still taste it. It tasted so good. Then when I was a teen, I thought about you constantly. I suppose I'll always love you."

Vera took Bret's hand. Unlike in the car, she clenched hard. "Where were you when I needed you?"

Bret said, "You know our lives went in different directions."

"I know. I know."

Bret was uncomfortable. It was leading to nothing good. To compound the problem, there was a flash behind him. He thought he saw that haunting image again shaking its head.

Bret said, "Did you see that?"

"What?" Vera said.

Bret said, "Never mind. I'm delusional. We better get some sleep. What about tomorrow?"

"I almost forgot; your friend is picking you up. I'll drive you to the airport. Then my birdie will fly away, never to be seen again."

Bret's stomach was fluttering. He prided himself with being able to have the right words. This time he was uncomfortable because he'd known her as a child.

It wouldn't get any easier because their bedrooms were next to one another.

After Bret took a much-needed shower, he lay down on the bed and looked at the ceiling. The estate provided a closet full of clothes, but he was still naked and thinking about what he could do for Vera. He laid there a while longer, hoping to sleep but couldn't. It didn't help that he could hear Vera crying though the walls.

When the sounds stopped, he was relieved. Maybe he would be able to sleep and think more clearly in the morning. He suddenly heard a soft knock at the door.

Before he could say anything, the door opened, and there was Vera standing in her bathrobe. The tears were still streaming down her cheeks.

"Bret, I've never asked for anything. Please be with me just this once before I die. I promise never to bother you again, and you know I always keep my promises."

She climbed next to him in bed. Bret felt conflicted. He was always loyal to Ani. But Vera had just saved his life.

"Ani baby, please forgive me," Bret said silently to himself.

Vera didn't want it to end. It was a marathon.

Bret was always prolific. Later on, he did put a stop to it. Bret thought he saw that flash out of the corner of his eye with a shaking head. He looked to the side, but it was gone.

Vera started to thank Bret. He cut her off and told her he didn't do anything he didn't want. They could now lie in a relaxed atmosphere and speak with a clearer mind.

Bret said, "If you ran, would your daughter go with you?"

"She's been telling me to leave him for a long time. It's no use. They have long arms and would find me. With no money and only art expertise, how could I support her?"

"What if I told you there's a place you could go where they couldn't touch you? It's a place where the weather is great all year round, the people are friendly, and the food is always tasty."

"I would say that's a fairy tale. There's no such place. Even if a place like that existed, I'd have to live on the streets. There's no free ride."

This was Bret's secret weapon. As Niz kept developing his island, there was one problem he hadn't solved yet. As times got worse around the world, museums and galleries were closing. They were selling and auctioning works of the great masters for pennies on the dollar. Niz was a big player and purchased so many items, he had to store them.

Niz wanted to open a gallery on his island. Since he had amassed great works of art and the people who lived and visited were all wealthy, it was an opportunity if he could find an art expert whose knowledge would be matched by their ability to run such an operation. Niz didn't like the applicants. They didn't have either the art expertise or the business knowledge.

After explaining this to Vera, he asked if she knew anyone who fit that description. It was clear he was being facetious. She smiled for the first time since the jet had landed.

"I guess you're talking about me. But would the island owner have me?"

Bret started laughing and said, "He's my lifelong friend and my mother's husband. If I explained everything to him, he would beg you to come. How long would it take to get ready to leave?"

"A couple of days. They'll wait at least a week until things settle down before they move against me. Tomorrow I'll replace the painting and get my daughter ready. My husband will be dead drunk on the floor."

Bret said, "Cameras?"

"The outside ones only are meaningful for things leaving the museum, not coming in. The room ones don't mean anything as I'm always taking things down for routine maintenance. I'll pull the switch in my office."

"We'll make arrangements with Steve tomorrow at the airport."

Chapter 6

Steve picked up Bret at the airport, and they flew back to Philly where they met Ani and Lisa. They immediately drove west.

Bret felt the family was biting off more than they could chew and everyone was getting tired, so he proposed changing their plans. Lisa was agreeable to just hitting some of the national parks in the western parts of North America before returning home.

The family made its way across the country. Lisa was disappointed she would miss the walking tour in Boston. The time and situation gave Bret pause. Although Philly was nice and the historical features were so interesting, they all agreed it was a good idea to head west. From Philly, they decided to go from Mount Rushmore in South Dakota south to the Alamo in Texas. The sparsely populated areas offered little danger along their north-south route.

They headed west with a stop in the new Apache state located in what was formerly part of Arizona. People were quite friendly and didn't want to speak about any political turmoil. Lisa was so happy with the handmade souvenirs.

Once in the western part of Arizona past the Apache state, they had plans for the Hoover Dam and the Grand Canyon. Once again Steve approached everyone with the same look as he had in the former New York City.

Steve said, "I hate to do this to you, but I need to borrow

Bret again."

"Is this really necessary?" Bret said.

Steve said, "It's of the utmost importance. It has worldwide implications and nothing to do with my clientele."

"Does this mean another little disappearing act for several days?" Ani said.

"I doubt it. The other parties involved are on a strict schedule," Steve said.

After breakfast at the motel, Bret went to the car while Steve stopped in his room and grabbed an attaché case. Walking out to the car, Steve threw the case in the backseat of their car, and the two men sped away.

"I didn't see that on this trip before. I saw the name Niz on it," Bret said, pointing to the case in the backseat.

Steve said, "My dad flew it in last night. I can't tell you the contents right now for your own protection."

That certainly piqued Bret's curiosity. Should the contents fall into the wrong hands, he wouldn't be held responsible.

Bret and Steve drove south and then farther west. It was over three hours since they'd left. Bret was getting concerned, and he called Ani to see how she and Lisa were doing.

Ani said, "Oh, Lisa's having a ball. She loves burro rides. I just had to stop a kid from pulling its ears. I pulled the brat's ear and asked him how he liked it. He just cried."

Bret said, "Were the parents angry?"

"The mother came over and thanked me. She said she had a tough time controlling her son."

After all these hours, Bret and Steve saw a sign indicating the Mexican border crossing was only a mile away. Bret asked if they were going to Mexico. Steve affirmed it. He also told Bret he'd explain the border crossing procedures when they got there.

They arrived at the border and turned into a huge parking lot. There were hundreds of cars parked in the lot. Bret noticed all the license plates were from north of the border.

The customs had two lanes going each way for the cars. It was Bret's first time at the border. He was curious why there was a line of people on the side crossing by foot.

Steve said, "Welcome to DD. That stands for doctors and dentists. You'll see why when we get across. Just tell the border agents you're here to buy drugs."

They left the parked car and got in line. Bret couldn't believe the cavalier attitude of Steve's advice. It sounded like something that would land him in prison.

After a time in the line, it was their turn. There was another shock. The agent gave a personal greeting to Steve with a smile.

Steve pointed to Bret and said, "He's with me."

Bret said, "I want to buy drugs."

The customs agent waved them on without checking their passports. As they walked through and entered the main street, Bret remarked how wild that experience was.

Now Bret understood the informal name of the city. The streets were lined with mainly two-story buildings. While there were some cantinas and touristy clothing stores, there were mainly enormous signs and banners with a medical name and prices for their services.

Bret said, "Cleaning and x-rays for five bucks? Are they real dentists or janitors impersonating them?"

Steve said, "They're the real deal. Many have American med school degrees. People come here who don't have insurance. The pharmacies sell expensive prescriptions for pennies."

As they walked, Steve said they were a bit early and had time to stop for lunch. He pointed over to a cantina that was one of his favorites. Although it was hot, the dining area was shaded and comfy due to the large ceiling fans attached to the overhang. They sat down.

Bret noticed several fairly young women giving neck massages to people sitting at the cantinas. Steve explained they make a couple of bucks on those. Many of them make an additional fee for sexual favors.

Steve looked across the street and said, "Oh no."

Bret wondered why Steve seemed disappointed. He alluded to one woman giving a massage. Steve said her name was Rosa.

"I hope she doesn't see us because she'll try to do business," Steve said. "Actually, she's a good girl . . . sometimes. She's just mixed up. Her grammar isn't great, but she can converse in English."

It was too late. She saw them and gave a big wave.

Steve said, "Let me do the talking."

Rosa finished with her customer and started to cross the street toward them. Steve put his case between his legs. This was something he didn't need now. She approached with a giant smile showing perfect white teeth.

Rosa said, "Stevie! We go somewhere? Rosa need loving."

Stevie said, "Come on, Rosa. You know we never do business."

"I know. But your amigo?"

Steve motioned, wanting to tell her something. She bent over, and Steve whispered something in her ear. When Rosa would hear something extraordinary, her eyes would open wide and bulge slightly.

As she listened, her eyes went wide and bulged. Then she nodded, stood up, and began to walk away, but Steve raised his voice. He got her attention immediately.

"Rosa, my wallet please?"

She returned his wallet while smiling coyly.

"My cell phone please?"

After she returned both items, Steve opened his wallet. He pulled out some money and gave it to Rosa. She kissed him on the top of his head.

Rosa looked at Bret and said, "I so ashamed. Stevie always good to me. He give me money for nothing. Rent due, business bad, and Rosa has no money. I so, so sorry."

As she walked away, Bret noticed her behind had an exaggerated wiggle like a pendulum. "That reminds me to get my watch fixed," he quipped. "By the way, what did you whisper to her about me?"

"I told her you had syphilis."

Bret feigned anger and said, "Gee, thanks."

They finished lunch and began to walk to the southern end of town. Where the road and town ended, there were few plants and just mainly cacti and desert. There was a paved single-lane road with three vehicles in the distance.

There was a stretch limo parked about one hundred yards away in the direction they were walking. It was in between two open army trucks loaded with soldiers. The soldiers had their rifles drawn and pointed in all directions. When Bret and Steve arrived at the car, a man wearing a suit got out of the back and held the door for his two new passengers. The man looked surprised.

"I wasn't told you were bringing someone with you. The

soldiers are because of increased cartel activity," the man said.

Steve said, "It's a safety precaution. He has clearance."

They entered the car. After telling the man they already ate, the man opened a hidden bar and said, "Have some tequila with me."

The caravan drove for about an hour in the desert. They finally came to a few buildings that were surrounded by walls and razor wire. On top of some of the buildings were machine guns mounted along with spotlights. The area seemed to be an army base.

They entered the compound and got out of the car. They were led to a windowless conference room with a large TV screen on the wall. A teleconference was set up. Bret was shocked to see who was on the screen at the other end of the connection. It was none other than Niz!

Niz said, "Hi, Bret. Sorry to keep you in the dark."

Several people were seated in the room. They were waiting for one more person. They overheard one of them say, "He's late."

When the door opened, the Mexican president strolled in and said hello. The attendees included his advisors, a representative from the CSA, and one from the USA. Noticeably absent was anyone from the PRSSA and anyone from the military. It was clear the Mexican president was in charge.

Steve opened the case and pulled out what looked like thick drawing paper. It was folded several times. When opened all the way, it was large enough to cover half of the table.

It was a map of the southwestern part of the former USA. There was something strange about it. There were markings such as solid and dotted lines and *X* markings evidently showing strategic points.

The president studied the map. He was familiar with its main ports from prior meetings. He put his finger at some points and traced some of the lines.

He looked up at Niz on the screen. "You have performed magnificently."

Bret didn't have to have intimate knowledge of the situation to realize this had something to do with partitioning—the addition and subtraction of land.

Bret didn't understand what two narrow strips of land indicated. One was running from Nevada to the Pacific. The other was running from Arizona to the Pacific. Both bordered each other and went through a section of the former California and the area newly acquired by Mexico.

Steve and Niz started making things clearer to Bret as to what those strips indicated. The president then spoke about the serious situation in Central America. While Mexico had elected a socialist president a few years back, the instability of the USA and the resulting bad economy in Mexico had the people elect a more conservative government.

The president was worried. Panama and Costa Rica were putting up a brave front. With the help of China and Russia, the closer Central American nations were allied with northern South America that had Marxist dictatorships. There was a reasonable chance they would fall in the near future. The next stop would be Mexico.

The president said, "This is a crisis. I don't want communists on both of my borders. Don't give me that garbage about the PRSSA not being communists. They've already been infiltrated."

With Northern California part of the PRSSA now and the northern neighbor of Mexico, Niz came up with a brilliant idea.

The USA had no warm water ports in North America. The only port the CSA had was Alaska.

With the help of cartography experts, Niz figured to give the USA a ten-mile-wide strip bordering the PRSSA to the north and the CSA to the south. He had another equal strip of land separating the USA and Mexico. The two strips would be wedged together and separate Mexico from the PRSSA by twenty miles. Naval ports would be built on the Pacific Ocean at the end of the strips.

Assuming the three countries present would ratify, this would all be accompanied by an economic and military pact. The present company felt this would prevent the current crises from getting worse and would recommend their governments ratify the sale of these strips from Mexico to the CSA and the US.

The PRSSA would scream loud, but what could they do? Their biggest nightmare would be the USA and the CSA forming an alliance.

The three parties were enthusiastic about the idea. Being surrounded by potentially unfriendly nations, Arizona now had a friendly border and access to the Pacific.

They left, and the army escorted Bret and Steve through the town because it was getting dark. Going back to the border crossing, the American customs agents also recognized Steve and waved them through. They crossed back, jumped in their car, and started driving. There were some loose ends to tie up.

"That large map stays in Mexico permanently. I made a copy of it on a flash drive for you to hold in case something happens to me. My dad has one also," Steve said.

Bret said, "I think CSA, USA, and PRSSA relations are

going to be strained for now. We had planned to stop in Hollywood next. Your opinion?"

Steve said, "Forget it. It's too much to chance with Lisa. Most of the artists and studios she wanted to see are moving away from there, anyway."

So far this trip had many of the pitfalls Niz had worried about. Bret wanted to talk to Ani about spending the rest of the trip visiting expansive national parks. There shouldn't be any danger other than wild animals.

Chapter 7

The family decided to head north to Yellowstone. Although Bret and Ani were barely middle-aged, they were pretty tired. Steve was taking over many of the driving duties as the couple slept in the back row.

They were going to spend three days in Yellowstone. When they arrived, the sights were varied and breathtaking. Whether it was a waterfall, thermal areas, or geysers, the adults acted like kids as they ran from attraction to attraction.

A report was broadcast about a tourist being injured by a bison. It was followed by a warning not to approach or otherwise disturb wild animals. Lisa's love for animals didn't stop her from wondering why anyone would approach a bison.

On their second day, they drove through an area known as the Bear-muda Triangle. Sure enough, they spotted a grizzly. It was large and munching on horsetail. This was a moment when Lisa could actually teach her family. She noted horsetail was a favorite of the grizzly and had important nutritional factors.

They were renting a log cabin right outside Old Faithful. Each day, as the others were resting, Bret would stand by the window, fascinated, watching it erupt in its timely manner.

After the third day, they were winding the trip down, and Bret was talking to Steve about their future plans. Steve would make arrangements for one of his personal jets to take everyone home.

In a little bit of mystery, Ani was standing behind Bret

smiling and winking at Steve. It was becoming obvious Bret wasn't aware of what was to come.

Steve said, "We're driving north to what used to be a reservation and is now a NASA state. They have a landing field on a ranch there."

Ani said, "I believe we ought to rest a few days before flying back. I think we can sure use it."

Lisa asked if they had horses there. She loved riding and was an expert. Steve told her they actually raised horses, but he believed their main source of income was cattle. With so much land, they could do just about anything with livestock.

Bret wondered what was going on. He switched with Lisa and moved to the front. He was wondering why Ani and Lisa were, at times, giggling in the back.

They passed a sign welcoming them to the Native American States of America. Steve announced they should be at their destination in about an hour. Steve called ahead to tell the unknown party to expect them.

They came to the property line, and the lush fields extended as far as the eye could see. This ranch was supposed to be for livestock. However, there was an unfinished ten-story building on the side. There were also piles of what looked like bathroom fixtures next to the building.

As they got closer, a group of people walked into their sight. There were at least a dozen, and some seemed familiar to Bret. They all started waving frantically. Bret was startled when he recognized them. They were Bret's old international friends from his time living in the mountain years ago.

They had been dispersed and given new IDs as part of the government's agreement of evacuation. Steve had tracked them down, and with Ani's help, they planned a surprise reunion for Bret. He didn't often show this much emotion. He broke down.

Bret didn't recognize everyone, but he knew he'd meet them soon enough.

Bret jumped out of the car and ran to his friends. Bret was first approached by his good friend Red Hawk. His tribe hosted Bret's group as the mountain was on their tribal land. He had two others with him.

Red Hawk said, "You've heard their names before. This is George, who formed the reservation economic cooperative. His business acumen was essential in dragging many of us out of poverty. By the way, he's also out first president."

Bret shook hands and said, "I'm impressed. Hi, George."

Red Hawk said, "And this is Chengua. He was Earl but legally changed his name to his traditional tribal name. His business expertise was essential to keep the conglomerate together. They're both here to meet about the casino, and we're affectionately known as the three chiefs."

Bret said hi to Chengua and shook his hand. They both smiled.

The tall building was a hotel and casino. The people on this former reservation barely made enough money to support themselves, and as the price of meat had fallen, most moved away to prevent starvation. All of Bret's friends visited as a surprise for him.

The remaining people voted for statehood in the NASA. As usual, George came up with a way for them to prosper. As a new nation, there were no restrictions. There was no casino within five hundred miles, and he wanted to build a vacation paradise for all ages. There were mountains nearby for skiing in the winter, and they were building a large water park.

There was more. George wanted a riding area for all the casino guests to rent horses. He even had a shooting gallery constructed. The list of planned amenities seemed endless. They even constructed an airport so people could come from anywhere in the world.

Needless to say, the plans also included traditional pow-wows, cooking areas, and reenactments of battles. There would be no place like it. The conglomerate was sitting on billions and would be fronting most of the money.

Bret had to excuse himself in order to make the rounds. He next wanted to see his closest friends, Alex and Lana. They had defected along with their children and had joined Bret's operation. They had since been moved to the northwest, but they weren't happy with the new PRSSA government.

Alex said, "We can talk about that later. There's something more immediate. Do you see those four men watching us? Try to avoid them. They're no good."

Bret saw them. He observed two younger men who were fathered by the healthier older man. The fourth man was severely handicapped with a pronounced limp and a useless arm. One of Alex and Lana's sons was engaged to the healthy one's third child.

"I cautioned my son to not marry that girl, but we'll see. You haven't seen him since he was a child," Lana said.

Alex gave them chilling details about the foursome's activities. Since Lisa would be around, Bret wanted a little more info about the men. The younger ones were part of the mob. They would behave, but it was best to stay clear.

The young pair's father was Yuri, who was called Yura. He

had done time overseas.

Bret said, "What did he do?"

"He was convicted of being socially close and got four years," Alex said.

"I never heard of that. What does it mean?" Bret said.

Socially close was their term for murder. The most punishable crimes were politically connected. Yura was still a bad guy but was behaving because he didn't want to get deported. The government thought it was better to let them out and force them to work. Better to get some work than none at all.

The handicapped person's name was Anatoliy but was called Tolik. He was Yura's brother. He was relatively harmless but very bitter.

Bret wanted to know how he got that way. Alex told him that during one of the brush wars, Tolik's unit was ordered to take a hill with a machine gun nest on top. Each time they were attacked, many were killed and wounded. The unit was almost decimated when they finally took the hill, only to find the enemy had escaped down the back.

"You can see the results," Alex said.

"It's horrible," Bret said.

Alex said, "It's worse."

Being good for little else, Tolik was asked to collaborate with the Soviets when he was younger. He explained he wasn't healthy enough. So he refused. They called him an American spy and sent him to prison. They kept him awake nights, and he weakened. He caught tuberculosis, and they gruesomely removed his lung under a local anesthetic. Alex said he has been heard saying one thing over and over: "I will never forgive and I will never forget."

As Bret walked around talking with everyone, he saw Red Hawk looking at Steve. Steve's mouth was wide open, and he was staring at a young woman who was speaking with Chengua. She had an unusual appearance. Her dirty blond hair and ice blue eyes were contradicted by her olive complexion. She was unusually tall for a Southwestern tribal woman.

"I think your friend was struck by lightning," Red Hawk said, leaning over to Bret.

"Maybe you're right. I just don't understand it. Steve's been all over the world. He never reacted like this."

Red Hawk said, "Perhaps they should be introduced. Just remember Chengua is a man of the old ways. In his tribe, women are more dangerous than bows and arrows. When it comes to courtship, a man can be beaten or killed if he does a woman wrong. The police can't help."

"I'll warn Steve," Bret said.

After the introduction, Chengua was surprisingly gracious. He immediately walked away so Steve and his daughter could chat. Close-up, she was even more of a statuesque beauty.

Steve told her his name. She was more evasive regarding her name.

"They gave me a name from our language. You'll have a tough time pronouncing it. It has a dual translation, either bright star or morning star. Everyone just calls me Star."

Steve apologized, but he had to remark about her attractiveness. She was surprisingly accepting of the compliment. She wasn't conceited at all. He also remarked that she didn't look Southwestern.

Star said, "That's because I'm a mutt. My mother is German, Italian, and French. It cost me."

"How so?"

"I was actually Miss Native America. But when I told them I was of mixed blood, I had to resign."

"That's a shame."

"Not really. Now I'm a plain old schoolteacher. Teaching is much more fulfilling than the pageant atmosphere."

When she asked Steve what he did for a living, he just said he was a rarities agent. He wasn't interested in talking about himself. He was more interested in her background. Her parents were from such different backgrounds. Steve was curious as to how her parents got together.

Star said, "My parents met when my dad went to college back East. I should tell you about him because he's sometimes not easy to understand. One minute he's in a rage and the next he's cracking jokes. He always says it's not important for one to understand me, it's only important for me to understand me."

"I wonder how he got that way."

"My dad was dirt poor. At the same time, Ivy League schools had Indian quotas. He had the grades, but he still had to live."

Waiting tables wasn't paying his bills. Chengua, who went by Earl back then, couldn't work two jobs and go to school. Someone came into his workplace and noticed his long hair and obvious ethnic looks. He asked Earl if he ever acted. When Earl said no, the man offered him a part in a local play. There were no lines. He was told he would dress like an Indian and say nothing.

The pay was a lot more than he was making doing menial jobs. One thing was immediately noticeable: Crowds would laugh every time he gestured. Sometimes he would stick out his tongue when the main actor turned around. The audience would be roaring.

One night, a man approached him after a show. He was a local agent. He told Earl he could make a lot more doing stand-up comedy. He was told to be himself and he would get help writing jokes.

Steve said, "Is it really a good idea to be so self-deprecating?"

Star said, "My father always says he will never trust a man who can't laugh at himself."

The chemistry was there. The planned short stop to rest for the family turned into longer than a week. Every day, Steve and Star were seen walking together and holding hands. Everything culminated at dusk one evening when Star approached Steve.

"I want to be close to you tonight. It's time," she said.

"There are eyes everywhere . . . even at night," he said.

She coyly said, "Not if we grab a couple of horses. I have an oversized sleeping bag. Nothing will stop me tonight."

A full moon was out, but it was still plenty dark. The stars seemed so close, almost like one could reach out and touch them.

They went to the corral and mounted two horses. They rode about a mile. Finding an extra soft patch of pasture, the romance was intoxicating. The bottle of wine didn't hurt either.

Most of the cattle were sleeping. They still heard one occasionally calling. The next hour was magical. Star didn't worry about prying ears so she could be loud. After all good things had to come to an end, they looked up at the stars lying next to each other.

Star said, "I am so happy. I will never forget tonight."

They were quiet for a couple of minutes.

Star quickly picked up her head. "Did you hear that?"

Steve rose up. "I did, but I can't see anything. It sounds like cattle running."

"No. Those are horses," Star said.

"Maybe we left the gate open," Steve said.

"Impossible. I secured it myself."

They agreed and listened. They heard the sounds again. It sounded like alternating galloping and running.

Steve said, "Aren't there wild horses around here?"

"Maybe, but wild horses sleep at night. If they were attacked by a predator, you'd hear screaming as well as running. I'm at a loss," Star said.

Steve said, "Let's just tell the hands tomorrow."

Chapter 8

It was almost a party atmosphere when everyone was having coffee in the morning by the picnic tables. The only person missing was Lisa. Every morning, Lisa would take one of the horses and go for a ride. The terrain was fairly flat, and she could be seen in the distance.

Steve approached the hands and asked about what he heard the prior night. They all thought he was hearing something other than horses. He figured they were probably right.

Screams rang out in the distance.

"Lisa!" yelled Ani. Fearing the worst, Ani grabbed a pair of binoculars that were always out on the table. Her hands were shaking. She yelled for Bret to look.

Lisa was being chased by a group of riders. They eventually surrounded her and started leading her away. One of them grabbed her and put her on his horse so they could ride faster.

These were the dreaded Purps. They got their name from the purple shirts they wore during their sadistic actions.

Before Bret and Ani could do anything, a group of hands were racing toward the abduction. They were shooting their guns in the air. The foreman cautioned Bret and Ani to wait there. The hands could handle the situation.

As the hands got nearer, several of the Purps dismounted and used their horses for shields while firing back. Outnumbering the Purps, the hands worked their way around the flanks and forced the remaining Purps to surrender.

It wasn't enough. Lisa was gone. The Purps had taken her into the heavily wooded mountain range. It would be useless to try to follow them.

Bret immediately called Niz to tell him the tragic news. Niz told him not to panic. He would grab one of his personal jets and arrive the next day.

There were four captured Purps. One of the hands brought four wooden folding chairs and the four Purps into one of the barns at gunpoint and seated them next to each other. Bret and Ani rushed to join the proceedings. This was a sticky situation since there were no police on this former reservation.

The Purps were all male. Three of them had nothing unusual about them on the surface. The fourth was different. He wore his shirt open and was covered head to toe with tattoos. He was a relatively large man. His head was completely shaven, and he wore an eye patch. He looked like a pirate from the movies.

Bret would randomly question them one at a time, leaving the bald guy for last. Bret approached the first one. "Where's my daughter?"

Before he could answer, the bald man shouted, "You tell them nothing!"

Bret walked over and looked at the second man, "Where's my daughter?"

The man looked over to the bald man, "But, Frank—"

Again, the bald guy shouted, "You say anything more, and I'll make sure you're through!"

Bret was ready to ask a different way to the third one. Before he could say anything, the bald guy yelled at the third man, "One word and you'll answer to me!"

It was painfully clear who was running this outfit. Ani's

patience was exhausted. She jumped in front of Bret, grabbed the bald guy by his shoulders, and started shaking him. "What did you do to my baby?"

The bald man just smiled. He then spat on Ani.

Bret had a knee-jerk reaction. He closed his fist and unleashed a powerful swing. He hit hard, and the Purp fell off the chair. He was bleeding from his mouth and spit out a tooth. Once they had reseated the Purp, the barn door opened. It was Alex. He motioned to Bret to step outside.

Once they were outside Alex said, "The Russians said you're handling this all wrong."

Bret was open to any kind of suggestion. Alex pulled out a crumbled piece of paper. It was written in Cyrillic, so Alex read it to Bret.

The note referred to rudimentary methods for interrogation. The first suggestion was to separate the prisoners. That could be accomplished because the property had multiple small steel sheds. Each had a small window and a light with a door that could be locked. The metal walls would be difficult to break through without making a racket and alerting everyone.

It seemed that each suggestion was progressive if the prior one failed. It read that the front two chair legs were to be cut two inches. While not painful, it would make the prisoner lean forward uncomfortably.

When moving a prisoner, it was best to tie him in a Burmese Tiger position. This involved tying the wrists and feet to a pole to carry the person in a way resembling an animal hung over a spit.

It also said the prisoner could be questioned to see if he was consistent. And not to reassure him to make sure he was on edge. The note continued, saying, "These Purps are likely not clever enough to make up consistent lies. Make sure the windows are covered as to assure the prisoner that he is defenseless.

"Make sure the guard has a weapon pointed at all times and is far enough away so the prisoner can't bolt and overpower him. Ultimately, you want the prisoner to see you as his only friend, confessor, father, or mommy." Alex had told Bret that Russian mobsters sometimes refer to a superior as mommy.

They kept reading the note.

"Next you can coat a ping pong ball with mosquito repellent. Force it into the prisoner's mouth and tape the mouth. The taste is horrible." Bret could return in a few minutes and threaten to do it again. He didn't want to do this now because the necessary pieces weren't available.

This was part of the third-degree expression. It came from the Irish Rebellion. The first degree let the subject know he could suffer pain. The second was showing instruments that could inflict pain. The third was actually inflicting pain.

"If the prisoner is still uncooperative, try some rope tricks." The ranch had plenty of that. "These methods are intended to cause discomfort rather than excruciating pain." Each shed had an exposed beam and could be used for some of these.

"The one-arm hang is simply pulling the person up off the floor just enough where the toes are touching the floor. This causes excessive fear of falling. A similar one is called the stork where the hands are tied behind the back and lifted as with the first method.

"Ulysses's Bow can become more painful than the previous. The rope runs along the back and is tied to the ankles, bending the head and legs backward. As the feet begin to relax, they'll start tugging on the neck, creating a choking feeling.

"A Ghurka Scissor is painful, yet nonlethal. It's easy to put a post in the ground and put the prisoner in a seated yoga position. One leg is wrapped around the post at the knee, while the foot from the other leg is placed behind the post. This creates knee and pelvic pain. It was at one time used in professional wrestling and called the figure-four leg vine and used as a submission hold."

There were other more painful ways such as electric shock, but the materials and time-consuming nature of it made the procedures impractical at this time.

"The whole idea is lack of comfort rather than excessive pain. Too much pain may make the Purp babble incoherently. Some people are destroyed mentally and may prefer to die."

Bret was astounded by these things. He was surprised the criminals could come up with such methods.

Alex said, "It wasn't the criminals. It was Tolik. He faced these things when he was falsely charged."

After Bret returned inside without Alex, Ani told him they were getting nowhere. They had tried the friendly approach and the rough approach. They had spent days trying to extract some type of useful info. They were unsuccessful.

Bret was approached by Red Hawk, Chengua, and George several hours later. Ani was with him. They were joined by a similar-looking younger man with long hair. Bret had seen him milling around. He had assumed the person was just a local. As it turned out, he was George's attorney and closest confidant, Sam. He always accompanied George to important meetings such as this. People called him Consigliere, a play on advisors from organized crime films.

George had an idea. Part of the education of his tribe included each young male taking a course in one of the ancient disciplines of tribal life. While most young men chose more exciting lessons like using a bow and arrow or fighting with a tomahawk, Sam had opted in another direction.

Since he was a child, Sam was different from others. He had heightened senses. He could hear and smell things that others couldn't. He also had a way of almost sensing what lay ahead in the near future. It was overwhelming, but he made it go away.

So, to best use his gift, Sam had opted for learning about tracking. It wasn't just following another living subject. There were many intricacies involved. He could of course, follow hoofprints. His sense of smell allowed him to guess the approximate age of animal residue such as horse manure and urine.

Sam could look at a broken branch or twig and sense the direction the animal was traveling and how long ago it had been broken.

"I got this gift by communicating with animals," Sam said.

Sam would at times speak to the animals. He was especially able to communicate with farm animals such as horses, cows, sheep, and goats.

While many people spoke to their pets, Sam was able to elicit reactions without the hand motions normally used in training. Some animals would react to his words in extraordinary and unusual ways. Others tried his words with no reaction. He would ask a person to hide a piece of food such as a carrot stick in an area where the animal never went. But once Sam whispered to the animal, it would go exactly to the location without trying to smell its way there. It was an extraordinary gift.

"Loosen the ropes holding the man they called Frank. They

are still tied but not too tightly and he could escape with some effort. Leave a horse near his shed. Call the guard away," George said.

Bret said, "It's too easy. Won't he suspect?"

"I think he's too stupid. He'll be in such a hurry, he won't be thinking of that," George said.

Sam and his horse would be hidden behind a building. They would watch Frank take off. Sam would wait long enough to follow him.

Bret said, "What if he gets too far ahead of you?"

"I'll give him a couple of hours. He'll be out of sight," Sam said.

"Are you sure you won't lose him?" Bret said.

"I've successfully tracked people and animals after a full day. Hopefully he will lead me to where they're keeping your daughter," Sam said.

They agreed. Bret went ahead and loosened Frank's ropes, claiming he realized they had been too tight. Sure enough, Frank took the bait. As they hid behind the building, they saw Frank come out and run off to the nearby horse. As they watched him disappear out of sight, Bret got somewhat edgy. Ani and George were a bit calmer.

Sam said, "Have patience."

After a few minutes, Sam finally looked at George and nodded. Sam mounted up and checked his horse for adequate supplies.

"Let's do it," Ani said.

Chapter 9

Niz arrived at the reservation the next day. Everybody was overjoyed because his logic and experience always came in helpful. Bret told him the bad news regarding the inability to extract info from the prisoners. Niz already knew there was no assistance coming from any authorities. He likened it to the Cold War. It would be similar to asking the Soviet Union and the USA to cooperate in police matters. That was a nonstarter.

Niz said, "I have to see about getting the governments involved. I'll try the three main players."

Niz started working the phones. He didn't inspire confidence. However, the pained look on his face an hour later didn't inspire any confidence. He had many connections before his retirement, but they were slowly fading away.

He would intermittently give Bret and Ani a look, put his hand up, and shake his head. He could even be heard yelling into the phone, which was completely out of character for him.

His first call was to the USA at the building that replaced the White House. He was kept on hold for quite a while. He was then passed around to multiple people. He was getting frustrated.

It reached the point where he couldn't be connected to the president. In the old days, the sound of his name would get an immediate connection.

"Please get a message to the president. I'm sure he will react to my name," Niz said.

While Niz had been an advisor to past presidents, the current president was a young politician and didn't buy into the old way of doing things.

The president had heard of Niz when Niz was secretly advising a former president. The last person on the phone returned.

"The president will not speak to you, nor will he see you. If you like, you can send your son and he can wait his turn to speak to the president after he arrives."

Niz hung up and gave Bret and Ani the bad news. That was strike one. He didn't want them to suffer, so it was on to the next call.

The reaction from the PRSSA staff was even worse. That president may or may not have heard of Niz. They refused to even try to connect with the president. Niz was told he was a busy man and could try next month or even next year, but even that was doubtful.

Next, Niz pinned his hopes on the CSA president. He made his next call. He wasn't able to speak with the president, but he was able to get a message to him. Niz finally caught a break when he was told the president would be at a place only a several hours' drive from the ranch.

Niz told the liaison to remind the president of the Mexican deal. That seemed to encourage the president. He finally got something good. The president agreed to sit for a few minutes with Steve. However, the liaison didn't sound confident, and that was a concern.

Bret's mom, Essi, insisted on flying to the reservation as well. Her only granddaughter's life was at stake. She spent a little time speaking with Bret and Ani while Niz was finishing the arrangements such as directions and passwords.

Bret and Ani were curious about the other passengers on the jet they arrived in. Essi brought Micah, his loyal pet. Essi felt his bonding with Lisa and sense of smell might help.

The female warrah was also brought. Her wolf-like species had become extinct. That was until a scientist developed a way to rebreed the animal.

He was the same scientist who brought Micah back. The original Micah had died during Bret's childhood. While successful cloning was around for years, this was different. He invented a manner of using Micah's corpse to import his being to the new German Shepherd dog. Whether one calls it a soul, spirit, or whatever makes a being special unto himself, he did it.

The scientist ran into trouble. He kept no records. All his secrets were in his head. His country wanted him to do this for a human even though he had previously worked with animals. He ran away shortly after the family made this trip, and Niz let him in Nizland.

Modern genetics proved the warrah was most closely related to the wolf. The warrah and Micah had previously mated and breed a hybrid and loving litter.

There was also a third animal, which arrived in Nizland after the family left on their journey. It was weird-looking to say the least. It seemed similar to a dog or wolf with a long snout but had stripes on its back similar to a tiger.

"What the heck is that?" Ani asked.

Essi said, "It's called a thylacine, a.k.a. a Tasmanian wolf. It's been extinct for over a century."

It was brought because Micah and the warrah accepted it and the three were bonded. Since loneliness could cause health problems, Essi thought it best to take it with them. It could also help protect the others should the need arise.

The thylacine suddenly let out a big yawn just like any dog. Everyone was startled. Looking straight at it, its nose and lower jaw were almost vertical.

Essi laughed. "I know you were all startled, but this thing can open its jaw an astounding eighty degrees. It's a kind soul, but it could easily envelope a human neck if it wanted to."

Niz hung up the phone and called Steve over. He apprised him of the situation. The president only had a little time and agreed to see him today.

"Get hold of Bret and get moving," Niz said.

Ani had to stay behind. It was agreed that one of the parents needed to stay at the ranch in case there was news requiring a decision be made. Since the president had already been aware of Bret's involvement with the land deal with Mexico, he would go.

They drove several hours. The area they drove through looked relatively arid. Yet they went through occasional thunderstorms. Bret was always thinking.

"I hope Lisa doesn't have to endure this sort of weather," Bret said.

Steve said, "She's likely high in that mountain range since they rode in that direction. The weather should be nice this time of year. The only thing she has to put up with is those lousy Purps."

After a few hours, they arrived at what looked like an army base. It looked similar to the meeting with the Mexican president, having several buildings surrounded by chain-link fencing topped with razor wire. The exception was two armored military vehicles next to the guard house.

They pulled up to the guard. When they asked for the president, he pointed at the road in the direction they were traveling. "He's at the smaller place. You can't miss it."

That was obvious since they were surrounded by low land. The vegetation was mainly tumbleweed. They drove to the place.

They reached the building and saw a helipad behind it with a helicopter containing an eagle symbol. The previous guard called ahead, so they were expected. After a quick search and metal detection, they were escorted to a small building and then into a small room. There were some suited men watching, some version of the old secret service. The president was seated in a small room. He asked one of the guards to leave.

"So what can I do for you?" the president asked.

Steve said, "Did you hear what happened to us up north?"

The president said, "I got nauseous when I heard."

Bret said, "I have no place else to turn."

The president stood up and walked around the room. He made sure the door was locked. He started looking up toward the ceiling and wrapped his hand around the back of his neck. "Exactly what would you like me to do?"

Bret said, "I don't know. I was hoping you had some ideas."

The president laid out the possibilities. He was making a representation of what could be done. Nothing sounded good. "We have to be realistic. I could send troops across the border and start a war. I can't do that."

The choices weren't good. They spoke of veiled threats. It was explained that it was a waste of time. One could never get anywhere with a regime like that when you played nice. They always wanted more. They would laugh at an offer of ransom.

"That PRSSA regime is less likely to speak with me than

everyday people like you. If you haven't heard, they already have foreign troops stationed in strategic spots."

Steve said, "It sounds like you're sending us packing."

The president said, "I wish there was something I could do. Intelligence says they're looking for a provocation. Your father did an admirable job working on the Mexican land deal with us. I'm not sure we could have succeeded without him. However, there are limits to everything, and preservation of the CSA and its citizens are my first priority. I'm so sorry I cannot be of more help."

Bret and Steve left feeling defeated. There had to be another way. The only thing they could do was to hurry back and discuss the next step with Niz.

Chapter 10

After their unsuccessful visit to see the US president, Steve and Bret phoned Niz to see what to do next. Niz did his usual calming speech and told them to get back ASAP.

They returned and found Niz had worked the phones again. He was trying to make some progress with the other two major nations of the split.

Niz said, "I'm afraid the PRSSA looks like a dead end. However, I was able to make a tiny bit of headway with the USA."

Tomorrow was the day the US president would see people in his temporary headquarters outside Philly. Niz had been able to at least get Steve on the list but was still treated rudely on the phone:

"You and your son are always looking for preferential treatment. Tell them they'll just have to wait their turn."

At least they had a spot where they could make their case. Niz was still pessimistic because of the awful attitude. Bret asked Niz for any hints as to what type of rhetoric could be used.

Niz was at a loss for words in this rare instance. They hadn't met because this president was a younger politician when Niz was retiring, and he could only guess.

After a moment, Niz said, "His reputation isn't good. He's stubborn, opinionated, and vengeful. He handles situations the opposite way that I would."

Niz had an impeccable reputation in the past. He felt it was all bad advice given to prior elected officials. The president was told not to listen to Niz. Now Niz quipped that this president's way was why the president was in such a mess politically.

Bret and Steve flew out to Philly. They were surprised at the amount of security at the airport and on the streets. There were soldiers everywhere with automatic weapons at their side.

Right away, there were difficulties. The GPS hadn't yet been updated with the locales of the new federal buildings. Most of the local population had no clue as to where the federal buildings were.

They were lucky they had a full day leeway. They drove in various directions. Each time, they were getting too close to the PRSSA borders and turned around.

Steve said, "This is crazy. Let's begin stopping in various commercial places. We can ask older people. They usually know everyone's business."

A few hours later, they still weren't having any luck until they stopped in a strip mall and saw a very old man sitting in front of a deli. It was a specialized deli with signs of sale items in the window—mortadella, soppressata, prosciutto, and braciole. They were hoping the owner could speak English.

Bret said, "Excuse me. Do you speak English?

"Better than you, Bub," the man said.

The man showed them an army cap with his unit number from when he was in the service. It turned out he was the owner and his sons were running the place.

He didn't know where any of the federal buildings were. They asked him if he knew where the White House was. He told them a couple of hundred miles south, referring to the old White House.

"I mean the new White House," Steve said.

"My sons can probably help. They had to go to the federal areas because this stupid president issued executive orders for new licenses, fees, the works. He's trying to dig up money any way he can."

Steve said, "I guess you don't like him."

The man laughed and said, "He can't count his coglioni and come up with the same number twice."

Steve started laughing. He knew the translation was a rude way of saying testicles. Bret looked confused, so they explained it.

The older guy asked why they wanted to go there. When Bret told him about his plight, the old guy had a disgusted look on his face.

"That's an infamnia," he said.

The man brought his new friends into the store and introduced them. Before they could ask any more questions, they were seated and given different samples of food.

"Try this conciato romano. It's imported and fifteen years old."

Steve took one whiff of the cheese and said, "It's older."

The old guy laughed and said, "I like you. Have some more."

One of the sons walked over with veal scaloppini, risotto, and polenta. The samples were more like a full meal. They enjoyed it just the same.

When they finally asked about the White House location, the son said, "You're going in the wrong direction. I'll tell you a shortcut. Just be aware the security is ridiculous with a lot of roads blocked."

Steve and Bret had full bellies and drove off. They arrived at a town near the new government buildings early the next morning. The traffic was terrible. When they eventually made it to the little town, the government had taken over; there was an immediate roadblock.

At the roadblock, they spoke to an officer. They said they had an appointment with the president. They were immediately asked for ID. They were given directions and had to pass through two more security checkpoints.

The temporary headquarters were nothing like the White House. It was unassuming. It was a good location. Was it being surrounded by high stone walls? It was easy to mount cameras and security personnel.

They were escorted to a large room that was full of people sitting in portable chairs. It was full of people. Bret and Steve were seated next to a standing secret service agent.

They began to worry if they wouldn't be called today. Steve looked up at the agent and wanted to know a few things. At first, he was ignored.

The agent then said, "We don't encourage communication between us. Not in the room, anyway."

Steve said, "I understand. I just want to know if the president will get to us today. There's a lot of people."

The agent said, "We'll cut people off outside very soon. Everyone here will get a chance today."

It seemed like years until they were called, but it finally happened and they were brought to an office. The president was seated and invited the secret service agent to leave.

The president said, "I'm very busy. What do you want?"

Steve said, "You know why we're here?

"Not a clue."

Steve was a little annoyed. He knew he should respect a man in that position. He still started getting abrupt because he wasn't feeling anything good was coming their way.

Bret said, "You didn't hear about my daughter's kidnapping out west?"

"I seem to remember hearing something. They took her across the border, I think."

"My daughter needs help."

"This involves three countries, none of which is mine. What do you expect?"

It seemed like a game of cat and mouse. It was pretty apparent that all parties present knew what the ultimate goal was. Yet the president seemed like he was playing a game. Still, Bret was hoping against hope.

Bret said, "We wanted to get your assistance."

The president said, "Why should I?"

Steve said, "The positive press will help you. Maybe you also just want to do the right thing."

"I'm listening."

Steve and Bret began to list suggestions. Some involved military interventions. Some involved negotiations. Some involved closer relations with the other nations that evolved as part of the partitioning.

"You want me to send the army?" the president chimed in. "Are you crazy? For sure, the PRSSA will think I'm siding with the CSA. You really want me in the soup."

Bret said, "All I want is dialogue."

"You sound like a decent man, whatever your name is. Nothing against you, but I'm going to direct my remarks to Steve." The president rose from his chair. He leaned over his desk while looking Steve straight in the eyes. "I hope the girl comes back unharmed, but the short answer is no. I will not lift a finger to help you or your father."

"What if it helps you—"

"I couldn't care less, and I'll tell you why. Your father is the reason I have ulcers. He was one of the main cogs of the secession."

Steve was shocked that it was even known. There were constant attempts to shroud the secession meetings in secrecy.

The president slammed his palm on the desk. "You're surprised I know about it? The fact is history is going to remember me as presiding over the destruction of the greatest civilization in the history of mankind."

"I'm sorry you hate my father. After all, he did help secure that land deal with Mexico."

"We have ports in Hawaii. The CSA needed this more than us. All this did was create stomach problems for me when I was trying to deal with the howling PRSSA. Did you ever think of that?"

"My father had peaceful coexistence in mind," Steve said.

"Is that so? Let me tell you something else about my future in the history annals. I will be remembered as the single worst president in the history of the USA. Now take your friend and get of here. You can go back to that island where you're hiding."

Steve and Bret were stunned. It wasn't common knowledge where they lived.

"You men look surprised. I was refused residence there. Can you imagine this for a sitting president? Now get out before I have you ejected."

When they left, both knew it would take a miracle to get the PRSSA involved.

"I guess we're fresh out of governments," Steve said.

Chapter 11

No help was coming from any official agency. Back at the ranch, concern was growing about Sam's failure to return. George always had a stoic manner, but his facial expressions gave it away. He was getting worried. He wouldn't wait much longer to organize a unit to go after Sam.

Bret and Ani were being boxed in regarding their decision-making process. It was becoming clearer they would have to attempt some sort of rescue.

Bret got a surprise when Nkuma walked over to him. He had just learned of the recent failures to get some kind of government intervention.

"I understand the PRSSA president won't see you. Why didn't you keep me in the loop?" Nkuma said.

Bret said, "I didn't think of it. We were trying to use Niz's old contacts to enlist some government help. The PRSSA wouldn't play ball."

"I believe I can get you in to see him," Nkuma said.

Years ago, the PRSSA president had been a volunteer for a peace effort in Nkuma's village. That part of coastal Africa was located in the heart of an area dominated by pirates. After Nkuma's father was murdered, both of them joined forces. They organized villagers and brought in some outside allies. The resulting violent confrontation rid the area of the pirates.

For a time, Nkuma and the now-president had become close friends. They eventually began to lose contact as Nkuma became disillusioned at his onetime friend becoming politically oriented. While nothing was ever official, Nkuma decided to sever ties with him.

Nkuma made a call. He insisted on getting word to the president using his name and asking for a meeting. It took very little time for the phone agent to say the meeting would be granted. He told the phone agent he would be bringing a friend, which didn't seem to be a problem.

Bret was elated. Now they could get the government of Lisa's present locale involved. Nkuma told him to temper his enthusiasm.

Nkuma said, "You have to realize something. Mutual acquaintances have told me he isn't the same man I knew. He's gone through some changes and not good ones. He's probably got an ulterior motive for seeing us."

There were no visual changes for New Africa since last time Bret had visited. Nkuma was surprised at the radical replacement away from European heritage, especially names.

Security was the same as everywhere else they'd visited. The only difference was this was the actual White House. The front was littered with soldiers. There were no traditional secret service people around. All guards and security personnel wore combat fatigues and carried automatic rifles.

They entered the White House and went to the registration desk. The attendant looked at Bret kind of strangely. The only people who normally met with this president were of African American ancestry as well as Caucasian or Asian diplomats and heads of state. People like Bret were usually unwelcome. Despite this, the attendant's demeanor was friendly.

When they finally got to see the president in his office, the president dismissed the guards and pressed his intercom button.

"I'm not to be disturbed."

He acted like a typical politician. He wore a giant smile. He shook hands. His grip was tight.

"Welcome, Nkuma, and a hearty welcome to your friend. Please sit down and have a drink with me to celebrate our reunion."

Nkuma's info was correct. The projection of a phony politician was almost nauseating. Nkuma and Bret still had to play the game even though it was apparent there was something going on besides a request to get Lisa released.

They initially spoke about philosophy, weather, and other benign topics. Nkuma started fidgeting in his chair, his straightforward personality finally getting the best of him.

Nkuma said, "We have to be honest with one another. We came for a reason. I suspect you have something to say to me too. Let's do that first."

The president said, "As usual, Nkuma, your forthright manner is refreshing. It's true I wanted to speak to you after all these years."

Bret asked if the others wanted him excused. Both responded he could stay in the room. He would try to keep quiet because he knew things might get tense.

"Nkuma, I haven't seen you in years. Yet I feel it's like yesterday."

"Let's cut to the chase."

"Fair enough. I need a strong-willed man like you. You're honest. You're intelligent. You're faithful. You check every box for someone in my administration. You will quickly make it up the line . . . Perhaps run for office as my VP, eventually."

"You have others. Why would you need me?"

"It's true. They just can't do for me what you can. When the going gets tough, I know I can turn to you."

"What if we disagreed? I fear your reaction would be very bad for me."

"Fear not. We can deal with that when the time comes. I would never harm you."

Nkuma thought for a moment. He was rolling things around in his mind. The president already played his cards—he was, sooner or later, going to sandbag his VP. Nkuma was suddenly ashamed for even considering it.

Nkuma said, "You know the way we both do things has diverged over the years. You would never be happy with my idealism. Frankly, I don't even agree with much of what you're doing in this new state," Nkuma said.

"I don't want you to be defensive, but I'd like to at least sell you the reason of what we're doing. The old USA had everything named after Anglo-Saxons or Native Americans. Perhaps a few from Asia. What do we get? Maybe a few streets with the name MLK? Now we are finally getting a piece of what we deserve."

"We've done okay economically."

"Come on, Nkuma. Forget about government programs. Outside of professional athletes and actors, how many Black people really make it up to the top rung of the corporate ladder? That's why a socialist redistribution program will give us what's rightfully ours."

"I hope my turning down your generous offer will not affect the reason why we came here," Nkuma said.

"I would've been happy if you accepted, but realistically, I expected your refusal. Now, how can I help you?"

"You're aware of my friend's daughter being abducted on NASA territory and being presently held in your country?"

"Of course I know. Those Purps have gotten out of hand. It seems you want me to get her released?"

"You're the highest official we can go to. Your word carries a lot of weight. Why not send an order to your VP? She's the governor of that state, after all."

"How little you comprehend about my stature in this."

"But I thought you—" Bret said.

"Listen for a moment. We are a fledgling nation. Some of this secession wasn't well thought-out. Our geographical border distances are too long. As such, I'm still trying to consolidate my power."

Bret and Nkuma were stunned at the frank admission of limited power. His statements made sense.

Nkuma said, "It sounds like you fear your VP."

"To a certain degree, I do. When the time is right, I will take her down."

"Can't you at least ask her to help us?" Bret said.

"I tell you what. As a favor to Nkuma, I'll call her now and see what can be done. If you could wait outside please."

The pair waited outside the office. They were called back in after only a few minutes.

"Her answers were vague," the president said. "She said she doesn't have power over the Purps. I'm not sure I believe her."

Bret said, "Do we have any chance?"

"She granted you a meeting in a couple of days. She said something strange though. I believe you have a friend named Steve? She wants him present at this meeting. Otherwise, it's canceled. I'm not sure what she has under her fingernails."

The results were not completely what Bret wanted, but it would engender some hope.

Chapter 12

The meeting with the PRSSA was a couple of days away. In that time, the family would try to be better prepared for what was to come. The biggest question was why the VP would request Steve's presence rather than just meeting with Bret alone.

One matter came to light. The VP's father used to be Niz's client. That had to be the circumstantial connection. The direct reason was still a matter of conjecture. Her father hadn't done business with Niz for many years and Steve had not done business with the VP nor had he ever met her.

A partial explanation was mired in a shadowy trial and imprisonment of her father. Even Niz wasn't able to determine the circumstances.

With all the intrigue, Sam's fate would play a large role in whatever future actions would be taken. Where was Sam?

Sam was still tracking Frank. In the days he was out, he never lost contact. Most people worry about loneliness. Sam never did. Nobody could explain how wild animals lost their fear when coming in contact with Sam.

Birds would perch near him. Squirrels would come close. The biggest shock was even dangerous predators never attacked when seeing him. As Sam searched, he would speak to the animals in as soft a voice as possible because he didn't know how far away his assailant was.

A separate compartment of Sam's saddle bag held some medical supplies such as disinfectants and antibiotics. He also had syringes. This would come in handy.

A mountain lion had been walking near Sam in plain sight since the first day. It didn't seem to be tracking him because it wasn't making an effort to stay hidden. There was no cat-and-mouse game.

Occasionally, she would be carrying a kitten in her mouth, not old enough to be considered a cub. Sam noticed it looked somewhat weak. It also appeared the mother was limping.

A few days in, Sam decided to try to make friends but kept his knife handy, just in case. He gave her a little food each day. Soon after, she finally allowed him to touch her. Being so close, he could see a deep gash and resulting infection.

Although Sam was an attorney, his tribal schooling gave him rudimentary medical knowledge. Even he was surprised when she allowed him to treat her and finally hold her kitten. A wild animal wasn't a pet, but she acted like one. After that, she would leave at times to hunt and nurse since her kitten wasn't weaned, and then she'd come back and resume her walking with him.

Over the following days, the kitten seemed to grow stronger. Sam surmised it was weak because the mother's injury prevented her from hunting and producing milk. They usually have a larger litter. Sam was pretty sure a male or other predator killed the other kittens. The mother was also getting stronger and disappearing for longer periods and became less dependent on Sam's care.

Sam finally decided to give the mountain lion a name. He made up a name. He called her Shmaska.

Sam tried to coordinate keeping track of Frank with being in touch with his new companion. Wherever they were headed, it became clear the Purp location was quite a distance.

Sam had been out over a week. He stopped by a mountain lake for some water. He saw a troop of mushrooms. He had been picking them since he was a child and could easily identify the good species. He went by the notion if you didn't know what it was, leave it. Today he was in luck; the mushrooms were chanterelles. Their shape and orange color gave them away.

Sam couldn't resist. They were considered some of the most expensive in the world. He sliced them at ground level so as not to disturb the underground network and began washing them in the lake. He envisioned a delicious feast later.

Sam suddenly stopped. He stood up and started looking all around.

He thought he heard voices in the distance. He was sure there was more than one. After a moment, he placed them. They were apparently coming from the other side of the small lake. He stood quietly as they seemed to be fading away.

Sam could have been imagining it. But with his penchant for discerning the sounds of the forest, he decided to mount his horse and ride on cautiously.

When he came to a fork, he had a decision to make. There were no tracks or other indicators that Frank had been there. He then looked closely at a small tree. There was a mark similar to an arrow that didn't seem natural. It was facing to the right which coincided with the direction he thought he heard the faint voices. He kept riding forward.

Sam finally came to a small clearing. As he looked down, his apprehension was confirmed. He saw enough hoofprints to know several horses were there recently.

Sam was torn. He recognized the possibility of danger ahead. He also was a man who always tried to do his best and his duty. He decided to proceed slowly.

He then came to another, slightly larger clearing. This one was different. At the opposite end were several mammoth boulders on each side of the trail. Each one was at least ten feet in diameter.

Sam said to himself, "That pass has ambush written all over it."

Knowing his odds, Sam started to turn his horse around. It was too late. Two men in purple shirts came out onto the trail from behind the trees. They had their guns pointed at Sam.

Two more appeared, surrounding Sam. One of the Purps motioned with his rifle for Sam to dismount. Sam had to comply. Escape was impossible.

A fifth man appeared from behind the huge boulders. He had no shirt. His skin was almost completely covered in tattoos. He was bald and wearing an eye patch. It was obviously Frank.

"You maybe thought my allies wouldn't come looking for me?"

Sam was silent.

Frank stared at Sam. He looked at Sam's long locks and high cheekbones. He recognized the stereotype. "An Injun? They sent an Injun after me?"

Sam held his tongue after the slur Frank threw at him. He wasn't going to take the bait. He would just listen to Frank's doggerel for the time being.

"What's wrong, Injun? Cat got your tongue? Maybe your ears are stuffed with tomahawks."

Determined not to mimic Frank, Sam decided it was a good time to start speaking. "I hear as well as you. My ethnicity is unimportant. I'm a man of peace," he said.

"A piece of what? You ain't number one, that's for sure. You look more like number two, if you know what I mean." The Purps laughed.

Sam spread his arms. It startled the Purps, and they pulled the bolts on their rifles.

"You can see I carry no weapons. You can tell your men to lower their guns."

"Enough of this garbage. Go look in his saddlebags."

One of the Purps went over and rummaged through the saddlebags. He displayed each item to Frank. The food and supplies, and the drug container.

"You a druggie?"

"Those are supplements and antibacterials."

The Purp pulled out Sam's knife. "You said you had no weapons. Yeah, right."

"I use that for cutting food and general chores. I've never used that on a person."

Frank was given a piece of food, took a bite of Sam's food, and spit it out. He took the rest and threw it to the ground and stepped on it. "This tastes like crap. I never ate anything like this. Maybe I stepped in it a few times."

It was time to attempt to converse about his reason for being there. He could see Frank was one step above a complete savage, but nonetheless, he would try to be logical. "I would like to negotiate the release of the girl."

"And what's in it for me?"

"Please tell me your terms. Everything is on the table. Money, food, drugs, you name it."

"With the release, who comes first, the chicken or the egg?"

Sam was trying to figure Frank's ultimate goal. It wasn't

going to be easy. He tried to give Frank his choice of which party upheld their end of the bargain first, but Frank was annoyed.

"The way this takes place doesn't depend on who's first. Either way, the result is your people shooting holes in me, and that ain't happening," Frank said.

"I'm willing to listen to any reasonable solution," Sam said.

While this tense conversation was taking place, Shmaska was watching in the distance. Her eyes were fixed on Sam. She hadn't seen a confrontation like this before.

Shmaska gave a very low growl along with a hiss. Both were inaudible at that distance. Her ears were pinned back. Her tail was shaking. What could she do against all the opposition? A cougar would normally run with the instinct for survival.

Frank abruptly cut off the negotiation. He walked away and walked back again. "You annoy me, Injun. You're going to be very sorry you put me through this trouble."

Back at the ranch, Bret and Ani were brainstorming with the friends. Suddenly, Wang rose and walked away. Everyone was perplexed. Bret got up and followed Wang.

Wang was known to have similar sensitivities to Sam. He attributed that to communicating with Chinese philosophers from the past several millennia.

Bret observed Wang had stopped and was facing the pasture and mountains in the distance. He was looking toward the route the kidnappers had taken and Sam was following.

"What's going on?" Bret asked.

"Sam. He was a peaceful idealist. He didn't understand the evil in the world. He thought reason could conquer all bad things. He could never grasp that there are wicked people who are barely human. He thought in terms of emotion. He never thought unfeeling beings existed," Wang said.

"Excuse me, my friend. Why are you speaking in the past tense?"

"Because when I look across those fields and pastures at the distant mountain range, I sense finality."

Chapter 13

Back in the town affectionately called DD, Rosa was working her usual massaging duties. She was more lethargic than normal. She felt a bit depressed.

Rosa was meeting Carol for lunch. Carol was a customs agent working on the north side. Carol wasn't even sure who her ultimate superiors were since there was some question about whether the area was in USA or CSA authority. But she was still getting paid in American dollars, which was all she cared about.

Carol was a single mother. She was middle-aged with short blondish hair. Her daughter had just lost her job because the restaurant she worked at went out of business. Carol's job was very important since she was the breadwinner of the family.

It was common for agents on both sides to cross the border socially. They all knew each other and had a cordial relationship. Many crossed the border just to have dinner at each other's houses as friendships developed.

Carol would take her daughter on shopping trips to DD. It was of the utmost importance to spend quality time together and continue bonding. She went frequently, and all the agents on both sides knew her daughter.

It wasn't unusual for Carol to have lunch quite regularly in DD. She loved the cantinas. Rosa had asked to meet her for lunch. Carol wondered if something was going on because they always met by chance, not appointment.

After they met and sat down at the table, Carol immediately

noticed something was off. Rosa was quiet. She would speak in yes and no answers.

Carol said, "All right now. Why the long face?"

"I miss Stevie."

"Who is Stevie?"

"He comes many times."

Carol started thinking. Rosa was describing Steve's outward appearance in detail. Rosa knew every detail right down to the way he combed his hair. It finally dawned on Carol.

"Oh, that mystery man?"

"Why do you call him that?"

"He's the only person since I've been working here who has a free pass to both countries. He's very unique."

"He says he's not married."

"Are you sure?"

"I think yes. He never use my body. Sometimes he just give me dinero because I no have enough to eat."

Carol wanted to let Rosa down slowly. She was sure it was just puppy love. The reality was a rich man and poor prostitute didn't end up together.

Rosa was insistent. "I want to see him."

"Hold the phone. I've been hearing rumors."

"What?"

"I've heard he's somewhere up north on some kind of ranch. It sounds like there's big trouble and the government is involved—"

"Stevie in trouble? I will give anyone who hurts my Stevie a low haircut." Rosa ran her index finger across her throat.

If Rosa got out of control, that would be a disaster for everybody.

"Calm down," Carol said. "Maybe he'll come visit soon."

"No. I got to get to my Stevie. He need me."

"How are you going to do that?"

"I cross the border. Maybe coyote take me."

Now Carol was smirking and shaking her head. This wasn't going anywhere good.

"Listen, sweetie. You'll most likely get arrested. Even if you don't, you have no money for a coyote. The last group they brought back had people saying they paid the coyote six thousand dollars each. By the way, haven't you heard people are dying from the heat in back of their trucks?"

"Maybe you can help me?"

"I'd lose my job for sure, Rosa. Then they'll lock me up and throw away the key. I need this job."

"I am sorry. You are nice. I don't want to hurt you. I'll think of a different way to get to other side."

Now Carol began to feel guilty. She had a rough stage in her life where she felt nobody cared about her. She began to think. Lunch was over, and Rosa got up to leave.

"Rosa, wait. I have an idea. I don't know why I'm doing this. I suppose it's time someone cut you a break. You know that quiet street around the corner? Tomorrow's my day off, so meet me there tomorrow at noon. Wear the same exact clothes. Pack a piece of luggage. Take everything you need because I think there's a good chance you won't be coming back."

After a big hug, they parted. Carol spent the rest of her workday planning. It was a simple plan, but her daughter would need to be involved and would have to approve.

Carol got home later and sat down with her daughter. She started telling her about Rosa's life. Carol emphasized there was really nothing in DD for her. Her chances at a better life there were almost nonexistent. Carol's plan was to temporarily swap places with Rosa.

Carol said, "You like Rosa, don't you?"

"Of course I do. Maybe there's a way I can help her."

"You hit the nail on the head. It's not legal. Are you okay with it?"

"Don't be silly. This is exciting. No matter what happens, we have each other. What's the plan?"

Carol would hide her wig under the car seat. It was pretty close to her daughter's hair color. Her daughter would wear a white top and blue jeans. Carol put her sun hat with the oversized brim in the car They would take two cars. The more Carol described it, the more excited her daughter got.

"This is like secret agent stuff. I love it."

Late the next morning, they drove toward the border. Carol's daughter followed, both cars turning into the large parking lot right near customs. They used Carol's car with them both in the front seat. They reached the checkpoint, and the Mexican agent immediately recognized Carol.

"Hi, Carol. Doing some shopping today?"

"No better way to spend my day off."

They were quickly waved through. When they were out of the view of customs, Carol dropped her daughter off at one of the blocks of stores. After buying something small, the bag would be visible. This would show the border guard that something was actually purchased.

After shopping for a bit, her daughter would cross the border at the walkthrough location. With a completely different group of agents, albeit knowing her, she would be waved through with no suspicions. Then she would casually return to her car and drive home.

Rosa was waiting down a side street with a piece of rolling luggage. The location was sparsely used and exactly where Carol wanted her. Her garb was exactly what Carol wanted. There were only a handful of people on the street, and they all seemed to be tourists.

Carol opened the trunk. Rosa threw her luggage in and then sat down in the passenger seat. Carol handed Rosa the wig and told her to put it on right away. Then she handed Rosa the hat with the giant brim on. Rosa had to lean back and to the side while covering her face with the huge brim. Rosa had to mimic being asleep. If there was no suspicion, it was unlikely someone would disturb a sleeping person. It helped that Rosa's body type was close to the daughter's.

They started driving to the border. As the car approached, Carol could see the man at the booth was one of her workmates. He waved and greeted Carol with a big smile.

"Hey, Carol. How's your day going?"

"It's nothing special. Anything wild today, like gun runners or something?

"Oh, sure," he said, smiling. "It's so crazy today, I might just take a siesta right here in the booth. Then again, my snoring might wake everyone else up." After a quick chuckle, he bent down to look through Carol's window.

Carol was getting a little nervous. Would he want to get a closer look at her passenger, even though he knew Carol's daughter was a frequent visitor?

He suddenly laughed. "I guess she's all shopped out. These young folks today don't have our stamina."

"Tell me about it," Carol said.

The agent waved them through. They drove away. That was a narrow one.

Once they were at a safe distance, Carol exhaled. "Okay, you can get up now," she said.

Rosa sat up.

"Open the glove compartment," Carol said.

Rosa opened the glove compartment. Inside was an envelope.

"Take that envelope out. It's for you."

"You're giving me something? I'm not good enough."

"Don't be humble. There's a bus ticket in there. There's also some money. It's should be enough for you to have food for a while."

"Where am I going?"

"The city is on the ticket. It's about one thousand miles north of here. It should leave you somewhere in relative proximity to your friend. I can help you no further. You'll be on your own."

They pulled into the bus station. Carol parked and walked Rosa to the terminal. They both had tears in their eyes as they hugged.

"I love you, Carol. I never forget what you do for me."

"Same here. I hope you never forget me. Come visit me someday."

"If Rosa stop running and become citizen someday, I promise I see you again."

They said goodbye, and Rosa walked toward the bus. Carol ran after her. She was now in a full-blown sob. She hugged Rosa once again, but tighter.

"Listen to me, Rosa. If you get married and become a citizen someday in the future . . ." Carol caught herself. "Never mind, it's not important."

"Bus is leaving. Tell me quick." Rosa wasn't having any of that.

"I beg you, Rosa. When you have a happier life with a citizenship, husband, and children, please come get me. Please take me with you."

Rosa licked her index finger and made an *X* on Carol's forehead. "That is mark of protection. I protect you forever."

Chapter 14

Niz had been doing his homework on the PRSSA VP. He discussed his findings with Bret and Steve before they left to meet with her. There were more questions than answers.

The biggest concern was why she wanted Steve present. He theoretically had little to do with the situation. They knew the VP's father had done business with Niz. But that was many years ago and Steve had never met her.

Most of the information they discovered was through the old contacts who were no longer active in politics. They weren't very kind in their descriptions. The VP had her father imprisoned for specious reasons. In reality, they found out he disinherited her and left his estate to her sister. Her sister was described as a kind soul who tried to help her family. The VP was a problem child who only thought of herself. Her sister told them she remembered the VP saying she wished she had died.

Added to all this, the VP was known as a pathological liar. She only respected people who were beautiful, important, or wealthy.

Niz said, "I've heard she'll try to come off as your best friend. Don't forget she's vicious and cunning. Count your fingers after you shake hands. Anyone who would do such a thing to her own father . . ."

"Timing is important. Debating is useless. I would hope the VP will give me a simple yes or no," Bret said.

"She wouldn't see you if she didn't want something. That's

the mystery," Niz said.

"I have almost nothing to give. I live on a distant island. I have modest means," Bret said.

Niz's last words were a warning for Steve to be especially careful. "She has the eye of the tiger for younger men," Niz warned Steve.

When Bret and Steve arrived in the city, they found the building where she was headquartered. It was about six stories and quite plain in light of her having a dual role as both governor and VP.

The security was different than the other places they visited previously. There were no military or suited guards. But there were several uniformed police officers walking around in front of the building.

When they went inside, there were also two officers at the reception desk and two more at the elevator. After being announced, they rode to the top floor. The lobby area had several antique chairs and sofas.

Steve said, "I recognize some of those pieces. They're expensive antiques. I suppose she really does have an eye for money."

They weren't waiting long when a fairly young man walked in from behind a closed door. He was tall with light blond hair. He had a darker tan, like he spent hours in direct sunlight. From behind his tight-fitting suit, it was clear he was muscular. His smile and pearly white teeth looked more like a model's than a political person's.

"I'm the VP's senior advisor. Please come with me."

Steve whispered to Bret, "Looks more like a beach bum to me."

He led them into a spacious office. The VP was sitting

behind her desk. She rose to greet her visitors. She was well dressed with a slightly stocky build.

"So I finally get to meet Steve," she said, correctly guessing who was who. "We know you're here to discuss Bret's plight. You're probably aware my father did a lot of business with your father years ago."

Steve said, "So I've heard."

"Then you've heard what a terrible person I am for locking him up."

"I judge people as I meet them."

"Don't give me that junk. Let me tell you what kind of father he was before you canonize him. When I was growing up, he was never there. He was, at best, a part-time father. He never even hugged me."

Bret said, "A lack of love is a terrible feeling."

"I'll tell you more. When I was six years old, I sat next to him. I asked him if we could talk . . . maybe a fairy tale or something. You know what he said?"

"I haven't got the foggiest idea," Steve said.

"He said, 'We have nothing to talk about. Go away. When you grow up, then we can talk about something.'"

Bret said, "In that respect, I feel very sorry for you. A child must always feel loved."

Bret and Steve weren't going to change the subject. They deemed it best to let her go at her own pace. She was candid about her father but not about her own personality flaws.

"Enough about my father. My advisor is just here as an observer. Everything you say should be directed toward me. Correct me if I'm wrong. You're here concerning the girl that was kidnapped by the Purps."

"My daughter," Bret said.

"And you want me to do something about it?"

Bret said, "Now that you mention it—"

"Don't be coy with me. I assume you want me to ride in like a knight on a white horse and demand her release."

Steve said, "We thought since they have the same political leanings as you—"

"Let me stop you right there. You know nothing about this group, the Purps. They are not socialists, communists, capitalists, or have any other political ideology. They're a mélange of criminals, mentally deranged people, and other antisocial types. They really have little value for life other than their own. I don't even know what they want out of life."

"I thought this was your bailiwick. You certainly have the might," Bret said.

"And what if they say no?"

"Can't you threaten them with arrest? You said they value their own lives."

"Oh, Bret. You really can't see the forest for the trees."

The VP rolled her chair back and got up. She turned around and walked toward the window behind her desk. It was an expansive window. She motioned with her finger for the guests to join her at the window.

"Now look down there." She pointed when they joined her at the window.

It was lunchtime, and there were crowds of people walking around. The street pointed out what was a main drag and had many cars. Across the street was a park with trees, walkways, and benches.

"Tell me something, gentlemen. How many people do

you see?"

Steve said, "I see hundreds. Including the park, maybe one thousand."

"What if I told you at least ten percent of those people were either Purp supporters or downright members? Many people buy in to their drivel. Some are well meaning like me. I'm a socialist who wants a better life for the downtrodden. They're just scum."

Bret said, "So you're saying that affects your decision-making?"

"If I went after the Purps, I would be placing a giant bulls-eye on my forehead and my back. I would likely be assassinated within a month."

"It sounds like you won't help me," Bret said.

"I didn't say that."

"I thought you wouldn't use your authority."

"I didn't say that either." The VP started explaining the reality of the situation. A show of force would likely mean Lisa's death, not to mention the VP's. "The Purps don't negotiate. They enjoy blood. I'm sorry to tell you this, but the only way to rescue your daughter is by raising some sort of guerilla force."

Bret said, "I thought of that, but I wouldn't even know where to begin."

"It gets worse. I hope you're aware of the tensions between the CSA and my country. Our military is everywhere. You couldn't get ten miles across the border without getting cut to pieces."

"Are you saying we would need a large-scale force to conduct this operation? That's like a war," Steve said.

"I'm saying the opposite. I can't permit such an incursion,

but I might be persuaded to allow a smaller force."

Steve said, "Can you expand on the so-called small force?"

"Let's say a maximum of one hundred personnel and lightly armed only. I mean no armor, no heavy machine guns, and no aircraft of any kind."

"But you said your army would cut us up," Bret said.

"What if I told you I would order our military to give you a free pass to reach your destination?"

Bret said, "Why are you being so benevolent? Why do I think there's a catch?"

"You're very perceptive." The VP opened one of her desk drawers. She pulled out a folder with papers inside. "I'm not benevolent. This is going to cost you. The top page is a summary, and the other pages have the details."

She handed Bret the folder. He started looking at the top page and put his palm on the side of his head. His eyes were open wide.

Her demands were astounding. The demands were broken down into cash, gold, silver, numismatics, and other collectibles. She gave the amounts of each cash transaction and instructions for which of various offshore banks the funds would be deposited to, along with their alias names and account numbers. The papers in the folder made everything clear.

"I don't have anything near this amount of money."

"Then get it," the VP said. "I want fifty percent within seventy-two hours. I want the rest upon completion of your mission, when your daughter is in your hands."

Bret was depressed. He would have given everything he had to get Lisa back. Steve asked Bret to look at the folder. His eyes moved up and down as he looked through the information. It looked like he was doing mental calculations.

"Eight figures is a lot of money, but okay," Steve said.

For Steve, it was as simple as that. The amount was a drop in the bucket for him. This was why this cunning VP insisted on Steve's presence.

"I'll make the transfer of the first half as soon as we get back to the ranch. My financial people will be informed with instructions when we leave you now. The second half will be transferred when we get back with the girl when we return to the ranch," Steve said.

The VP immediately frowned. She started pointing her finger at Steve. "Oh no, you won't. You'll have the second half ready as soon as you leave on your mission. When the girl is in your hands, you'll immediately make a call and get the transfers done. Those are my terms. Take it or leave it."

They had no choice but to accept her terms. Steve's nose was itching once again. They weren't thinking about the difficulty of putting a rescue together. For now, they just had some hope.

As they left and entered the elevator, Bret thought he saw a flash from behind. He turned quickly. There was nothing there. He thought he saw that haunting image, but it was gone too soon. All he made out was something shaking its head.

The VP was still in her office with her advisor. He was surprised she would do anything for capitalists, even with gaining a monetary reward. She kissed him passionately.

"I can't comprehend why you're helping them. You seem agitated. I'm worried about your blood pressure," the advisor said.

"I'm not worried about my blood pressure," the VP said. "I'm worried about my bank account. Who says I'm helping them? You're a smart man, but you still haven't learned how to cope with the big picture. Let's go back a bit, shall we? That president on the other coast used me to get votes. He never liked or wanted me. Right now, he's planning on getting rid of me either by political blackballing or worse."

"I don't understand the connection with the kidnapping," the advisor said.

"Stay with me. Even if I survive, my political career will be ruined. Since my father skunked me, I'll be out on the street starting over. This is besides losing you."

"I wouldn't—"

The VP said, "Stop with the charade. You aren't with me because of my looks. When the man upstairs gave out beauty, he was out to lunch for me. You're only with me because of my power."

"Why are you hurting me?" he said.

"Forget it for a sec. Let's get back to the subject. That money is a nest egg for us. I can gracefully leave. Do you think Steve and Bret are the only ones who can hide on an island? The president won't care as long as we're out."

"I see what you're implying."

She said, "That money ensures you won't leave me. You won't have your looks forever."

"I'm sorry you doubt my love, but I still wouldn't help them."

She said, "You're not a good listener. I said I would let them get to their destination. I said nothing about returning."

"It depends on who wins the battle for you to succeed," he said.

"No it doesn't. When the battle is over, we will turn our troops on the winner and annihilate anyone left on either side."

"And the Purps here locally?"

"Word will get back that the invaders killed them and our heroic forces tried to save them. We'll be heroes and even the CSA won't say boo because of their provocation."

"You're such a schemer. Anyone who tangles with you has it coming. I guess that's why I love you. But what about the girl?" he said.

"Who cares? She's small potatoes."

Chapter 15

George would take his binoculars and look out toward the mountains several times each day. He was gradually losing his stoic manner. His concern for Sam became more overt. He knew Sam would try to send a message with any news. The only possibility was the bad signal that phones had in this area. Even satellite phones would be dead in spots.

Bret and Steve had returned to the ranch and gathered the group together to start brainstorming. Bret and Ani still held out the slight hope that Sam could come back with good news. But they knew the chances were slim due to the excessive time Sam had been away. George waited in his room and moped.

Bret was outside by the picnic tables and saw the foreman running toward him. He had almost a panicked look on his face. "One of my hands just called. They have a badly injured man strapped to a horse. They're bringing him in now."

Everyone had their binoculars watching for the arrival. Bret and company immediately left to meet the returners near the corral. They spread a blanket on the ground. The hands gently removed the man and laid him down.

It was Sam. He was barely recognizable with all the cuts, bruises, and swelling. He was mumbling incoherently. He was delirious.

Alex and Lana worked feverishly. Lana had a lot of experience with trauma cases. She spoke in Russian to Alex. Alex looked at Bret. He clenched his lips and slowly shook his head.

The prognosis was clear. There were massive internal injuries and likely a fractured skull.

Bret tried to be tender while asking Sam what happened. Nobody could understand what he was trying to say.

"No, Shmaska. Get away."

Bret looked up and said, "What's a Shmaska?"

"Save Shmaska. Don't. No, no, no. Please, Frank."

George arrived. He was out of breath after running out as soon as he'd heard. He was closely trailed by the other two chiefs. He looked at Sam and took a moment to catch his breath. He finally spoke in his usual calm way. "Who did this to you?"

At this point, Sam's voice was only a whisper. He was very weak. He at least was able to imply Frank did the damage.

"No, Frank. Save Shmaska." Sam said.

George said, "Shmaska has been dead for many years, Sam. Your pet cat died when you were a child. Please hang on. Try to think."

It was no use. Sam expired. His eyes were open, and Lana gently closed them.

George finally lost his composure. He dropped to his knees and covered his face, sobbing. "My son. My only son. Look how that evil man butchered you. Please join your mother above and tell her I'll be joining both of you after my unfinished tasks. Maple Sapling, Flint, and the Sky Woman will protect you."

Everyone was stunned, including the chiefs. George had never told anyone on his business trips that in addition to Sam being his lawyer, he was also his son.

Red Hawk told every person present to please leave. Chengua would join him in taking care of George. When they walked away, George regained his composure. Having been widowed,

George was left to do everything on his own.

"I will make arrangements to have my son brought back east. I want his funeral to take place near his home. Now I have to make a call."

George called Jack, his law partner. Jack was more than an attorney to George and Sam. When Jack was a child, his parents were killed in an automobile accident. He had no living relatives. With Jack being the same age as Sam, George and his wife decided to take Jack in and raise him. They thought it would be good for Sam to have a permanent playmate.

Sam and Jack did everything together. They went to law school together. They even dated sisters. Being related through marriage would have been a dream. Alas, it would never happen.

When George informed Jack of Sam's death, he was met with stunned silence. Then Jack began to cry.

George said, "Take a moment and then please pull yourself together. Braves don't act that way. I need your help."

"Anything. You know that."

George asked Jack to make funeral arrangements. He then described the circumstances of Sam's death. Once again, Jack was silent for a moment. Then he reacted.

"Give me two weeks. I will attack with one thousand men—"

"Stop. You're letting your emotions cloud your judgement. This isn't the wild west. Revenge, if any, will be conducted on my terms and my time frame. We're limited in how many we send. We don't want to start a war."

George gave Jack all the details of the circumstances that led to Sam's death. He elaborated on the kidnapping and his role in a possible rescue attempt.

"Now that my son's spirit is in the other world, the girl's

survival and rescue is paramount. You can help."

"Just name it."

"That archery club you belong to uses long bows and practices often?"

"Correct."

"Weren't several of them in the US Army mountain division and trained for such terrain?"

"Yes, and they are expert marksmen."

"I suspect part of the rescue will involve near-silent actions. Long bows aren't practical here. Can they use crossbows effectively?"

"They can pick their teeth with them."

"Would they be willing to join us in the task at hand?"

"You don't even have to ask. You're a legend among our people. There isn't one of them who wouldn't lay down his life for you."

While George and Jack were talking, Bret was meeting with all his friends from the mountain. They all respected Ani as well. The circumstances had changed. It seemed the VP was right. It was becoming apparent a more aggressive approach would be necessary.

Wang had correctly predicted a bad ending to Sam's journey. He was the first to speak. He liked to quote ancient Chinese philosophers. "It may have been a long time ago," he summarized, "but what this man said holds true today. The translation is roughly that you cannot win a civilized war with savages. You must meet fire with fire. They must be met with the same cruelty."

Bret was a pacifist, but after seeing Sam, he understood well. Everyone there were amateurs for conducting the likely violent events to come.

Ani spoke about the need for mercenaries. Bret was cautious. He read that mercenaries were not easily controllable, their loyalty was questionable, and their adaptability didn't always work.

Bret said, "We don't have any trustworthy leaders with the correct background."

"What's plan B?" Ani asked.

There was no answer. Getting trustworthy people with fighting experience was a daunting task. This group almost needed idealists.

Wang said, "I can start. There are friends who illegally came here from China. They settled in the Chinatown section of San Francisco. I trust them one hundred percent."

This piqued Bret's and Ani's interest. The question was their ability to fight.

Wang smiled at his answer. "They were part of special military units in the PLA. They were sent to various areas to deal with supposed counterrevolutionaries. My friends could no longer take the death and destruction."

Wang's friends recently had a severe issue. The PRSSA became close to China. As such, they agreed to start returning those who came illegally. Wang's friends kept in contact. Wang had medically treated their families when they were all young.

Now that the process of return had started, they decided to flee California. They were heading east.

"Right now, they're temporarily not far from here. They would be happy to join us. Fighting evil is now in their blood," Wang said.

Perhaps their numbers were only a handful, but that was a start. It started a chain reaction.

Most of Bret's friends from the mountain had a similar beginning in their medical field, albeit in different areas of the world. As young doctors, they would go to poverty-stricken villages and offer their services for free. This was especially true in areas stricken with a potentially deadly epidemic.

Before the group continued expressing ideas for Lisa's rescue and contributing personnel, Ani excused herself. She made a phone call and started walking toward the airport.

Alex said they couldn't offer personnel. The only ones available were the Russian mob guys presently at the ranch, and he didn't recommend them.

He did offer some chemicals he developed while working in a lab for his native land. His lab had been charged with making substances for espionage purposes, and he had managed to smuggle out some samples.

One was a severely debilitating laxative. Another was a deadly poison. Once it entered the bloodstream, the heart would stop in three seconds.

As each friend spoke, it became perfectly clear that Bret would have to go with each one to potentially fetch the future guerillas. He wanted to make sure they were acceptable for such a dangerous rescue.

Carlos said he thought he could help, but it would be tricky. His idea was to get some indigenous Amazonian men known as Shuars. The conquistadors called them Jivaros because of their fierceness. When Bret asked how fierce, Carlos spoke about their success in fighting off invaders for hundreds of years, including the conquistadors.

Some of the Jivaros, including Carlos's friends, remained either isolated or semi-isolated. Over time, they adopted some modern ways, along with using some modern materials. In other ways, they were still quite primitive. Bret and Carlos would have to fly to South America to enlist them.

Nkuma also had some friends. They were much closer, living in Virginia. Bret would have his own problems there. They disliked anyone of European extraction and were still citizens of their various African countries. They too had problems. They were enemies of the PRSSA president, and being so close to the capital was hazardous for them. The one saving area was that Virginia was still part of the USA. The PRSSA would be in a bad position if they attempted harm on USA soil.

Nkuma hoped he could convince them to join if they met Bret. They were temporarily living in the USA and part of a worldwide network of cells who were waiting to be called to overthrow the tyrannical despots leading their nations.

Hans wondered if there was any interest in bringing forth some knights.

"This isn't the crusades. I didn't realize there were knights left in Germany," Bret said.

"They're not in Germany. You and I will be flying to Latvia," Hans said.

Hans had gained everyone's interest. He was speaking about the Brotherhood of Blackheads. They were at least six centuries old. For centuries, they were defenders against invading armies such as the Muscovites.

They were mainly wealthy merchants. As such, they were able to practice fighting all the time. When they wore their armor and displayed their swords, nobody wanted to fight them.

"To this day, they have strict rules. You're fined for cursing at a fellow member and fined a larger amount for striking him,"

Hans explained.

Pramesh also had a group in mind. He wondered if anyone was familiar with the Gurkhas. They'd fought for years in special units of the British army even though they were from the Nepalese region.

"They're pretty good, huh?" Bret said.

"The Brits say if someone says they're not afraid to die, they're either lying or they're a Gurkha," Pramesh said.

Bret thought it would be quite a long trip to Nepal. Pramesh allayed his trepidations. He said they were retired from the British army and had settled in England.

If all these small groups were brought together, Bret envisioned a formidable force. Unfortunately, their numbers would still be far short of the one hundred the VP had said she would allow. This was important, as Bret had no idea of the Purp strength.

Bret wondered how to organize such a diverse group, let alone devise a workable plan. He thought it best to go step by step in light of the clock ticking on Lisa's life.

Bret was holding out hope that the daily interrogations of the captured Purps would yield some assistance with finding where Lisa was being held, along with info pertinent to the Purps.

He walked away from his friends and started looking for Ani. Steve was sitting with Bret, so he didn't know either. He asked everyone he could see without results.

She wasn't in her room. She wasn't near the corral. He wondered if she took a walk in the pasture, but the binoculars yielded no results. The fact was, she was gone.

Bret knew Ani was too level-headed to try a rescue on her

own. Besides, the horses were all accounted for. The only way would be if she were to sprout wings and fly away.

Bret discovered he was partially right when he saw Niz.

"Did you see Ani?" he asked.

"She commandeered one of the jets and said she was going to get some help."

Bret noticed Niz was upset about something. He had a tear in his eye. He started thinking. He had been so wrapped up in the events, he realized he hadn't seen Essi since he returned from the meeting with the VP.

"What's wrong? Is it Mom?" Bret said.

"Yes. Your mom suffered a stroke. I guess this Lisa business was too much for her."

"Is she okay?"

"Yes, she's resting comfortably in a hospital not too far away."

Now Bret had another problem. He wanted to go see his mom in the hospital.

Niz hugged Bret and said, "Take stock of the situation. Time is running out on Lisa. You have to take care of that first. If your mom sees you, she might get more upset and have another stroke. I think she'll be okay and released soon. I'll fly her right back to the island."

The pressure was finally starting to get to Bret. As the expression went, "Laugh and the world laughs with you. Cry and you cry alone."

Bret went back to his room and had a good cry.

Chapter 16

The mystery of where Ani disappeared to was solved when she called after her jet had landed. She had flown to Long Island to speak to an acquaintance she hadn't seen in years. She decided not to fly into the five boroughs as there was news of the continued turmoil she had seen when they were there. There were also reports of constant harassment of airport passengers.

The man she wanted to see previously lived in Queens and now resided east of there in Suffolk County. He had had no qualms about inviting her to his new home. He was known as Bags, which was short for Money Bags, owing to his frugality. He was a rising star in his family and was now promoted to caporegime, which gave him substantial power and influence.

His present place in the upper middle-class part of the area was easy to identify. The color and style of his Mediterranean home stood out among the standard colonials in the neighborhood.

Off-white stone fencing with balusters and balustrades surrounded the home. The home itself was a similar light-colored brick. There were religious statues in front.

Bags had previously explained to Ani why so many Italians had similar homes with so much masonry and less wood. He told her that wood was sparse in Sicily and that's why so many immigrants from there were masons by trade.

Bags's wife answered the door and hugged Ani. She met Ani years ago when Ani was invited to their previous home. They developed a bond when Ani spoke about her time growing up in an orphanage and treated Ani like a daughter.

Both Bags and his wife had been upset when Ani spoke about the pedophile director abusing some of the girls at the orphanage. Thankfully he never touched Ani because he was afraid of her fighting back. She told them that he was the cause of the death of her closest friend and how she named her daughter after her.

Bags labeled it an infamnia to Ani. Bags used the terminology quite often. Shortly after that, the former director died under questionable circumstance while he was in prison. Bags and his wife had been upset back when Ani told them of the director's actions years ago.

Bags walked down the stairs while still buttoning his shirt. He was very informal with Ani. After they hugged, she noticed the dining room table was set.

Ani said, "I'm so sorry. I didn't know you were having company."

Bags said, "We're having some people over. My wife already set a place for you. You're never a bother. She's making enough food to feed an army."

His wife retreated to the kitchen, and he invited Ani to sit with him. He already sensed Ani had a problem. Ani reminded him of his promise to go to him if she ever needed help.

"You need some dough? That's no problem."

"It's a little complex."

Ani proceeded to give Bags details of the kidnapping. He listened intently.

"It sounds like you need some muscle."

"Well now, that you mentioned it . . ."

"I'll see how many buttons I can spare. Go help my wife, and I'll make some calls."

Ani was a little concerned that Bags would be discussing something as illegal as using buttons on the phone. She knew a button did hits. When she expressed her concern, he waved his hand dismissively.

"They haven't tapped La Cosa Nostra phones in years. Except for our system of justice, we're in legitimate businesses now. They have their hands full with the Russian, Latino, and Chinese mafias."

"What about the buttons?"

"They're happy when we clean out the bad blood. The only reason they ever bothered us was money related. I mean gambling, unions, drugs. It's always about money with the lousy government."

Ani was somewhat relieved. She went to the kitchen and was immediately overcome by the smell of food. It was intoxicating.

Ani said, "I could gain ten pounds just by the aroma."

"Have a seat and pour yourself some wine. The bottles are uncorked. I'm letting the reds breathe for a bit."

Ani saw four bottles of the finest Italian red wines. There was a Barolo, Barbaresco, Brunello, and Amarone. Ani had a weakness for Brunello and poured half a glass. "I feel terrible not helping. Isn't there something I can do?"

"The veal, meatballs, and sausage are all in the oven. The tomato sauce is cooking on the stove as well as the Marsala and Sorrentina sauces."

"There must be something I can do?"

"I tell you what. There's three boxes of pastries in the

refrigerator along with a couple of cakes. You can put them on the large plates over there on the counter."

"Of course."

"While you're at it, here's a cup of tomato sauce with a spoon and some slices of semolina bread. I know you like seeded Italian bread."

One thing Ani had learned was the Italians had a habit of spreading tomato sauce on Italian bread and snacking on it. She busied herself and made sure she didn't eat too much of the bread. She didn't want to get too full to enjoy the main meal and dessert.

Ani couldn't believe the assortment of desserts. She saw sfogliatelle, pasta ciotti, pasta cross, rum baba, and cannoli. If that wasn't enough, she saw a pizza di grano and a special large cake.

"Is this what I think it is?"

"Yes, it's zuppa inglese. The bakeries don't want to make it anymore because it's too much work. It took me two days. The Strega makes it heavenly," Bags's wife said.

In between the work, Bags's wife was snacking on a rum baba. She cut a piece and brought it to Ani.

"It's too much for me. Try some."

Ani had a little. "Wow. That's powerful. I'm glad they put some baba in the rum."

After a short while, Bags summoned Ani. There was still plenty of time before the company would arrive. They sat down, and Bags scribbled some notes on a piece of paper and handed it to Ani.

"Don't worry. I'll burn this when you leave."

Bags had written the names of the team he assembled.

She looked over the list. Ani was still worried. There were so many things that could go wrong. "I know I shouldn't ask questions, but my daughter's life is at stake. Would it be okay to know a little about these folks?"

"Sure, ask away. Don't be ashamed to reject anyone. You'll notice I went outside the family some. They're not all Italian, but I think they're what you need."

"I don't know how to say this. What if someone gets out of hand?"

"It won't happen. They all report to the Kid.

"Someone so young?"

"You're funny. He's not young. He owns funeral homes, so we call him Kid Horizontal. They wouldn't dare go against the consigliere, or they would have to deal with the pezzonovante."

"That's a relief."

"I'm telling you, they're all almost choir boys. None of them will turn a saint upside down."

Ani noticed some familiar names from her vending machine days. She recognized Dinny, DS, and Mr. Low. She sort of remembered Froggy because he walked with a hop.

"I see Sally the Shiv. A woman?"

"Salvatore. He's good with a knife in case you have some close-in disagreements. He can draw and hit dead center at ten feet before someone can raise their gun."

"Sammy the Spider?"

"We call him that because his last name is Webb."

She kept looking through the list. "Okay, I'll bite. Who is Bootintheass?"

"He's Pat Murphy, the cop."

Murph was originally a city cop. For unknown reasons, he

decided to transfer to the transit police. He was given one job and one job only. That was to guard an aircraft hangar at the international airport, which affectionately became known as Murph's turf.

In the old days, Murphy would chase kids away when they were up to mischief in a place they shouldn't be. He would always say, "Get out of here, or I'll give you a boot in the ass."

Kids always greeted him by saying, "Hi, Officer Bootin-theass."

Ani smiled at the story but kept her eyes on the list. "I'm not sure how Sonny the Sailor is pertinent," she said next. "We're not going near any large bodies of water."

"He got that from always going to Little Neck Bay and stealing boats. Nobody knows why. He never robbed banks or nothing. He just loved stealing boats."

"Voila Vinny?"

"He blew a safe once while the department store was still open. He hid the loot inside a TV. He walked out carrying the TV and told security the TV belonged to him. He got the name because he made money disappear."

"I'm not sure I like this one. His name is Gooey."

"He was out of the sun for a while. He behaves better now. Let's just say he did things with his hands the church didn't approve of."

"He went to jail for that?"

"Nah. In his stupid days, he robbed a bank. He was a guard. When there was a shortage, they would bring the tellers in the back room away from the vault. It would be open because the bank was closed at the end of the day. In those days, there was a direct line to the FBI inside the vault. He sneaked in with a hatchet and chopped out the phone line."

"How could he get away with that?"

"He didn't. They locked him up and threw away the key."

Ani came to the last two names. She was surprised at their ethnicity and background. It seemed contraindicated. "Goniff Goldstein. I never heard a first name like that."

Goniff was a Yiddish word for a thief or a crook. He was a doctor for the railroad. When someone was lazy and didn't want to work, they would go to Goldie.

He would look in medical books for diseases that hadn't afflicted people for hundreds of years. Sometimes he would make up names for diseases that hadn't been invented yet.

"He sometimes does me favors. He knows how to use a syringe effectively," Bags said.

"I think I read about this last guy, Arson Abe. Didn't he once burn his own place down?"

Abe Levy owned a large variety store with a warehouse behind it. The complex had an area where everything was attached like a strip mall.

People would see Abe pull up at night and load his truck. Everyone thought he was making deliveries. He was really just emptying out his inventory. He then torched the place.

The insurance payment would have been substantial. There was a snag. He had so many fire code violations that the insurance company wouldn't have paid a dime. This was exacerbated by his getting fined several times during inspections.

Abe was a brilliant manipulator of fire. He was an expert at fooling fire inspectors.

In this case, he broke into the adjoining supermarket. He was able to make the fire look like faulty wiring in their freezer section. Their freezers were only a short distance away from the wall adjoining the two stores. There was still enough space to make it easy for the fire marshal to determine that was the origin.

Abe was able to funnel the fire through the wall, up the shaft into Abe's crawl space, and down the shaft to his store and warehouse. With fast-disappearing accelerants, the building was destroyed before the fire department knew what hit. Abe got hit with some heavy fines, but the insurance payout was enormous.

"This is a nice story, but why would I want to use a guy that could burn down half of the Pacific Northwest?" Ani said.

"Because he's not a pyromaniac. He's a professional arsonist. He knows how to marginalize fires. He even invented a substance that will put itself and nearby burning areas out."

"Even so, are you sure these last two Jewish guys are a good fit for this job? The fighting might get pretty hairy."

"Fear not, Ani. These two are battle-hardened veterans of the wars in the Middle East. They can accomplish what you need quickly and efficiently."

Ani couldn't say no to any of Bags's suggestions. She did have a concern, though. "I don't think I have enough money to pay their fees."

"The money isn't your concern. I'll take care of it. This is a contingency. They don't have a contract." Bags reached into his pocket. He brought out a fistful of folded currency. The wad was several inches thick. He handed it to Ani.

"I can't accept that from you," she said, waving her hand at the money. "You've helped me so much already."

"There's six big ones here. You know better than to say no to me. Let's just say it's a rescue gift for your daughter."

Chapter 17

Bret was flying with Nkuma to a small airfield in northern Virginia. They wanted to recruit some of Nkuma's friends. It was a rural area not too close to the PRSSA. They would be going to an African cultural festival.

There were merchant tents as far as the eye could see. Several stages were constructed for entertainment by musicians and dancers. It had a separate field for the very popular battle reenactments.

Nkuma was strangely quiet on the trip. Bret could see his mind was churning. Bret finally wanted things out in the open.

"There are several things you need to know. Getting assistance from these people is no slam dunk," Nkuma said.

Bret would play along with any request from his buddy. He was all ears.

"You've never asked me why I always refer to the continent rather than individual countries. It's because we identify with our heritage. Our people spread across several countries. We have what you would call a chief or king, and he is our leader. When not speaking English, we speak a Bantu language. That's why we are Africans, not identifying with any nation," Nkuma said.

"Thanks for telling me that. I always want to show the proper respect for people."

"The man we are seeing is the king. He is exiled here. The big caveat for you is his not being particularly thrilled with helping a Caucasian. We'll see how it goes."

Nkuma invited Bret to walk the grounds and enjoy the festival. While Bret did that, he would make contact with the pertinent people and set the meeting for when the day's festivities closed at the end of the day.

They separated, and Bret began walking the multiple rows. He enjoyed meeting the various merchants. They were all from overseas. He found their accents and manner of speaking refreshing.

Bret didn't feel out of place. The visitors were all different races. He became more and more curious about the goings-on as he walked. There was weaving, crafts, pottery, and woodwork.

It wasn't a surprise that the tents that attracted the most male crowds were those with the weapons. A fearsome-looking man in one of the tents was dressed as a traditional warrior. His face was painted with chalk and red ochre.

He stopped Bret and said, "Come in. I'll give you a good deal on an iklwa."

Bret had no idea what an iklwa was. The man pulled out what looked like a spear. It had a broad steel blade and a wooden shaft.

"If you buy one, my wife will decorate your face for free."

"It's okay. I'll pass on that. I'll just take the spear," Bret said.

Bret was a little self-conscious as people would look at him carrying the spear and giggle. But it was worth it; it would be a great decoration for his house.

Aside from the refreshment stands, Bret wished he had time to stop in every tent. There were so many things he hadn't experienced before. The common thread was everyone was more than friendly.

He stopped by a place where a woman was selling herbals. He didn't even try to pronounce some of the item signs. Bret was curious. "Do these have Western equivalent plants?"

"Very few. Most of these do not grow outside my continent. Some have a chemical analysis unlike anything else in the world," the woman said.

"I assume they have medical benefits as opposed to food uses?"

"That's not my field. You can probably find some of them in the food tents. They're not as pure as mine. I can cure many illnesses."

"I see you have one locked up," Bret said, pointing over to a cabinet with a glass window.

"It's very rare. I have used it both topically and internally to cure cancer. Governments have resisted on both sides of the ocean. I was warned by a pharmaceutical company to stop. They can't use it because it's natural and can't be patented."

"So it's just for show?"

"I can sell you some. But it comes with a warning that it's merely a food additive with no medical benefits, et cetera."

Bret was getting eager to purchase something. He had visited very few sellers and already was carrying several purchases. Fortunately, the woman gave him a large shopping bag.

Bret was limiting his eating of the traditional food. Their taste was so different from what he was used to.

Now that he had a large shopping bag, he had room for other purchases. He walked by another booth and saw an ornate basket he thought Ani would love. He knew she wanted something to display flowers on the kitchen table. He bought it.

He saw another tent with a crowd. The worker inside was

making and selling pottery. He loved knickknacks from other lands on some shelving in his personal den. Another purchase.

As he kept walking, Bret finally realized people would constantly meet him in front of their tents and try to entice him in.

One woman put some beads around his neck. "That's for a man. Come in, and I'll give you a bargain on a fancy one for your girlfriend or wife."

Bret couldn't resist. He spent hours looking and buying. He was carrying two large shopping bags and a spear when Nkuma finally located him and smiled.

"It looks like you bought everything in this fair. Why don't you leave something for other visitors to buy?"

"I have to admit, my arms are getting tired," Bret said.

"Give me a bag, and we'll put everything in the car. Then we must sit and talk. We have some issues."

"We're not meeting with your friends?"

"We are. There are just other problems."

"Not that Caucasian issue, I hope."

"Unrelated to you."

During the time when Nkuma was growing up, he lived in a poor village. His family was so poverty-stricken, he never had a toy to play with.

Nkuma studied hard to hopefully work and put himself through college. His big break came when he received an offer to attend medical school in England at no cost. He thought it was an excellent opportunity to help his family.

After med school, he returned to his village being overrun by pirates. His father was an idealist. Although he had nothing, he wouldn't give in and was executed. Nkuma joined other young men and fled to the jungle. They were determined to rid the area of this scourge.

There were skirmishes, and the pirates found themselves in an untenable position, so they left. At great cost, the village was finally free. It took several months, but it was worth it.

As the village was rebuilt, Nkuma felt one great shortage was medical equipment. So he joined two others in forming such a company. They would work on both sides of the Atlantic.

Each person took on a specific role. One was a fellow villager who would handle sales in Africa. Nkuma would handle USA sales, and the third was an American of the same heritage who volunteered in Nkuma's village. He would run the daily operations, especially finances.

They hit the jackpot when the company received a grant of $75,000 from the US government. Being a grant and not a loan, it was free money.

It didn't take long, however, before they were unable to pay for their medical equipment costs. The money dried up, and the money trail was unknown.

The blame game began. Nkuma was forgiving and was convinced the American had just made bad investments. The villager accused the other of stealing the money.

"That's when I met you, Bret," Nkuma said.

"It's a sad story. I'm glad we're friends.

"It doesn't end there. We will meet later with the villager partner. He's my king. Our relations were tenuous for a time, but we smoothed things over. You know the third guy."

"I don't know many Africans. Who is he?"

"He's sitting in the White House."

That explained why they were enemies. Nkuma thought his friend would be in danger being so close to the capital.

"They won't touch my king as long as he's in the USA. It would be a fatal mistake, and the president knows it."

Bret said, "So there's others here with him?"

There were several others at the festival. They were part of a worldwide network of cells. They were waiting for the call. Once they had enough power, they would go back and overthrow the wicked rulers in several countries. They envisioned a mass revolution like the world had never seen.

"That's quite a story. Your personal relationships are okay?"

"From the business, yes. Now, there's another situation. There's a woman," Nkuma said.

Being the same age and from the same village, she was an inseparable playmate of Nkuma's during childhood. They did everything together. She grew to be one of the top models in Africa. She was tall and slim. They thought they would be married someday.

Bret said, "It wasn't to be?"

When Nkuma came back from medical school, she had changed. Her father never thought Nkuma was good enough. Her fame also spoiled her. She developed an eye for opulence. She was seeing the young king. She believed her fortune and the queen title were the ultimate achievements in life. She even joined the revolution.

"While she's still part of the revolution, her king is no longer a love interest. They have a platonic relationship. She's here today," Nkuma said.

"You think she could help in getting my daughter back?"

"It's hard to say. Frankly, it will be awkward when I see. I'm afraid my disdain may cause me to use the wrong words."

"Can we have our talk with him without her?"

"Impossible. She's always by his side."

"Okay, let's see how things play out. That seems to be all that we can do."

"I agree. There are just too many variables to cover every contingency."

They decided to relax a bit and watch the battle, which was the last event of the day. All the visitors were anxious about this.

They got to the area where the battle would take place. The people participating in the battle were decorated in face and body paint and wore headbands.

"If I get into a barroom brawl, I want those guys on my side," Bret remarked.

"Well, you know some of them are in this cell. I'll introduce you. I think they can scare the heck out of the Purps . . . especially if they dress this way."

The battle they were about to see was a reenactment of a battle between the Zulus and Xhosas. Bret asked about the yelling. Most charging during a war had men giving high-pitched screams.

When the reenactment started, the men started yelling in a very low-pitched yell that sounded like they were saying "Oooooh."

"What is that yelling?" Bret asked Nkuma.

"They are yelling a word in our Bantu language. It means death."

Even though the battle was a reenactment, they used real blades. One attempted slash got too close and injured the recipient. The man was bleeding and shaking his hand. He retired for medical attention.

Soon, the battle was over, and it was time to go to the

king's tent. Nkuma had briefed the king earlier in the day. It was an oversized tent, and there were several men along with the woman Nkuma had spoken to Bret about. She immediately hugged Nkuma, but he didn't return her hug. He merely put his hands on her waist.

She whispered in his ear, "I love you."

Nkuma whispered back, "Ours is a love that can never be."

She released with a shocked look in her eyes.

"Shall we get to the subject at hand? I believe everyone is aware of the situation." Nkuma spoke abruptly.

The king looked at Bret. "I trust Nkuma has informed you of my hesitancy to help people of your ilk," the king said somewhat dismissively.

"He is a special man. His daughter is only a child. Do you not have any feelings? At one time, you would lay your life down for a child," Nkuma said.

"He may be special, but he's Caucasian."

Bret was getting more angry than nervous. "Listen to me, Black man. I bleed red blood just like you. Our internal organs are the same. If we don't learn to live together today, there will be no tomorrow."

"Okay, listen to me, White man. Centuries ago, the Europeans came to Africa. With them, they brought darkness. They stole our people, possessions, and our natural resources."

"That was then—"

"It's no different today," the king said, cutting Bret off. "The only change is their putting Black pimps in charge to do their dirty work for them. It's no change whatsoever."

Nkuma said, "This debate is going nowhere. I would like to make a procedural point. You used to have a solid, logical mind.

If you can't comprehend the validity of what I'm about to say, then I will take my friend and leave peacefully. I dare say I will most likely die helping my friend."

"Please make your point."

"I see your men acting like heroes out there by putting on an act. You're not even close to readiness for a real battle. Try going into a battle with those Marxist troops in Africa. They'll eat you up and spit you out. This may be your only chance to get some real experience."

The king was quiet for a moment. "I appreciate your comment. I must ponder."

The woman had been silent. Now she unexpectedly interjected. Her voice was fraught with emotion. "How dare you reject one of your subjects?" she said, pointing her finger at the king. "Nkuma has been loyally on your side your entire life. He even supported you when that stupid business went bad. He sent that wicked man in the White House packing. If you refuse to help, I'll lose all respect for you. I will take a gun and go help Nkuma myself."

Her speech sealed the deal. Another handful of fighters were coming west.

Chapter 18

Bret's group of helping rescuers was growing. He was still far short of the number allowed by the PRSSA VP, and he needed all the help he could get. He now had two stops to make in Europe. The first was with Pramesh in England. When Bret was done there, he would call on Hans to join him in Latvia.

There were the usual problems when he arrived in England. Pramesh lost touch with his Gurkha friends. He knew their last location was a small town heading north toward the Scottish border.

The town would be easy to recognize. The streets were lined with Indian and Pakistani stores. Pramesh's friends had served in the army with a unit populated with nationals from these countries.

After their service, the Gurkhas couldn't go home. Their places had been overrun by China. They were fortunate enough to get their families out. The other Gurkha convinced these Gurkhas they would be accepted in this English village.

"That thing you said about people lying if they say they're afraid to die unless they're a Gurkha . . . what about loyalty? I understand they're fierce," Bret said.

"They're well known for that," Pramesh said. "There's another tale that mentions a Gurkha and an employer. If a Gurkha works for you and you ask him to stand in one place, he will still be standing there twenty-four hours later."

They entered the town and parked. They walked around

the main street looking for an indication of the whereabouts of Pramesh's friends. There were more shops than they expected so they started asking people if they knew who they were looking for.

Nobody seemed to know. Pramesh finally started describing their looks by running his fingers across his eyelids. He was indicating their smaller eyes, which were more akin to people from the Far East.

One man acknowledged the description. He actually nodded and pointed to the end of the main street.

"You mean the knife guys. Go to the end and turn right. You'll see their office and factory."

It sounded like the Gurkhas were the owners. This surprised Pramesh. They entered a small lobby and spoke to the receptionist. She asked if we had an appointment.

"Just tell the owner Pramesh is here."

She picked up the phone. She spoke with someone and hung up, looking surprised. "He said to tell you to sit down and don't move."

The door to the back area had a glass pane. They could see the owner coming. He wasn't walking. He was trotting. The greeting was just as eager as his gait.

"I'm so happy to see you, Pramesh."

There would have to be some allotted time for reminiscing. Bret resigned himself to enduring the personal small talk as they sat in the lobby.

"I'm a bit surprised at the size of your operation. How did this happen?" Pramesh said.

When Pramesh's friend came to England from the army, he needed a job. That was before settling in this town. He went to an employment agency. After speaking with the agent, the man went in an office. The door was left open.

"I heard him speaking on the phone. It was shocking when he told the other person he could hire me because I wasn't too dark. I felt so bad."

The head Gurkha spoke about it to his old army friends. They received about the same treatment. He suggested they go into their own business to succeed here. The other Gurkhas didn't know what to do.

"I had little else besides my clothes and my kukri," the owner said.

Bret said, "I'm sorry to interrupt. What is a kukri?"

"It's something between a knife and a machete. I'll show you."

He drew his kukri from the scabbard on his hip. It was relatively long with a wide blade and a bend in the middle, almost looking like a human arm.

"I carry it with me. It is not quite legal, but the Brits don't bother me."

A few days after Pramesh's friend discussed the job rejection with his friends, a man saw the kukri and offered to buy it. It wasn't for sale. He asked if there were any others. The head Ghurka's friends had several. The man directed him to go to a local gun and knife show scheduled in a few days.

Even with a high price point, the kukris sold out in a matter of minutes. Since the Gurkhas knew how to make the knives, they bought a small forge. They couldn't sell them fast enough.

The Gurkha was then approached by someone who had an import/export business. He not only wanted to finance a factory for mass production of kukri knives, but he also wanted to manufacture other items such as the special Gurkha pants, useful in both hot and cold weather.

"So here we are. Everybody in this building is family and friends," Pramesh's friend said.

Bret and Pramesh were extremely impressed with the success story.

The Gurkha looked at his cell phone and checked the time. "I'm meeting a Pakistani friend for lunch. He just moved to this town. In his younger years, he was captain of the world champion field hockey team. Why don't you join us? I think you'll enjoy the stories of his travels."

They all met at an Indian restaurant on the main drag. The waiter took one look at the Pakistani and ran in the back. He came out with the owner and the chef, both of whom were carrying cameras. Between the pictures and autographs, the food was flowing. The owner never expected to meet such a celebrity. Naturally, there would be no charge for lunch.

Bret asked the player about his experiences. During his time, India and Pakistan were the top two teams in the world. The political differences didn't matter. Both teams were friends.

During the world championships one year, India lost in the quarterfinals to an inferior team from Germany. He knew something was wrong.

The player said, "I went to the Indian captain and asked what happened. He said the German coach sent a bunch of hookers the night before and kept the Indian team awake all night. I told my coach about what happened, and the night before the finals, the hookers showed up again, but the coach was waiting and sent them away. We won."

"So those shenanigans really do happen in professional sport, huh," Bret said.

"The German captain was so angry, he swung his stick and hit me across the bridge of my nose. Look at my scar."

Bret now understood when the Gurkha spoke about the interesting stories that Pramesh had alluded to. He was anticipating the next one.

"Things got serious with Russia. My prime minister was crazy for field hockey and set up a three-game exhibition to secure friendly relations."

"I didn't know they even played field hockey there," Pramesh said.

"There were pretty bad. I was ordered to lose one game and tie one game. We were allowed to win one."

Bret said, "That's really hard to do."

"I had to play so poorly, the newspapers back home printed I was drunk during the game. My father even called me and asked what the hell I did. I told him I had the flu," the player said.

"That's quite a story," Bret said.

"It didn't end there. In the Moscow hotel, I woke up in the middle of the night. I smelled a flowery odor. There was a bouquet of roses on the table. It wasn't there when I went to sleep. The Russian captain told me it was someone who didn't deliver on time and was probably afraid of getting in trouble. He just used a passkey or a secret entrance."

As they spoke, the player even made a funny reference to an overweight dictator in Africa. Estimates were he weighed about four hundred pounds. He invited the team to dinner after a match.

"You know how big a leg of lamb is? He ate three of them by himself," the player said.

Bret asked if he had ever been to America. He told him he would be welcome.

"The Americans offered me to coach the national women's team. I would never teach anyone our techniques. Even the coach has no say when the match starts. The captain is in charge during the match."

Lunch was over, and Bret, Pramesh, and his friend headed back to the company. The owner gave them a factory tour first. Some of the kukris were made in mass production. The very expensive ones were handmade over a forge.

The clothing machines were fed by these massive spools. They saw a box with some shirts and pants.

"What are those?" Bret asked, pointing to a box with some shirts and pants.

"Those are rejects. We get a lot of money for our pieces, and quality control is very important to us," Pramesh's friend said.

"What happens to the rejects?"

"We donate them or sell them at shows as second quality. People love discounts."

Bret and Pramesh were surprised at the shoemaking operation. It was an odd combination of manufactured products.

"Our shoes are a little different. Nobody wanted to make them to our specs without killing our profit margin. So we make them ourselves."

They passed by a huge bank-like walk-in vault. The owner said they should go inside.

"You might be wondering why we need something like this. We make special kukris for the wealthiest people. The vault contains gold, silver, diamonds, emeralds, rubies, and sapphires."

The owner opened the vault. There were several cabinets

with small drawers, which contained the gemstones. Larger drawers held precious metals. There were also a few kukris with obvious gold handles.

There was one kukri that stood out. It was hanging on the wall and had a variety of gemstones on it, including some very large diamonds. The handle was made from precious metals.

The Gurkha said, "I see you looking at this elaborate one. There's a lot of platinum besides the gold and silver in the handle."

"I can't imagine the value of this," Pramesh said.

"It's priceless. There is only one other kukri like it in the world."

The royal family commissioned this as a gift to the late queen. The Gurkha was picked up in a limousine and driven to the palace, where he personally presented it to her.

"It must've been an honor. Did you feel uncomfortable?" Bret said.

"Why would I? She was my queen."

Finally, the three men went back to the office to discuss the real reason for today's visit.

Pramesh explained what happened. "I was hoping you could offer my friend some assistance. Now that I see you're cranking this operation day and night, I hesitate because it would mean taking time off."

"You're right that we keep the operation going almost twenty-four seven. People have been working six and sometimes seven days. I was actually thinking of closing down for a short time to give everyone a break," the owner said.

Bret said, "This would be no picnic. It might be harder and more dangerous. That's no vacation."

The Gurkha directed Pramesh to his door and pointed toward someone. He had his shirt off and was quite muscular.

"Do you remember when you came to my village during the epidemic? There was a young child. He was puny and almost dead. The sickness almost ate him alive. He was my son. That's him standing over there."

Pramesh did remember. He marveled at what the child had become.

"You saved my son's life, and please don't think for a minute I'll say no."

"What about the others?" Bret said.

"You don't understand Gurkhas. They all still have army fever. It may sound gruesome, but they still thirst for battle. Any or all of them will be happy to join you."

Bret looked at the wall. It was full of medals. Pramesh had already told Bret that Gurkhas were the most decorated minority in the army. No matter how much the heat was turned up, the Gurkhas' numbers could not be fazed.

Chapter 19

Bret and Hans flew into the Riga airport in Latvia. They were going to meet an old friend of Hans's. He was quite elderly. The man was good with languages, speaking Latvian, Russian, German, and Lithuanian in addition to being fluent in English.

Hans was giving a little background of the Black Heads to Bret. He already spoke about their founding six centuries ago to protect against invaders. They morphed into an organization of knights and swearing to do righteous things. That's why Hans was hoping to enlist some of them.

"How do you know so much about them?" Bret said.

"Haven't you guessed? I'm one of them," Hans said.

Bret was a little confused since Hans was not Latvian. There were some Black Heads in Estonia and Lithuania. When the Soviets took over, they made the Black Heads illegal, and many fled to Germany. When the Soviets fell, many of the children and grandchildren came back.

The two men met with Hans's friend. Bret thought he looked somewhat frail. They shared their situation. The man told them it was too early in the day to meet with his people. He would spend the extra time giving Bret and Hans a tour of the city.

He was widowed but wanted to speak of the experiences both he and his wife had when Latvia was still part of the Soviet Union. Bret had a thirst for knowledge, especially that which wasn't broadly reported.

As they toured around, the first thing Bret noticed was the number of places that were boarded up. It seemed the economy wasn't so good.

Hans's friend said, "We had a population of three million in Latvia, with one million in Riga. They officially say there's one million in the whole country. I believe they're lying. There's maybe sixty thousand. Even the president said that at this rate, Latvia will cease to exist in twenty years. I hear there's a deal brewing to carve up Latvia between Russia and Germany. The big sticking point is a place on the coast called Ventspils. It was a Soviet naval base, and they want it back."

He spoke about the difficulties under the Soviets. His father was a German POW, and after World War II, Stalin called the POWs traitors and put them in labor camps. His father was sent to Vorkuta, which was above the Arctic Circle.

"My mother moved there to be with him," he continued. "She worked a plow just to survive."

They strode past a four-story building. It appeared to be a college as young people carrying books were coming and going.

Hans's friend said, "That's the Riga Polytechnic Institute. Both my wife and I went there. I wanted optics, and she wanted to be a doctor, but the Soviets needed structural engineers. The ministry sent people here.

"She used to run from work to the lecture hall with no time to eat. She would sit next to a nice Ukrainian man. He would open his attaché case toward the professor so he couldn't see inside. There was always a half sandwich he would save for her.

"Behind them sat three females. They were ethnic Russians. They constantly made fun of both of them because she was a Jew and he spoke Russian with a heavy accent. He was so soft-spoken that they didn't realize he worked at the ministry and was plenty dirty.

"He turned to my wife and unemotionally said, 'Do you want them to be away?' My wife asked what he meant, to which he said, 'I mean, do you them to not exist?'

"My wife understood and, of course, said no. The Soviets would send a car, and nobody would ever see them again. Their families could say nothing."

"Was he kidding?" Bret said.

"In the Soviet Union, you never, ever kidded like that. This was serious."

Bret nodded and was quiet.

"She was so smart," Hans's friend continued, smiling as he spoke of his wife. "She should've won the gold medal in middle school. I believe you call it valedictorian in high school. They forced her to voluntarily lower a class grade. They did this because she was a Jew. They handed all females flowers at graduation. She refused to take hers."

"Religious problems?"

"Here, it was a nationality, not a religion. Her internal passport was stamped JEW under nationality." Hans's friend paused for a moment, before continuing. "When she was seven, she couldn't eat lunch at school. She would have to run home to give her father an injection. He was a handicapped wounded war veteran."

"What about her mother?"

"She was working double shifts at her job, sixteen hours a day. Her father only got a seven-rubles-a-month military pension. It wasn't even enough to buy some bread and meat. When my wife was eight, she went to the dentist. At that time, they used a low-speed drill and had no anesthetic. She was screaming."

"Crying from the pain?" Bret said.

"She wasn't crying. She was screaming at him because he wasn't doing what she told him to do. Can you imagine an eight-year-old child today trying to teach a dentist how to work?"

They passed the Black Head building, which was now a museum. Hans's friend showed Bret the bottom stone. It was so old it was somewhat sunken into the ground. The Black Head's patron saint was Saint Maurice, a Black Egyptian.

The man then told a story that made Bret sick to his stomach. Her mother and handicapped father had to run away because the war was raging. Her mother had just had a baby son. They ran to middle Asia, but there was no food. So her mother dried up, and her baby brother starved to death. Her father had to bury him on the side of the road like a dog.

"These are the realities your newspapers didn't print," the man said.

They walked a little further. All were silent for a few moments.

"My wife was also very talented," the man continued, lightening the mood. "They wanted to send her to Moscow to vocal school because her voice was so good. But she refused with the excuse she had to help her parents. The real reason was they wanted the students to sing Soviet patriotic songs, and she didn't want to do that. She was also athletic, a speed skater."

They walked past another building that had been a railroad repair center. "She worked here," the man told Bret. "The inside actually had an open area several stories high so locomotives could be hoisted for the repairs."

Railroads were a bigger deal there in the Soviet Union than in Western countries. Everything about railroads was controlled by the military. It was illegal for a map to even show the location of railroad stations.

"Any trouble?" Bret said.

"The real trouble was with the architects. I was in the same situation when I designed bomb shelters. The engineers and architects never got along."

"I would think they wanted the same thing."

"Architects thought about beauty. We thought about practicality and what actually worked."

He told Bret about a time when his wife designed moveable stairs to work on various parts of the train. The architect wanted to close the sides because they said it was too ugly. She countered that the trains couldn't be worked on if the sides were open. The workers had to be able to extend their arms.

Their argument got heated, and they went to the director. That was a very high position, and you had to be well-placed in the government.

"Who won?" Bret said.

The director was annoyed, and his response to the architect was quite blunt. The answer was clear. He wanted the open stairs. The director had said, "What do you want next? Do you want to put flowerpots on the electric meters?"

That gave Bret and Hans a chuckle. Bret was enjoying his education.

"Were her friends like her?" asked Bret.

"It's strange you ask that. She only had three close girlfriends. She never wanted friends like this because she hated the government. Their families were heavily involved with the government.

But things just happen in life.

"My wife brought her first friend home as a child. Her father recognized her and asked, 'Is she the one we see on the military parade stand?'"

It turned out her friend's grandfather was the first president of Soviet Latvia. Her father wasn't happy, but what could he do?

The second friend's father was a colonel in the army. High-ranking officers held a special prestige there. The father was always nice to the daughter's friends, except he constantly told them to never talk to anyone outside of their apartment. More than most, it seemed both civilians and army personnel feared him.

Out of fear, nobody spoke about the second friend's father. It was clear he was either a KGB or GRU agent.

The third friend of Hans's friend's wife was an idealist, always building communism. When she grew up, she worked in the records department in the personnel office in Riga. Even a collaborator couldn't hold a job like that. She was definitely one of theirs.

The third friend was an ethnic Russian. After the Soviet breakup, the Latvians did not treat ethnic Russians well. When she went to apply for her pension, the truth came out. The woman in the pension area said the third friend was code 12 and that was KGB."

"It is strange how my wife cared for her friends, yet they all stood for everything she hated."

They walked over toward the train station. The man said they would take the train to the last stop.

"I wanted to stop by the sea, but the beach is still closed because the Russians were dumping nuclear waste and some of the barrels started leaking."

On the train, the city soon became countryside. It was completely flat with just forest trees and fields.

Bret noticed a small house next to the forest. It was all alone, with no other structures in view. "Who lives there?" Bret asked.

"It's the man who takes care of the forest. He's not what you call a ranger."

Hans's friend told Bret that starting with the Soviets and later the Latvians, the man was given the job of keeping the forest clean. The man would clean out the twigs, leaves, and anything else on the ground. If the trees were too dense, he would cut them down. In Soviet times, he was allowed to grow crops for himself on the property.

"That's why you have forest fires in America. We have never had one. The only problem was once when a cat lynx jumped out of a tree and bit a man on the neck and killed him. The Soviets sent in the army and exterminated every last one of them."

They were nearing the end of the line when they passed by a large memorial with flowers around it. Bret was curious and asked the man about it.

"That's honoring the largest three-day mass murder in the war. Twenty thousand were killed and not with gas. They were shot. My wife discovered the site in the forest, but someone else took credit."

There was a group of about forty people who went to look. Even though the Germans did the slaughter, the Soviets wouldn't allow it because they officially said it was Soviet soldiers murdered. The truth was many were children.

"As is typical with Latvia, it was cold, windy, and rainy.

Everyone went home except my wife, her father, a former soldier who thought he saw the massacre during the war, and another man. My wife was only fourteen.

"After spreading out and walking through the forest for a time, she sunk in mud to her ankles and flopped into a hole. It was one hundred meters wide. She was surrounded by all the bones."

The man took out his wallet and showed Bret a picture. It was a shovel stuck in the ground. There was a child's skull sitting on top of the shovel.

Bret wondered who took credit for finding the site. It seemed like such an important event.

"It was a woman in charge who went home because it was too cold to look. Many of the people from that group were arrested. Her phony excuse was she dropped the list on the train and the KGB found it. She later went to Israel and founded the Soviet-Israeli friendship committee. She was obviously a collaborator."

"That's quite a story," Bret said.

"There's more. The head of the group said in her autobiography that she found the site by following some highly unusual flowers. My wife made those flowers out of cloth to mark the area."

They reached the end of the line and hopped off the train. There was nothing but forest.

Bret said, "Where are we going now?"

"Into the forest we go. Our destination is a castle."

Bret was asking about a castle hidden in a forest. It seemed unusual to him.

"There are many such castles in forests all over Europe.

Children often find the ruins when they are playing in the woods."

After about a half mile, they approached their destination. The castle was anything but ruins.

"Our brotherhood restored it after the Soviet breakup. Unfortunately, the twentieth century has taken its toll. Each generation of children and grandchildren lose interest. We don't have many Black Head descendants left."

They were met at the gate by a smiling man. It was a shocking scene from the Middle Ages. He was wearing a suit of armor, complete with a sword, and carrying a helmet.

They were escorted into a room where a group of middle-aged men were seated. Younger men stood in the back, lining the wall. They too were in armor but standing at ease.

Bret was happy to see all the young men spoke English, unlike their fathers who were seated. The young ones greeted Bret in English. Bret would keep quiet as this meeting would have coded speech. There was always concern about spies being present.

Hans and his friend spoke in Latvian to the men. There was some noncommittal gesturing and talking.

After some time, Hans looked at Bret and said, "It looks like they want to go along with us. The young ones are eager to see a battle."

"They aren't in the military?"

"They hate governments and politics of any kind. You might call them anarchists, in a good way. They side with none, be they fascists, communists, or any other political entity. Their saving grace is they do what they think is right. That's their oath."

"This sounds too easy," Bret said.

Hans said, "You're clairvoyant. They do have a strange request."

"As long as they take orders, I'll be very lenient."

"Along with automatic weapons, they want to go into battle wearing their armor."

"So do they wear flak jackets under their breastplates?"

"They do."

Bret thought for a moment about their request. He then smiled.

Bret said, "Imagine the fear in those Purps when they see these guys coming at them with swords drawn along with their rifles. Tell them I'm in with their desire."

Chapter 20

The rescuer force was growing. Bret's last recruitment trip was going to be with Carlos. Bret was hesitant. There were more questions than answers on this one. There was concern for introducing, what Carlos referred to as, South American Indians to Western civilization.

During Bret's other trips, Ani was trying to figure out the details of what the rescue force would be up against. So little was known, but Ani did her best figuring out the probabilities.

Ani assumed they weren't likely to hold Lisa in any kind of city. It was too dangerous with too many intermingled enemies. The same went for suburbs and even small towns.

She theorized they were holed up in a small enclave that was defensible against any group except an army. She also thought Lisa was too valuable a hostage for them to do serious harm to.

Looking strictly at numbers, they were still far short of the limits imposed by the VP. That also played an important part of her thoughts.

"We need enough personnel to essentially surround wherever this enclave is. At the same time, we can prevent them from sneaking Lisa out," Ani said to Bret as they were going over whether they had enough people and the right types.

"What does this tell you now?" Bret said.

"Carlos is waiting by the jet. I say we try to recruit that batch of South American Indians. We need more people. If they ultimately prove unsuitable, we can leave them behind."

"I studied them a little while you were away. They can walk almost silently in the woods. We may be able to use them to sneak up on our opponents. Now, get going," she said, motioning to him that it was time to leave.

Carlos tried to give Bret some background during the flight. The conquistadors called them the Jivaro tribe. They referred to themselves as the Shuar people.

Some had had contact with the European descendants. Many had not. This particular tribe was seminomadic. They still made structures for homes, and they had adopted a few Western ways.

"Don't be surprised if you see a few shotguns," Carlos said. "That's their weapon of choice for battles against neighboring tribes."

"Don't they hunt with those?"

"The shotguns are too noisy. In the jungle, they still prefer blowguns."

Bret looked at some pictures of the tribe that Carlos brought. Their dress was almost a contradiction. Some of their clothing was quite colorful and some simple and primitive.

The tribe used some pots and pans that Carlos brought to them years ago. Their pottery was also European as Carlos showed pictures to Bret.

"They speak no English. A few speak Portuguese or Spanish. Mainly, they speak their Indian language. It's a good thing I'm fluent, although I'm a bit rusty," Carlos said.

Like so many of Bret's other friends, Carlos volunteered his medical time during an epidemic many years ago when Carlos was a young doctor. Some of the tribe members were suspicious at first, but he saved many lives. It wasn't all one-sided. The shamans were experts in South American herbs, and they all worked together.

"Those herbs are pretty powerful for many diseases," Carlos told Bret.

"Yes, I've heard stories," he said.

"Did you read about that American woman with stage four uterine cancer? The Western doctors gave her a few months to live. She came down to the shamans, and they cured her."

"That's amazing."

"Now she's the sole distributor of many of the rare herbs in North America. Unfortunately, the government is giving her a hard time."

"If something works, why stop it?"

"The drug companies can't patent a natural substance. Their best hope is to regulate it. Then they can control it. For now, she has a hold on her business."

Some of the plants were common in different parts of the world. Others only grew in South America. Bret had traveled extensively, but this trek would be unique.

When their jet landed, they had a few places to go first. Carlos had made arrangements for a special pickup, an off-road capable truck. Bret wondered why.

"I ordered some large boxes of food and supplies. They are mainly freeze-dried, so they're not perishable. They use them for emergencies," Carlos said.

They drove outside of the city toward a very rural area and stopped at a warehouse where Carlos's order was waiting for him. An older guy was finalizing the deal and was happy to see Carlos. Although limited, Bret's knowledge of Spanish still allowed him to get the gist of the conversation.

"He was so happy to see you after so many years," Bret said after Carlos finished talking with the man.

They loaded the pickup, and it was off to the next stop. Bret noticed the terrain was getting more than off-road. They were driving on a trail covered in wild vegetation.

"We're heading to the river," Carlos said.

When they got to the river, there was a vehicle with a boat trailer. A man had already unloaded an airboat. He gave them earplugs. They boarded the airboat.

"That giant fan gets really noisy. It can be deafening at times," Carlos said.

The man handed Carlos the key, and some workers loaded the airboat. There was barely enough room for all the boxes.

"If the Shuar men agree to come with us, the remaining tribe members will need food for the families since there won't be any hunting with the men gone."

They went slowly along the water. Midway, Bret noticed a huge snake. He asked, wondering if that was an anaconda.

"Don't worry. It hates the fan. It looks like it's a caiman, anyway."

"I'm glad we have the fan," Bret said, relieved.

"I still wouldn't put your hand in the water. A piranha might take off a finger."

They finally approached a small clearing. What looked like two canoes were partially sticking into the water. A nearly naked older man was standing and staring at the airboat.

"I think I know him," Carlos said.

The man broke into a big smile. He was missing a few front teeth. It was obvious Carlos was welcome. The two men greeted each other with a Western-style handshake.

Carlos had a pretty good command of the tribal language. He explained to everyone that Bret was a friend. The Shuar escorted his guests to their village. Everyone came to greet them. There were mostly females present as the men were hunting. They would wait for their return for help to unload the boat.

As Carlos had said, Bret noticed shotguns standing in front of their huts. There were also some spears. It looked like the women were preparing to cook dinner with whatever was brought back.

It was already late. The men finally returned, showing sadness because they were empty-handed. Their sadness turned to glee, however, when they saw Carlos. One told Carlos they had gone far today and if the same happened again tomorrow, they would have to consider moving on.

Carlos also felt sad. The man said tonight would be difficult for the little ones without enough food. He was ecstatic when Carlos explained what was on the boat. The men immediately went and brought back the boxes. They acted like they were getting a gourmet meal.

Bret didn't want to say anything. He was afraid of what Carlos's friend was wearing around his neck. He was wearing a necklace containing three shrunken heads. He asked Carlos what that was all about.

"It's an old custom. They still have skirmishes with other villages. A shrunken head supposedly protects them from the spirit of the man they vanquished."

"Isn't it illegal?

"It's been illegal for years. The government has a 'don't ask, don't tell' policy. They try not to interfere with the Indigenous people as long as it stays with them. The Shuar don't bother people in the so-called civilized world, so it gets left alone."

A while later, Carlos's friend told Bret he wanted to give him a gift of one of the heads. Carlos quickly intervened and told his friend that Bret's government wouldn't allow it but thanked him.

When they arrived, Bret was looking at some of the men standing around a fire. It looked like a broad leaf was being held over it. The leaf had some sort of substance in it. As it heated, a syrupy liquid formed.

The men started immersing what looked like twigs in the goo. These weren't ordinary twigs. They were straight and shaved down to a point. Some were longer than others, but it seemed like there were two basic lengths.

Carlos saw Bret watching and leaned over to him. "They're making curare darts for their blowguns," he said.

"Isn't a curare dart deadly?"

"They use them for hunting and other reasons. Their killing speed is determined by how pure they make the curare. The long ones are for killing animals. The short ones are for killing men."

The women boiled some water to make the food the two men brought. Bret was thankful he would have the type of food he was used to. The conversation would slow while they ate as Carlos was translating for Bret.

At one point, Carlos shook his head and waved his hand. Bret wanted to know what that was about.

"He has a daughter. He wants to match her up with you."

"Oh no—"

"Relax. I told him your wife would shrink your head."

It was a good laugh. Bret wondered when the conversation would get serious and asked Carlos about it.

"Take it easy," Carlos reassured. "Tonight is public relations. We'll get serious tomorrow after the hunt. They want us to go with them."

"I wouldn't know what to do."

"They know you're just an observer. Go with the flow."

They started out early the next day. The long walk through the rain forest was a bit tiring for Bret. After half a day, they saw something moving up in a tree. A dart was shot with the blow dart. It was too high to tell if something was hit.

Carlos said, "That's a howler monkey. It's a big part of the Shuar diet."

"Yuck," Bret said.

The animal was using branches to go from tree to tree. Another dart was blown. They thought they hit the monkey as its movements got noticeably slower.

When the monkey stopped moving from tree to tree, they knew it was dying. One of the men started scaling the tree. Bret was amazed at the speed he climbed.

After bringing the monkey down, they tied its arms and feet to a long branch so they could carry it on their shoulders. Bret told Carlos to figure out a way to decline eating the food. Carlos just said to make believe he wasn't feeling well.

Back at the camp, the Shuar men weren't happy with how far they had to go for their hunt. They would discuss it after Bret and Carlos left.

The following day, everyone was in good spirits. It was time to talk business. Many of the villagers had never ridden in a car before, let alone a jet.

Carlos wanted to start off slowly. He would be addressing his friend the leader, with the three shrunken heads. He mentioned to him that they needed a favor. While speaking, the leader had a smile.

The leader said, "Carlos cure the sick, he bring us food. We will always do all I ask from my people."

The reaction was a bit grim when Carlos said it would involve leaving the village for some time. Carlos thought the food supply would be more than enough.

Things got a little better when Carlos told them the purpose of their need was to save a child from bad people. The leader was listening. The most surprising reaction was the leader's enthusiasm at being able to fly like a bird on a jet.

Carlos asked for volunteers. He promised everyone would return well before the food supply ran out. He calculated enough food was given to feed the tribe for months. It was just a matter of getting their agreement to go. He hoped for a dozen men.

Only one man protested. His woman was pregnant. Carlos told him he had brought some medical supplies and would quickly teach the remaining tribespeople how to keep an eye on her.

The leader was no longer speaking. He was staring at the person in dissent. The look in his eyes was nothing good for that man. There was finally a reaction from the protester.

The man looked at the leader, slapped his thigh, and spoke.

"He said, 'I go,'" Carlos translated.

Chapter 21

Bret made his last effort to secure more troops. The total was still short of the allowable number. Ani was still guessing if what they had would be enough.

"I suppose we'll have to make do with what we have. It would be sure nice to have some more force," Ani said.

George had gotten Jack and his archery men. Red Hawk enlisted the same friends who made sure there was safe passage for the mountain residents many years back.

They hadn't spoken about it before, but the one person who hadn't contributed was Chengua. He had a volatile temperament and had militant beliefs for similar situations.

Chengua was essential for the building of what George called the Indian Cooperative during the reservation times. Yet Chengua was vociferous regarding his willingness to take up arms should the USA renege on any treaty. Nevertheless, he was a righteous man.

Ani went to update Niz. Bret heard a similar rumbling to the south as Steve had said he'd heard when Lisa was kidnapped. He thought it sounded like wild horses again.

Bret grabbed his binoculars. He was astonished at what he saw. There was a group of men riding side by side. They were barechested with long hair and war paint on their faces.

Chengua came up and put his hand on Bret's shoulder. "How do you like my friends?"

Bret didn't know how to be polite. He thought it best just

to be blunt. “I appreciate your trying to help, Chengua. But this isn’t the 1880s. The Indian wars have been over for many years. They rode their horses from the south?”

“Of course not. They drove up with horse trailers. They just wanted to make a splash.”

Seeing scabbards with automatic rifles and one talking on a cell phone brought Bret out of the time warp and back to the present.

“Who’s that frightening-looking guy in the middle? The one talking on his phone.”

“That’s Cho. He’s my accountant.”

“He doesn’t look like a CPA.”

Cho wasn’t only a CPA. He was also one of the few taxation experts for all the new nations. Bret asked about his name.

“His name in Joseph. When he was young, his grandfather had trouble saying Joe. It sounded like Cho and that stayed with him.”

The men on the horses rode up to them and immediately joined with the other men from the cooperative. Bret joined Ani and Niz.

Ani said, “They’ll be good working together. I’m not so sure about the rest of that mélange of people you brought from different parts of the world.”

Niz was asked if anyone had seen Steve. He was vital for their brainstorming efforts. They asked around and even Star hadn’t seen him for a couple of days.

“Steve used the same expression as Ani when she flew away. He said he was going for some help,” Niz said.

This surprised Bret and Ani because he flew a small jet. It was large enough for only a couple of extra passengers. They wondered what he had in mind.

It didn't take long. A couple of days later, they heard the roar of the jet engines overhead. Steve was coming in for a landing. He was always clever, so the anticipation was grating on them.

The plane landed. Since the airstrip was at a distance, they watched with their binoculars, eager to see who was with Steve. Three people exited the plane. They recognized Steve. The second was a man wearing camouflage fatigues. His baseball-style cap was pulled low, so the brim was partially covering his face. The third was the pilot.

"I'm pretty sure I don't know him," Bret said about the man in the baseball cap.

"Me neither. Wait, a minute. There's something about that bouncy gait I recognize," Ani said.

They got closer. Ani was intently watching. Then it suddenly hit her like an explosion.

"That's Jim! This should be good."

Jim was formerly Ani's superior in intelligence gathering. At the time of Bret and Ani's escape from the mountain years back, Jim was the person who facilitated the safe release of Bret's friends They all met in the field.

Not trusting the government, Bret and Ani had devised their own clever escape while leaving information that they had both perished. Jim was in for a shocker.

The men approached the group. There was just silence. It was as if Jim knew all along. Steve had also filled Jim in on what happened with Lisa.

"You don't look surprised. Did Steve tell you?" Ani asked.

Jim said, "He didn't need to. Do you think I really bought into that junk report about Bret committing suicide and Ani getting eaten by a bear?"

"So what are you doing here . . . thank God," Ani said.

Ani was still good for a laugh. Bret was wondering what good Jim could do other than be an extra fighter.

"Why did you come?" Bret asked.

"Do you remember your pharmacist in the mountain? She was that attractive single mother with a young daughter," Jim said.

"Of course I do," Bret said.

"Well, they're now my family. I figured it's the least I can do," Jim said.

"I wish you were able to do something with figuring out how to rescue my child. I guess not," Bret said.

Ani said, "Hold on, babe. Jim's a decorated war hero and an officer. He has plenty of experience in strategic and tactical planning."

Bret pointed out the ragtag bunch in the distance. Each group was training separately. The language barrier and culture kept them separated.

He said, "I wish there was something you could do with them. Notice how separate everyone is. Even if you come up with a rescue plan, how do you mold them into one unit?"

Jim said, "You don't. It's not necessary. You give each group a specific task. As long as they'll take orders from me, it'll work."

Bret and Ani were elated Jim would take charge.

Jim had been devising a rescue plan in his mind while on his trip to the ranch. He had ideas. Jim also lamented about some serious problems.

"I understand you haven't been able to extract any info from your prisoners," Jim said, taking off his backpack and setting down a rifle and briefcase he'd been carrying. "That's a big problem. Tomorrow, I'll get things going with your guerillas and then we'll sit down with the contents of my briefcase."

No matter how carefully Jim laid out his plan to Bret and Ani, there were three essential pieces of info missing: the detailed layout of the Purps' hideaway, where it was located, and their strength in numbers.

Jim had already briefed Steve on the danger of the mission. He knew Ani trusted him and would go along with almost any suggestion. He was concerned about sharing the details with Bret because of his pacifism. But he knew the contents of his briefcase could sway him.

Since it was late in the day, Bret decided to let Jim and Ani reminisce. Then they could all start fresh in the morning.

Ani was eager to learn about the agency since she'd left. She also wanted to know about their mutual acquaintances. "Have things changed much?"

"You wouldn't recognize the place," Jim said. "Most of the people you knew are gone. They were either forced out or retired."

"How about you?"

"I'm sort of the last man standing. I've been hearing things. Anyone connected with that mountain incident is a target."

"That's the thanks you get for all your devotion. I'm glad I got away from there so many years ago," Ani said.

"I'm not worried about me. I'm concerned about my wife and child. Don't forget, they were part of that mountain incident. It doesn't matter. I have them safely stowed away in a secret place. If I survive this journey, I'll join them, and we'll start a new life. If your old sparring partner can make it, so can I."

"Who's that?"

"Scott, your training partner at the agency. He was incompetent," Jim said.

"I know I rode him pretty hard about his obesity and other bad qualities. I was just trying to get him to give himself a sense of dignity. His family's money kept him there for a while," Ani said.

Scott had to leave the agency. He was in really deep. Jim tried to help, but he was too far gone.

Jim said, "Do you remember that undersized shirt he always wore? His stomach was sticking out, and it said something about big guys always get all the girls."

"I do. That was pretty creepy."

"It was true, except all the girls were underage by several years. He beat one of them and got caught. Scott had to resign from the agency," Jim said. "Even his wealthy family couldn't save him this time. There was a trial. The judge and jury couldn't be bought. He made a plea deal. Part of the plea deal was he had to get a job. This was his only way to serve his prison sentence.

"The problem was nobody would hire him since he was a convicted pedophile. He was close to getting sent up the river. So his family decided they would put him in business. It was the only way. He could show phony pay stubs to his probation officer if business wasn't good."

Ani said, "What could he possibly do? I always thought he was good for nothing."

"His family knew he was pretty good with his hands. He liked all aspects of contractor work. They set him up with all the add-ons. He had tools, two trucks, and bogus reviews."

"What kind of contractor?" Ani said.

"They started him off as an electrician. He could barely screw in a light bulb. Soon he decided he wanted to learn more and prove he was the real thing. He crossed some wires and burned someone's house down. Insurance temporarily saved him, but the electrician idea was finished. He had to declare bankruptcy because the insurance was short of the claim.

"Scott had all the basic hand tools. Carpentry was his next attempt. But he was very sloppy. He never understood the expression 'measure twice and cut once.' He got some jobs, but many of his pieces didn't fit together. He tried to build a home, but it looked more like what you would see in a horror movie," Jim said.

"Did he get better with time?" Ani asked.

"He didn't have the chance. He almost sawed off three of his fingers."

"What did he try next?"

"He tried his hand as a plumber. He faced the same problems. He was good enough to unclog drains but little else. His family was running out of ideas."

"So plumbing didn't work?"

"Actually, it did," Jim said. "Although Scott had little imagination, he finally came up with an idea. He was near the state border and would cross it regularly for work. It was time for a rebrand. His family gave him some money for advertising. He took out ads and became the interstate plumber. People didn't understand that any small contractor who bills himself as interstate anything is suspicious."

Ani said, "It got him some business?"

"Yes, and he didn't stop there. Scott's family had friends

in Canada. They convinced the friends to let Scott replace a faucet. It took time because it kept leaking, but Scott finally got the system dry. Now Scott bills himself as the international plumber. More and more people bought into his advertising, and he finally got his business off the ground," Jim said.

"So now he has a good business?" Ani asked.

"Wait, it gets better."

"Scott always wanted to take a trip into space. With private companies funding it now, his family bought him a ticket even though it was at enormous cost. He figured out he could be first at something. With the trip, he billed himself as the interplanetary plumber. That was enough to garner some media attention. They ate it up, and his business boomed. He was able to hire competent plumbers and sit with his feet on the desk, smoking a cigar."

"He finally had some success. That's good," Ani said.

"There's more," Jim said. "Scott read some scientists believe Einstein's laws might be broken. With that in mind, he went to the media. He said he wasn't satisfied with just plumbing in this solar system. Now he could go faster than the speed of light and become the interstellar plumber."

"And they bought into that?"

"He's become a darling of the media. Some think of him as an idol."

Ani thought the story was over, but Jim kept going.

"The media couldn't wait for his next adventure. He had one more trick up his sleeve. Scott had been reading about wormholes. Those are theoretically possible portals connecting different parts of the galaxy. He thought, why stop now? So now he's billed as the intergalactic plumber," Jim said.

"That's quite a story."
"You'll love his simple slogan."
"What is it?"
"Even aliens need a plumber."

Chapter 22

The force that Bret and Ani constructed was now complete. It would be up to Jim to come up with a plan and get the most out of this diverse group. They were all as different as night and day.

Bret turned as he saw that flash again. This time, he was a little quicker and thought he saw a figure with a head bobbing up and down. But it was too blurry and gone in an instant.

Jim decided he would try to give the group some combat and endurance training first. The trek through the mountains would be extremely exhausting. He decided to speak to each subgroup individually about their potential duties.

The easiest training would be the groups headed by the three chiefs. Most of them had served in the military and could train together. There would be very few differences.

The early removal of any advanced scouts or guards near the Purp location would need speed and precision. When Jim found out about the chemicals Alex had, he felt George's archers would be perfect for the task. Since the volume was limited, his backup would be the Shuar and their curare.

The three chiefs were also perfect to lead their men into battle and also be able to restrain them when necessary. They understood well that Lisa's safety was paramount.

Jim was also aware of Alex's strong lab-developed laxative. He would use some of the men to lace the Purp water if possible. This was by far the largest subgroup. Jim would leave it up to them as to how they would distribute their forces in a surrounding manner.

Jim wanted to keep it simple for the Shuar people. Carlos would be their interpreter.

The Shuar liked the idea that they would probably use blowguns per Jim's orders. Carlos also informed Jim of how light-footed they were. Jim thought they would be perfect for a sneak attack.

"These men can get within a few feet of their target, and nobody will know what hits them," Carlos said.

Jim wanted to know the fatality rate for the darts and the speed of death.

Carlos spoke to the men and came back to Jim. "They prepared a heavy concentration. While death isn't instant, their target will think they got pricked with a twig. They will become unconscious almost immediately and never wake up."

Jim noticed the Shuar had some large covered woven baskets lined up next to each other. "Is there a significance to those things? They'll take up space."

"The baskets are full of snakes. They're used to scare their adversaries," Carlos said.

"Venomous?"

"Just constrictors. Imagine how you would feel being surrounded by a bunch of large snakes."

Jim understood the snakes could be used as a distraction and throw the Purps into a panic. This tactic had been used successfully by the Shuar in the past.

All that was left was to make sure the Shuar would wait for a signal to use their blowguns, snakes, and shotguns.

"Someone has to be with them to translate orders into

English," Jim said.

Carlos said, "I'll be there. They are very good at following procedures."

It was also relatively easy with the Gurkhas. They were training on their own before Jim arrived. Their leader explained to Jim that they could be used in any area of the operation.

"My guys and our bellies are aching to get back to military-style events," he said. "The Gurkhas are well aware of what they can do and can't do. They're hardened by those battles across the pond."

Jim moved on to the Latvians. The Black Heads were actually dueling with their swords. Jim was concerned about their sense of reality. Hans was very reassuring. He knew everything about their order.

"Trust me. Those swords will come out only as a scare tactic. They spend a great deal of time in the forest practicing marksmanship. Do you see the round medal that guy is wearing?" Hans said to Jim. "The man had competed in the biathlon at the last Olympics, which was shooting combined with cross-country skiing. There weren't any mountains in Latvia, so everyone was a cross-country skier. He's a dead shot."

Bret told Jim there could be a slight problem with the Africans. They hesitated to take orders from him. He knew they wanted to go home and fight eventually.

"If you think you can just do what you want, you'll get lost up there. Then we'll have our own guys shooting at each other. Come on. Use your heads," Jim said.

The Africans didn't have any formal training before. They liked the idea of discipline and relented.

The most informal group contained the guys Ani brought

back with her. They weren't used to regimentation except those that had done time. Jim decided and told them they could be a semi-independent backup unit. Sort of like a reserve.

Bags's men also had an assignment to move through the brush after the attack began and clear out the unfriendlies. Jim didn't want too much aggressiveness.

Kid Horizontal had a stock response. "We'll make nice if they will also."

"And what if they don't?" Jim said.

"We'll crawl up their asses and come out of their eyeballs."

Jim gave enough instructions for all groups to run some drills. He wanted everyone to be in decent physical shape. Next, he stopped at the hotel to grab his briefcase and then headed to where Bret and Ani were.

They were sitting at a picnic table when Jim walked up. He sat down and laid his case on the table. He needed to have a frank discussion with them.

"Are you going to show us what's in your case?" Bret asked.

"In a minute. I need to discuss something else with you first. How are you going to haul the supplies on this trip? When added together, that's a lot of weight," Jim said.

"I didn't give it much thought."

"Let's back up. You can't use a motorized vehicle. Electric vehicles will run out of juice. An internal combustion motor will be too noisy, and the gas odor will tip off the bad guys."

Bret said, "Maybe the horses?"

"Horses can't do it. In World War II, horses and vehicles were useless in the Asian jungles. The US army used mules. They can carry lots of heavy stuff. Before Steve brought me here, I took the liberty of ordering some. They should arrive in a couple of days."

"Remember, this was the reason why Jim was an ideal fit for this excursion," Ani said to Bret.

Jim wasn't finished. "I look at this motley crew and see many of them can't ride. How will you transport them?"

"We were thinking a wagon," Bret said.

"Oh yeah? Those paths in a heavily wooded forest are barely wide enough for a horse or mule. Try again."

"Come on, Jim, . . . give," Ani said.

"Along with the mules, I also ordered some special transportation. They were surplus and not being used. The only cost was shipping," Jim said, with a solution.

He was speaking about special narrow wagons. They were barely wider than a horse. The wagons were also fitted with a floating axle and oversized tires to dampen the sound.

"These wagons will carry supplies and people. They can be drawn by either a mule or a horse."

Ani said, "That's why you're here, Jim. You figure out even the smallest details."

Jim finally opened his briefcase and took out three folders. "These are the dossiers of our opponents."

"All of them?" Ani asked.

"No. I only have detailed information on the top three people. The rest are just toadies, but still dangerous, nonetheless. They won't fight without their big shots though, so you don't need to know as much about them."

Jim gave a quick rundown of the minor players. He spoke about them being antisocial types. Some were career criminals. Most just couldn't accept the direction of society. A common thread was amoral beliefs. They felt the end justified the means, even if it involved felonies.

"The one factor I find unusual is one type of person who seems to join often. Schoolteachers," Jim said.

Ani said, "What is the connection?"

"Nobody really knows. I know some of them had disciplinary records due to their trying to impress ideas on children, which ran far outside the curriculum."

"The VP told me the Purps were basically criminals and mentally unbalanced," Bret said.

"I'd say it's a fair statement," Jim said.

It was time to go into the dossiers. Each folder had a bunch of information relating to one particular person.

Ani said, "You have hard copies of everything. Why no disk or flash drive?"

Jim's answer was quite logical. These were the originals in the records center. He had clearance to examine all documents. He couldn't make copies because every computer had an alarm, as did the copy machines. His biggest problem with taking the originals was the plethora of cameras.

"An old magician friend taught me some sleight of hand. I moved papers in and out, like a card shark shuffling a deck and fixing it. The cameras caught nothing. I put garbage back in the file cabinets."

The first folder had information on a guy named John. The name was translated from the language where he was born. He was the leader of the cell of Purps that had Lisa.

"So he's the creep that had my daughter taken?" Ani asked.

Jim said, "I don't think so. He's currently in prison on some serious charges. The VP found out. Since she's also the governor, she immediately pardoned him because she wanted no problems from the Purps. He's due to be released tomorrow, which is why it's important we do our homework on him."

John had a spotty record. He was a carouser and liked to party. When he first got promoted, he changed completely. He acted like a dictator. He was short in stature and some said it caused little man syndrome.

"What kind of things did he do?" Bret said.

"He got weird. He called his managers into a meeting. Then he promptly got angry, got out of his chair, turned off the lights, and walked out. He left everyone sitting in the dark," Jim said.

John would insist phones were ringing when they weren't. People ridiculed him by saying he was hearing bells. He even kept secret files on people.

"John really lost all respect when he tried to fire a thirty-year honored employee for false reasons of sexual harassment. One guy complained John was looking behind the pictures in his office. Nobody knew why," Jim said.

"As time went on, he was allowed to visit the country he was born in," he continued. "They previously closed the borders when Marxist rule took over. He came back a paranoid wreck. He was always looking over his shoulder. He wouldn't speak to anyone unless the door was closed. Even benign topics like sports and weather were met with suspicion. He would eventually just lock himself in his office. He only came out for bathroom breaks. He even brought his lunch.

"We saw similar people like that in intelligence. Quite often, an unfriendly nation would plant drugs on a visitor and arrest them. They would say either they collaborate or they'll spend a lot of years in their horrible prison."

"How did he get in with these maniacs?" Ani said.

Jim said, "After his trip, he changed his political ideology. Eventually he was forced out for reasons, and he formed a unit of the Purps. I'll detail when we go over the next person."

The next person was a woman named Josephine. Everyone called her Josey. She was married to John.

"For a long time, she only dated married men," Jim told them. "Then she would tell the wife and intentionally break up the marriage. Office personnel nicknamed her Succubus after the female demon. She met John at work. This time, their affair blossomed into his leaving his family.

"She also has this strange way of addressing John. She never calls him by name. She only says 'my husband.'

"Josey was the office spy. She told lies about a lot of people, even those she liked. She got in pretty deep on a sexual harassment charge, in addition to her other charges.

"Most of the time, her charges have some validity. The sexual harassment charge was one of her attempts to extract money. She knew even if a guy was innocent, he was guilty. She accused this guy who refused her advances. He had a reputation of always helping people and practically being a saint. All the women in the office lined up against her."

Ani said, "Is she that pretty?"

"Not really. By her pictures, I'd say mildly attractive at best," Jim said. "When the investigators started looking into her background, it worried her, and she dropped the complaint. She also got the two women who testified against her laid off. Retribution is alive and well. By this time, she turned her love interest to John. He was married with kids.

"Nobody knew why she was with him at first. Then the truth started trickling out. Salesmen weren't getting paid for their travel expenses. The money that Josey diverted was being issued to a bogus name in cash.

"Josey had roped John into her scheme and now they were caught. John left his wife and children. They were married as soon as they left their positions. Word spread quickly, and it was impossible for them to get any kind of well-paying job. The corporate network was on fire with them in the center."

"What's her significance other than being his wife?" Ani asked.

"She's number two in the organization, and many of John's ideas for hurting people come from her. This is especially true with other women, especially if they're pretty," Jim said.

"I hope she doesn't physically hurt Lisa," Bret said.

Jim said, "Now we come to the last main player, but certainly not the least. Meet Frank. He is the number three man. Everyone is so scared of him, including Josey. Especially because he pictures himself as number two. Some say he does look more like number two, if you get the pun.

"Frank's a real sweetheart. He's got a rap sheet a mile long. We think he's the guy who chopped up Sam.

"The earliest they can trace Frank's childhood is to when he beat two local pets to death. They couldn't prove it, but they were pretty sure he also did a hit for a local mob boss as a teenager.

"He did and still does a lot of drug dealing, and he did some time. He led a significant number of Purp raids on businesses and farms. On one of them, he locked the doors and windows. He burned the house. The neighbors said they could hear the cries from the family, especially the children. Frank was supposedly laughing. He has no value for any life other than his own—"

"Why are you telling us all these terrifying stories?" Bret interrupted.

"Because you're a pacifist," Jim said. "You need to really and truly understand what we're up against. If you want my unvarnished opinion, these Purps have no interest in letting Lisa go alive."

Ani said, "Oh no—"

"I think they'll hold on to her as long as they think she might be useful. With John leaving prison, that should buy us some time."

"Where does this all leave us?" Bret asked.

"I'll tell you," Jim said. "Forget about the movies where someone sneaks into a heavily guarded area and sneaks a hostage out. That just isn't the way it goes. It'll get bloody, real bloody. Lives will be lost. I pray it doesn't happen to our side."

Chapter 23

Today was the end of John's sudden pardon from a long prison sentence. Josey was waiting for him outside the penitentiary walls.

Josey had not visited him during his incarceration. John had given strict orders for no Purp to visit. His paranoia was working overtime. He was sure the visitor logs would be monitored. John didn't want any connection with his Purps.

Josey was surprised at the size of the complex. Even though it was considered one of the largest prisons in the northwest, she hadn't realized its immense size. There were at least a dozen buildings that she could see.

When John came through the gates, he stopped and looked around. He saw Josey leaning against the hood of their car, smiling. The car itself was an older sedan with a lot of scratches and small dents. They only used it to run errands when they left their hideout area.

They hugged and kissed, then got in the car and sped away. It would be a several-hour ride. Josey was driving. She asked John about life inside the prison.

"I got a good dose right away," John said.

He told her how he was paraded through the corridors with cells on either side. They hadn't swapped out his street clothes yet. The other inmates were hollering at him. He heard expressions like, "You see those shoes? They're mine" and "You see that shirt? It's mine."

Josey said, "That's frightening. Did they hurt you?"

"There was an occasional fight. I held my own."

John was temporarily put with the general population. The correction officers were called COs. There were some hardcore criminals in that block. But it was only a matter of time before they were moved.

"Some of those guys made Frank look like an angel," John continued.

Josey wanted to know about the CO attitudes and how they treated the men in the different jails. The jails each had a different purpose. Each one had a nickname given by the COs.

"They called jail 'four gladiator school.' That was mainly Latino teens and gang members. A lot of them were able to fabricate knives in the various shops. They would brag about their desire to get back out on the streets and take someone else out."

"Nobody stopped it?"

"They thought it was a way of thinning the herd when one of them got killed. It cost the taxpayers a lot less to bury someone than feed them. Sure, they investigated. But they swept it under the rug. The relatives didn't care. Every time there was a jailbreak, the relatives would call within a few days and say, 'Come get him. He's crazy.'"

"People broke out?"

"All the time. They just don't publicize it," John said. "I was fairly friendly with the cellblock called the Old Folks' Home. They were mainly older guys who just wanted to play cards and serve out their time. Some weren't bad. We'd talk about life in general and the past. They wanted no part of politics.

"I felt sorry for some. They would talk about their children and grandchildren. They would show me pictures. I felt sorry for the guys.

"One guy said he killed a guy who raped his wife. He spoke about being a loving husband and doting father. He had never been in trouble before. He told me he had a pretty good job. But one bad move and he lost everything."

"You mean they couldn't parole him?" Josey asked.

"For murder? He's lucky they didn't give him capital punishment."

"So they have a death house?"

The politicians referred to the entire prison as a progressive prison. They allowed the condemned in the death house to choose their own form of death. Old age was not an option.

"I'm surprised famous and well-connected people weren't bothered," Josey said.

"They had two jails for them," John said. "One was for the bad boys. The other one was for the average Joes who were in the news. Those guys had to be kept away from the bay boys, or they'd be taken out pronto."

"Did the average Joes live better?"

"They were just isolated. A CO took some chalk and wrote HOLLYWOOD and VINE on their cellblock. He joked he would sell maps to their cells, just like in old Hollywood.

"There was a second cellblock for famous people. It was much smaller and included the most important politicians and highest-ranking mob bosses. Their rooms weren't fancy, but they had a few big ones for multiple people who knew each other. It had a small kitchenette too."

"They were allowed to cook?" Josey said.

"They never ate prison food. The good stuff was smuggled in. They ate better than people on the outside. The COs were bribed. I saw lobster, filet mignon, booze, the works."

"I find that hard to believe."

John said, "Check this out. Occasionally, they could be seen carrying golf clubs. They would be taken by a prison bus to the golf course. I even spoke to one of them once."

"What did he say?"

"He had quite a plan. He would allow himself to get caught for something minor. He couldn't get sentenced to more than a year. He said he was tired of his wife nagging and needed a break. They even let his girlfriend pay conjugal visits. He justified it by saying, 'This way, I don't resent the old lady so much.'" John let out a small laugh.

"I wonder why," Josey said.

He was distracted for a moment and was silent. Then he said, "I was thinking about Almond Joy."

"What's candy got to do with it?"

"That's what the COs call the crazy house. You know, Almond Joys got nuts, Mounds don't. Everyone knew most of them were sane. They were just trying to get out on a mental. They didn't even try to hide it unless an official like a deputy warden was around.

"One guy was on bail and waiting for trial. He walked around the streets in just his underwear and shoes. To make it worse, he accused everyone of stealing his shoes while he was still wearing them. It worked. He knew he would be rehabbed a lot sooner than if he got a normal prison sentence.

"They even had a conference room. It was used at least once per week."

"What for?" Josey asked.

"The unions and mobsters would hold meetings there. It

was safer and more private than the outside. They would say, 'Walls have ears, but not here.' It was lucrative for the COs."

"They had money inside?"

"Money was exchanged outside. They also have a commissary. Families send money, and the regular prisoners get credits so they can buy some goodies. Pecan pies are the most popular. They can never keep enough in stock. The problem is these guys always get mugged on their way back to their cell just for a stupid pecan pie."

"Did the COs just look away?"

"I was with a CO when he spoke to a few of the crabs after a mugging. He said, 'I don't understand you guys. Why don't you just share the pies? I think I'm gonna make a video game about this. I'll call it something like "Get Back to Your Cell Without Being Mugged." There'll be a guy with a baseball bat down one corridor and a guy with a knife waiting in another.'"

"This is so funny. I guess I shouldn't be amused. You sound like you talked to the COs often," Josey said.

"We spoke a lot. I gave up on trying to recruit all the lunatics for the Purps. The next thing you know, you and I would be found with our throats cut."

"You spoke about different people. Are there any other types? This is interesting."

John said, "There was only one ethnic group that nobody messed with. They were the guys from eastern Asia.

"Saturday evenings were movie nights. All of the prisoners loved Kung Fu movies. We were allowed limited requests, and they always loved the battles.

"The rest of the prisoners were convinced every Asian was a martial arts expert. Even the killers didn't harass them.

“There was one CO who I was fairly friendly with. On one hand, he loved his family and showed pictures. On the other, he was very unhappy with the job situation. His captain was nasty and mean. The union didn’t help him at all.

“Each time there was a sick-out, he was forced to work a double shift in that bad environment. He would be overly tired and couldn’t defend himself. He was even told at the academy, ‘If you’re taken hostage, expect to be killed because they have had zero cases of rehabilitation in this place.’”

Josey said, “He didn’t have a weapon?”

“They can only carry when they’re transporting criminals outside,” John said. “They’re not allowed to carry weapons inside. They only have a panic button. If things get out of hand, they call the hats and bats. Those are the riot guys with helmets and long batons.

“One day, this CO came to me and said it was his last day. I wanted to recruit him, but it seemed unlikely because the CO had a conservative outlook. The CO had a melancholy look, and I felt bad. I wondered what happened.

“One of the no-goods had gotten the cuffs away from another CO outside the blocks and started beating the CO. Handcuffs are pretty heavy.

“Being the only other CO in that block, he jumped the prisoner and subdued him. This CO was less than six feet but weighed over two hundred pounds and was all muscle.

“Having subdued the criminal, the CO was called down to the administrative office. He assumed he was going to get a commendation for saving the other CO’s life. He was wrong.

“Instead, he was told he was in trouble. He reiterated what had actually happened and a CO’s life might have been lost. He had saved the man's life.

"The investigator was unmoved and said, 'Yeah, but you didn't have to break the prisoner's collarbone, arm, and jaw while you were doing it.'

"That was the end. He was quitting. He told me he used to work in printing and was going to transfer to the printing shop in the Department of Sanitation. The last thing he said to me was that he wasn't going to miss the food. People don't realize it, but the inmates cook for the COs also. It's not great but not bad either."

"Isn't there a fear of prisoners spitting in the food or tainting it?" Josey asked.

"They wouldn't do that. They're watched. If they get caught, they get assigned real punishment—heavy type of work, like a road crew being chained like a dog."

John had no problem relaying these stories and had many more. But he was more interested in what was going on at their hideout. "I'd like to know what's going on at our enclave," he said.

Josey changed the subject. They spoke a little longer about plain vanilla topics such as the weather.

John asked again. Once again, Josey changed the topic.

"Come on, Josey. Are you going to tell me what's going on or not?"

Josey finally relented. Getting John angry was not the way. She would have to disclose everything.

"We had a little incident." she said.

"What kind of little incident?"

"Some of the Purps did a cross-border raid."

"What? I authorized no such action. Do I even need to ask

who did this?" John said.

"It's Frank's deal. He scares me, my husband. He's already claiming he's number two and wants to eventually take over."

"He only looks like a piece of number two. I'll deal with him later, like I do with all my enemies. I hope he got us a lot of supplies and didn't kill anyone like at that farmhouse in that prior raid."

Josey said, "That's the problem. He changed course and kidnapped a teenage girl. His men brought back nothing except her. I'm not sure what to do with her."

"What do you mean by 'his men'?"

"Frank was captured along with three others. He escaped, but the others are being held captive."

"We need every man we have. Maybe I can work out where they're part of the deal to release the hostage. We should get a pretty penny for her," John said.

"There's a complication. Evidently, the family sent some guy to negotiate. Frank described him as an Injun. I don't know whether he is from that former reservation where the raid took place."

"That numb nuts did it on a former reservation? They'll have an excuse to attack us. What happened with the guy? Maybe we can work with him."

"Frank told us the guy annoyed him, so he beat him to a pulp and sent him back on a horse. The way he described the beating, I doubt that guy survived," Josey said.

"Frank screwed this up royally. I don't understand how . . . I guess I'll have to take care of it. In the meantime, I don't want the kid harmed."

"I slapped her around a little bit."

"Oh no. Not you too. How little?" John said.

"She has some bruises, but she'll be okay. I just wanted to keep her in line."

"You've been hanging around Frank too long. Don't you realize if they find out you've been using her as a punching bag, they'll come after us with everything they've got. They might even risk a war. Use your head."

"Do you want to try to rescue the three? Maybe they can tell us the negotiation plans," Josey said.

"I could use them, but they're a sunk cost. Thanks to Frank's muscle brain, we have less options. Unless I miss my guess, they'll look at that beaten guy that Frank did the number on. They may get desperate and try to come and save her or attack."

"What should we do?"

"I'll annihilate them if they try something foolish. They can't overcome our numbers with just a family and ranch hands," John said.

"I hope they didn't get any of the governments to go after us now."

"I doubt it. We would've heard something or been destroyed by now. I know that the PRSSA VP won't move against us. She's too smart."

John and Josey were getting close to the end of the line for their travel by car. They had long since left any city or suburban areas. There were just open fields and a steep elevation in front of them. Their old car was no match for the impending mountain.

They pulled onto a dirt road and drove for a couple of miles. It ended at an abandoned farm. This was a good place for them to switch modes of transportation because it wasn't visible from the main road.

A Purp was waiting outside the barn door. He opened it, and Josey drove the car inside. It would be stored in the barn.

Nobody would find the farm. The land was overgrown with weeds, and the value was practically worthless. They took out some horses that the Purp had brought for them. They mounted and started their ride up the steep mountain incline.

John said, "When we get back, let's inventory food and other supplies first. Assuming we have enough, we'll put all our energy into resolving this hostage matter. If we're lucky, we can come out of this smelling like a rose."

Chapter 24

Jim's training exercises for all the groups were showing good progress. He was working the psychology part also. They needed to believe they were doing something important for humanity.

Ani and Lana had their morning coffee together each day at a picnic table by the ranch entrance. From where they sat, they could watch the trainings in the distance with their binoculars.

"Look down the road. It seems somebody is walking toward the entrance," Lana said.

Ani picked up her binoculars and looked down the road. Still a good distance away, she saw what looked like a young woman dragging a piece of rolling luggage.

Ani said, "She looks young and pretty. I wonder why she would come here. I better intercept her and try to get rid of her."

Ani walked to the entrance. She knew strangers could make a mess of things if word got out about the training. A few minutes later, the young woman arrived at the entrance. Her face was sweaty. She had obviously been dragging the luggage for a long distance.

"I'm sorry, young lady. This is private property. It's closed to the public," Ani said.

"I'm not the public. My name is Rosa. I've come to help Stevie. I hear he has trouble."

"There's no Stevie here." Ani thought for a moment. She was trying to place who the young woman was talking about. "Oh, you mean Steve."

"I hear someone hurt him. I will give that hombre a low haircut." Rosa ran her index finger across her throat.

Now Ani had another problem. She surmised Rosa had a romantic interest in Steve. He could usually be found holding hands or arm in arm with Star. It was a potentially ugly situation.

Rosa dragged her luggage past Ani and walked to the picnic table without being invited. She really did need a rest. "I rest a little. Then I find Stevie," Rosa said.

Lana said, "You must go now." Lana was known to be abrupt at times. She wasn't as diplomatic as Ani.

"I'm not gonna leave until Stevie is safe."

Ani decided any kind of small talk could delay her seeing Steve with Star. Buying time, Ani started asking Rosa where she came from and how she got here.

Rosa had taken the bus with the ticket Carol had gotten her. Carol didn't know the location. However, Rosa had bad luck. She was dropped off in another state.

Out of money, Rosa had to work for a couple of weeks and vowed not to return to prostitution. She started talking about different jobs she had. She could only work for cash and had gotten some work as a day laborer.

Rosa would lay sod and do heavy labor. She was extremely strong for her size. There wasn't much salary, but it paid for food and a temporary flop.

Sadly, the amount of work dried up, and the landscaper couldn't use her anymore. Next, she found a Mexican restaurant. This had good possibilities because she spoke Spanish. She was willing to do any duty.

The idea came to a halt when she was asked for a green card

or social security number. Being a fairly large restaurant, she saw many workers. She was brash to the owner.

"You tell me all these people are legal?" Rosa laughed.

"You understand things. I will tell you what. Everyone uses the same social security number. The tax guys don't care as long as they get their money," he said, feeling her sincerity and desire to work.

Rosa now had a decent job. It was legal, and the tips from Americans were much higher than she ever received in Mexico.

But once again, after a week, trouble followed Rosa. She saw two men dressed in a questionable manner arguing with the owner. One grabbed him by the shirt collar. The man said something and let the owner go.

When they left, Rosa approached the owner. He was a kind older man. As he listened to her, his eyes welled up. He said they were gangsters, demanding money that he didn't have.

"I help you fight them. You nice man. You give me job," Rosa said.

"You can't fight them. They will kill you."

"Give them my pay. You just feed me, and I work for free."

The owner cried and hugged Rosa. He would never do that to Rosa. He waved his hand and thanked her, but he would figure something out.

The owner didn't have the money, and the gang refused to wait. Rosa came to the restaurant the next day and saw the remains smoldering. They burned it to the ground. The owner was sitting on the concrete steps with his elbow on his knee and fist against his cheek.

He told Rosa it was too much trouble to be in business. Maybe someday, but not now. Before saying goodbye, Rosa said she would someday help him get a new restaurant.

"I want job at ranch," Rosa said now. She said she would do anything including cooking, washing, and cleaning toilets and made it obvious it wouldn't be easy to get rid of her.

Ani feared what would happen next if she stayed.

"Why all those men fighting?" Rosa said, looking in the distance.

Ani's fear was coming true. She changed the subject. Rosa could ruin everything if she leaked the project. "Lana, see if you can find out about a job," Ani said. She could then take her time letting Rosa know about Steve's situation.

Ani escorted Rosa to one of the finished hotel rooms. Once inside, Rosa jumped on the bed.

"So soft . . . I feel like princess."

"You can stay here once we get you a job."

"If I stay now, I sleep forever. I look for Stevie." Rosa rushed past Ani before Ani could stop her.

Once outside, Rosa ran to an area where there were more people. Ani also ran but was lagging behind. There was a reason why Steve and Star were nicknamed the crowbar couple. It was because it took a crowbar to get them apart.

Rosa suddenly stopped. As was her habit with something unexpected, her eyes bulged. Another of Ani's fears came true. Steve and Star were in a romantic embrace.

Rosa gave out a brief yell, turned, and ran past Ani back to the hotel.

Ani had to think about damage control. When Ani got back to the hotel room, Rosa was lying face down on the bed. She was sobbing heavily. Ani sat next to Rosa and rubbed her back.

"Stevie no love me. He love other woman."

"We can't always have what we want. I love my husband, but he does dumb things sometimes."

"I no good for nobody. I wish I not born. I only good for selling my body."

Ani was astonished. Now she understood Rosa was a prostitute. She had always respected Steve. Now she wasn't so sure. It was hard to believe Steve doing that.

"Steve was a client of yours?" Ani asked.

"We never have sex. He just always give me money for nothing when I have none and rent due. He so good to me."

Ani was relieved. She felt guilty for even suspecting Steve. "Yes, Steve is quite generous. He spreads it around like the Russians were at the shore."

Ani started talking about her childhood. The moment she mentioned the orphanage, there was an immediate bond. Rosa was disgusted when she heard about the man who sexually assaulted her friend.

"In Mexico, if man did that, hombres would cut him to pieces."

Ani wanted to know what Rosa would like to do with her future. Even though she wasn't educated, once you got past the grammar, Rosa was very intelligent.

Rosa said she liked working with animals. She especially loved farm animals. She could hug anything with a hoof for days. If she was given a horse, cow, goat, and lamb, she would be in heaven.

It was no wonder she wanted to stay at the ranch.

"You know there's plenty of handsome men out there—" Ani started.

"They want sex because I have pretty face and good body.

I never do that for money again. Maybe I join convent."

"You shouldn't make hasty decisions. I'm glad to see you have respect for yourself. You mentioned feeling like a princess before. There are plenty of men who would love you and treat you like a princess."

"So hard to believe."

"There are men working at this ranch. They work very hard and were born in the same country as you. Maybe I can take you to meet them."

"It no matter. I honest girl. They find out I hooker and they throw Rosa in the garbage."

"You have to have more confidence. I will fix you up if you like."

"Why you help me?"

"Orphans have to stick together. I hear them talk. They badly want a wife and children. I can ask the foreman if it's okay to speak with you."

Ani had impeccable taste when it came to clothing, hair, and makeup.

Ani told Rosa to look in the mirror. Rosa looked and groaned. She felt she didn't look very good.

"That's the last time you'll look in the mirror before I'm done with you."

"Maybe you make me look good like you."

Ani ran to her room and got her cosmetics bag, along with some other supplies. She wasn't a hairdresser, but she had enough knowledge to know she could make Rosa look stunning.

Ani started with scissors and a hair wash. She knew Rosa would look great with bangs. She also took a little off Rosa's shoulder-length hair. She had some spray color, so she frosted

Rosa's black hair with some lighter streaks. Next she looked online at the latest styles and made sure she accentuated Rosa's best features with the cut.

Rosa wore way too much makeup, almost imitating a clown. Ani knew if she made it right, Rosa would look great, since Rosa already had pearly white teeth and a killer smile.

"Okay, I chipped off that lacquer you called hair spray. Now I'll scrub off that war paint," Ani said.

Rosa was beaming with excitement. Nobody other than Steve had treated her so well. She was beaming even without seeing the final product.

Ani cleansed and moisturized Rosa's face. Next, she put a little blush on her cheeks. Rosa already had a great complexion and Ani didn't want a pancake look. Her eyeliner had been too thick, so Ani replaced it with one thin line.

Ani then replaced the dark blue eye shadow with an almost natural look. Ani thought the way Rosa had been wearing it made it look like someone punched her in the eye.

Last was a small amount of mascara. Rosa already had long lashes, and Ani's technique made them look naturally longer without caking.

Ani had a personal dislike for lip gloss. She felt deep red lipstick or even pink would be distracting. Rosa already had full lips and only needed a little color, so Ani put on a little of an almost nude-colored lipstick.

"Okay, we're done," Ani said.

Rosa looked in the mirror, and her mouth dropped. Her eyes gave her bulge. She turned and hugged Ani tight. "Nobody in my town look like this. You do it like movie stars."

Ani was honestly proud of herself. She took a picture of

Rosa. She wanted to get comments from others, especially Steve. She would admit she was trying to make him jealous.

"Let's talk a walk. I'll introduce you to some of the men," Ani said.

Rosa was excited. Ani held her hand, and they walked toward the corral. The men were leaning against the wood fence and facing the two women. The foreman had his back to the women and sounded like he was scolding the men.

"I heard some of you speaking in Spanish. How many times have I told you the only way to get somewhere in this country is to speak English. I don't care what you do when you're off duty. For now, I want to hear English only."

Rosa stopped. The foreman's voice sounded familiar. He had an unusually deep voice. His back was turned toward the women.

"Ramón?" Rosa said.

The foreman turned around and looked at Rosa. He looked perplexed. "I'm sorry, young lady. Do I know you?"

"I Rosa. You remember the little girl who walk from the orphanage every day and you were the boy I watch at your father's ranch?"

"Rosa? Rosa? Rosa!"

The ranch was at least one thousand miles from Mexico. Rosa used to go see the animals she loved as a child and always watched Ramón, who was a teenager, more than the other hands. His father had put him in charge as a teen.

Ramón was always authoritative, but in a nice way. He wasn't normally at a loss for words. This time, he was. They both exchanged the line about what they were doing here.

Ramón dismissed the hands, so he and Rosa could sit and

talk. Ani took the opportunity to excuse herself. Rosa thought he would have owned his father's ranch by now.

"He refused to give me a piece of the business, even though I was doing everything."

Ramón threatened to quit. He didn't think he was being treated fairly. His older brother already had ten percent.

"He was a lazy slob. He never worked."

His father called the bluff. He still refused, and Ramón left.

"Couldn't you go back someday?" Rosa said.

"Rosa, it has to do with religion. Ours is different than most in Mexico. My father sat for a week in mourning. To him, I am dead. There's no return. That's why I left Mexico . . . forever."

It was getting time for Rosa to tell her story. She was faced with a conundrum. She could feel a crush was already developing for him. If she lied and he found out, it would likely be over before it started. If she told him the truth, he would probably not respect her and it would never even start.

"I wonder why you're so hesitant," Ramón said.

She was acting as if she had something to hide.

"I'm a big boy. I can take it."

Rosa decided to tell Ramón the truth. It was better for love to develop naturally. If it wasn't to be, it wasn't to be.

As Rosa shared her story, Ramón couldn't hide his shock. It wasn't anger. He was more stunned. "Why did you do such a thing?"

"No money. No food. No jobs. No nothing. Rent due. Would you want me to live on the streets and beg? Would you want me to kill someone for their money? I can't. I go to church."

Ramón was more shocked at Rosa's aggressive answer than how she lived. He could see she was tired of people looking down on her. “I learned many years ago to not moralize. If I was in your shoes, I probably would have taken a gun and robbed a bank.”

“So you not throw me in the garbage yet?”

“How can I? After I finish work, we should have dinner together and take a nice walk in the moonlight.”

The ranch had a second crowbar couple.

While the trainings were going well, Jim was somewhat concerned about some details that were still up in the air. He summoned Bret and Ani for a heart-to-heart chat.

"We still have some problems that aren't going away. If we don't get some idea of the location, we could be lost in those mountains for a month," Jim said.

He felt the worst-case scenario of his other concerns could be overcome to some degree. He thought long and hard about details of the Purp forces.

Jim explained that he thought the VP tipped her hand a bit with her arbitrary force restriction. He felt the Purp numbers were somewhat smaller than they suspected earlier because they weren't a trained force and so are normally not a tight unit.

They had previously discussed his concern regarding the type of location they would be heading into. He was convinced now more than ever that the Purps were in a more rural or even desolate area. Based on the dossiers, it would make no sense for a megalomaniac like John to rule around a contaminating population.

Bret said, "Would a few more days of speaking to the prisoners help?"

"I'm hesitant to do that. Our group is ready both physically and psychologically now. I've seen these factors diminish before a combat situation. I'm also getting the feeling the Purps might be growing impatient. That John has a habit of overthinking,"

Jim said.

Bret said, "Maybe you can question the prisoners."

"I'm not sure it would help. Ani and I worked in gathering outside information. Neither one of us is trained in field interrogation. I'm sure professionals within any government could get something out of them, but that isn't forthcoming," Jim said.

"We're going in circles," Ani said. "We trust you and that you can save our daughter's life. You've never had a problem making decisions in combat. You're the answer man. Just tell us what you want to do and we'll say yes or no."

Jim always appreciated Ani's forthright manner and her clearheaded ability to think on her feet. It was difficult to answer Ani's question. Without more specific info, he knew Lisa's chances weren't good.

"Let me keep it simple," Jim said. "We need to gather everyone in the hotel auditorium. This will be a final attempt to come up with ideas for extracting info from those no-goods. We'll then question them one last time. Even something little could help."

Bret and Ani knew Jim's capabilities. It was too late not to trust his instincts. They agreed to haul everyone in.

Ani said, "What if this doesn't work?"

"Either way, we leave tomorrow. Hopefully, we can get some help from a higher source. Praying never hurts," Jim said.

They all separated to call everyone on the ranch to the meeting. The night before, Bret had another dream about the mysterious figure. He hadn't been to get past the blurry image all morning. All he could discern was almost a nodding motion of what appeared to be some kind of head.

Bret found Alex and told him about his discussion with Jim.

They kept chatting as they walked together to find the others.

"You know, maybe we should invite the Russians to give us some tips on interrogating," Alex said.

Bret said, "I thought you told me to stay away because they're criminals."

Alex corrected himself. Tolik, the handicapped man, was just bitter. He really didn't have a criminal past. He was just good at bringing everyone's mood down.

"Do you think he can help?" Bret said.

"I don't know for sure," Alex said. "I do know he has been on the receiving end of a violent interrogation. Perhaps he remembers the techniques they used on him."

"We can include all four of the questionable characters," Bret said.

The auditorium had seating for at least one thousand. Since the group was small, everyone could sit close to the stage. Bret, Ani, and Jim sat on the edge of the stage with their legs dangling over.

Jim gave a candid synopsis of the present conditions. He was careful to compliment the group on their hard work and accomplishments so far.

"We need all of you to think. Some of you have seen the prisoners. They're running a stiff opposition. We are going to make a final attempt to loosen their tongues. Either way, we're leaving tomorrow," he said.

Jim then threw the meeting open for ideas. He asked that people raise their hands to be recognized, so there wasn't a lot of confusing crosstalk. It turned out it wasn't necessary, as there was complete silence.

Jim said, "Please, anyone?"

One of the younger Russians raised his hand. Alex, in particular, was hopeful, but he remembered this guy was a criminal. He let the guy speak.

"Do you want these prisoners to disappear?"

"I'm afraid I don't understand," Bret said.

"I mean, do you want them to be no more?"

The other young Russian started laughing. It was obvious he just wanted to kill them.

Ani immediately poked Bret's arm and motioned for him to come with her to speak privately. They got up and walked to the side of the stage out of earshot of the group.

Ani said, "Did you hear that? I've met some psychos in my day, but these guys are the champions. If we take these guys on the mission, Lisa's a dead girl."

"I agree. Let's just give them guns, leave them behind, and tell them to guard the ranch. I think they'll like that," Bret said.

Bret and Ani returned to the group and sat down on the stage. The group was still silent. Their hearts began to sink. Tolik finally raised his hand.

"Please explain the procedure you've already used during your questioning," Tolik said. As Bret explained, Tolik gave a dismissive wave of his hand. "You'll never get them to talk that way. I'm afraid you Americans don't understand the Soviet manner of dragging out information."

Bret said, "You mean Russian?"

Tolik said, "Soviet or Russian . . . it's the same."

Ani said, "You think you can get them to talk?"

"I can force them to falsely admit to raping a child. For now, I'd like to borrow your Black friend and Spanish friend."

"I am not Spanish. I am South American," Carlos said.

Tolik said, "Spanish or South American . . . it's the same—"

"No, it's—" Carlos said.

Bret said, "Gentlemen, please . . . We need to remember we're here to save a young girl's life."

The men calmed, and Carlos and Nkuma got up and walked to the back of the auditorium. Tolik hobbled behind them. Their conversation wasn't audible. Tolik was doing most of the talking. He was shaking his head violently. He was also gesturing, pointing in various directions and waving his one good arm.

Bret, Ani, and Jim looked at each other. They didn't know what to think. Then Alex reminded Bret the lighter methods, like sawing off the front legs of the chairs, were Tolik's ideas.

The three men returned to the front. They were nodding.

Carlos said, "It might work."

"It just might," Nkuma said.

Tolik announced in a loud voice, "I will have what you need by the end of the day."

Tolik explained the rest of the plan to everyone and then the people involved in the task immediately went to work. They left the auditorium to gather materials they would need to speak to the reluctant prisoners.

The first group to interrogate the first prisoner was the four Russians. They walked to the shed holding one of the Purps. They carried several items. One of the young guys carried a chain saw. The other carried what looked like a doctor's bag. A black marking pen was sticking out of his shirt. Yura carried a rifle, and Tolik carried a pen and sketching pad.

They walked in to the shed and told the guard to wait outside. They put the bag on a table, took out some instruments—scalpels, suture, a torch, and other items commonly used by surgeons—and neatly laid them on the table.

Tolik said, "So, my friend, I hear you are reluctant to give us the information we desire."

"Go fly a kite," the Purp said.

Tolik didn't understand the expression. He hobbled around the room. Everything he said and did was measured. "You know a little girl's life is hanging here."

"She can drop dead," the Purp said.

Tolik said, "You're making it difficult for me to pity you."

"Go make doodoo in your hat."

"That's disgusting." Tolik looked at the others and said, "Strip him down to his underwear."

The Purp was surprised as they started taking his clothes off. Being in restraints, he started resisting. "You're going to rape me now?"

Tolik said, "Shut your filthy mouth."

One of the young Russians took the black marker and drew a circle around both thighs. He then encircled the upper arms in the same manner near the shoulder.

"What are you doing to me?" the Purp asked.

Tolik ignored the comment. He showed the Purp the pad. And attempted to give him the pen.

"I need you to tell me your home location and how many of you there are."

The Purp laughed. "Is that all?"

Tolik smiled. "No, that's not all. I want you to draw your neighborhood, top view, and all details about what each building is."

"Yeah, right. It'll be a cold day in hell—"

"Last chance, tell me. If you don't, we will remove your limbs, one by one until you do. Should you still refuse, I will cut out your tongue. You will live the rest of your life like a tree stump, unable to communicate. If you change your mind, you better not lie. We will compare your notes to the others."

The guard outside heard the roar of the chain saw. He then heard deafening screams. He wanted to open the door, but Yura refused him entrance.

The Africans went to the unused plumbing fixtures next to the hotel. They borrowed a bathtub. Nkuma had them dress in the garments they used for entertainment. They gathered dried branches and twigs. They spread them out behind the shed where another Purp was being held. They put the tub on top of the wood scraps and filled it with water then lit the wood on fire.

They told the guard to wait inside as they wanted to talk to the Purp outside. They took the Purp's shirt and pants off. The Africans looked fierce. They were bare chested and had paint on their face. The designs scared the Purp.

Nkuma spoke to his friend in their native language so the Purp wouldn't have a clue. He carried a pen and pad just like Tolik.

"What's all this? I mean, the water heating in the tub," the Purp said.

"Isn't it obvious? You're on their dinner menu," Nkuma said.

"I don't like this. We are stereotyped enough. There are no cannibals in our country," Nkuma's friend said uncomfortably.

The Purp had no idea what they were saying.

Nkuma said, "Just put on an act like you do at the festivals."

"I haven't got the foggiest how to cook a man."

"Just use your imagination."

With that, the friend took a spear. He approached the Purp and gently nudged as the point touched the Purp's stomach. He then smiled, exposing his gold teeth.

The Purp groaned. He looked like he was ready to cry. The other Africans approached him, holding large rocks and told him they were going to tenderize him.

"Please tell them to stop," the Purp said.

"I can try only if you give me your location and numbers with drawings of the area where you are holding the child," Nkuma said.

"I can't. Frank will kill me."

"It's your choice."

The bathwater was now boiling. Nkuma motioned for the men to pick the Purp up and dump him into the boiling water. The Purp was wrestling with the restraints.

"You're lucky they didn't cut out a piece to sample before they cook you."

The guard inside heard loud screams. Nkuma started walking away as the Purp lost it and began to panic.

The third Purp was going to meet Carlos and the Shuar people. There would be no language difficulty as they could only converse in their native language.

They all brought their shotguns and sat them against the walls. Like the others, they asked the guard to leave. The Shuar put various knives and blowguns on the table. Then they laid out multiple shrunken heads. Carlos had the pen and pad of paper.

Carlos said, "I think it's time for you to draw a picture of your setup and tell me what I want."

The Purp was initially defiant. He was confident he wouldn't be harmed, like in the previous questionings. "I'll save you some trouble. Why don't you take those savages and get the hell out of here," he said.

"I see you're a nasty man. I hope you understand what you're saying. They're not as forgiving as me," Carlos said.

He then said something to his friend and pointed toward the Purp. The Shuar walked around the Purp and looked at the back of his neck He took his index finger and ran it from the bottom of the neck vertically and stopped at the top of the skull.

"That tickles. What's he doing?" the Purp said.

"He's just showing me where the cut is made," Carlos said.

"What cut?"

"He has to remove the inside prior to shrinking your head."

"You're not serious."

"You can see he has three of them from the battles he fought. He wants to give me yours. I'm sorry, but it's painful before death."

The Purp started shaking. He was taking it seriously now. Sweat was rolling down his face. "Please tell him to stop."

"Why should I? I can see now you won't give me the info regarding your Purp location," Carlos said.

"Never. I guess you'll have to cut my head off."

Carlos wasn't buying it. He told his friend to make a slight prick in the back of the neck. It would hardly draw any blood but would be enough to cause a burning feeling.

The outside guard heard the screaming as the Purp was convinced.

After the three interrogations, Tolik went to find Bret, Ani, and Jim carrying the three pads. When he made eye contact with Bret, he immediately gave a thumbs-up.

The trio couldn't hold back their excitement. Jim did a quick scan over all of the information Tolik brought and was elated when the info and drawings matched up.

Bret said, "Did you harm them?"

Tolik said, "They are wounded in pride and dignity only. You better send someone to clean their areas. They made a mess."

Bret said, "What?"

Tolik said, "The stress made them treat us to their bodily functions."

"I have to work with this new info now," Jim said. "I'll be done tonight. We'll pack tomorrow, sleep tomorrow afternoon, and leave after sunset."

Chapter 26

Jim was still working on the strategic and tactical plan the following morning. That left Bret, Ani, and Steve to coordinate the preparations for the excursion.

Ani had a keen mind for numbers and detail and was in charge of the inventory. She carefully calculated the amount of food, water, ammunition, and other supplies needed with the allotted space.

Jim guided Ani regarding the weight loads the mules could carry. That would leave enough wagons for the subgroups to have their own.

Some groups wouldn't need a wagon. The three chiefs' men were already experienced riders and wouldn't need an entire wagon for their supplies. Those who had never ridden a horse would be sitting in the wagons.

Ani thought it best to take the three canids in her wagon, along with a sample of Lisa's clothes. Micah had some tracking ability, and he might be able to locate Lisa if she couldn't. The warrah and thylacine could be helpful in an undetermined way.

Ani was preparing the canids when Bret approached her. He was saying how she never ceased to amaze him. She could see, though, he had an ulterior motive and wasn't happy.

Bret said, "I was thinking about our future. It doesn't do Lisa any good if one or both of us perish. It would really make more sense if you stayed behind."

"Are you on drugs?" Ani said.

"What did I say that doesn't seem logical? A child's mother must survive."

"You need to think more positive. I hope you realize I can take down a lot of the men on this trip. Remember my martial arts."

"Martial arts will do you no good when a bullet comes whizzing at you."

They were both intelligent enough to avoid a full-blown argument. People were watching, and neither of them wanted to destroy any morale and hurt the cause.

"Is there any way I can convince you not to go on this dangerous mission?" Bret asked.

"Think of it this way, babe. I carried Lisa for nine months. All of my life's essence is inside her. I know you love her too and she's a daddy's girl. If she's alive, I can't let them harm her any further. She's worth more than my life. I hope you understand."

Ani's speech put Bret in a corner. He strongly believed his words. He also realized nothing he could say would deter Ani from making the journey.

Jim was nearby. He wasn't trying to eavesdrop, but he heard the sum and substance of their disagreement.

Walking up to them, he said, "I'm sorry, Bret. I have to go along with Ani on this one. She worked side by side with me for years. I know her capabilities. I pray she survives, but we need her abilities as well as her level head."

Bret was outnumbered. It was against his better judgement, but he decided he would no longer make a fuss.

Jim had the plan in place. He decided to see how the mules were being packed. In other wars, mules were required to carry enormously heavy weaponry. That wasn't the case here and was an advantage. Other than large water barrels, the mules could carry just about anything else. The next heaviest items, such as ammo cases, were relatively lightweight compared to the mules' prior jungle uses.

It was beginning to look like there would be plenty of extra room in the wagons. So much so, Ani asked if they needed all the wagons.

Jim said, "You should know better than that. There are always unexpected space needs. What if we have to carry someone who is wounded? Don't we need a space to lay them down?"

This was why Ani was so glad Jim had come. He had experience with small details. Of course, there were always last-minute problems that had to be addressed. But this time, space wasn't one of them. There was even enough room for the Black Heads' suits of armor.

Steve took a break from loading and sat with Star. She was abnormally quiet. He would speak, but she wouldn't answer.

"Cat got your tongue, or are you just mad at me? Did I do something wrong?" he asked.

Star heaved a big sigh. She could see he wasn't understanding her body language. "You really want to make this voyage. Is it really necessary?

"I'm no coward."

"Look at these other guys. I've watched you fight. You couldn't whip cream with a propeller. One man more or less won't make a difference."

"I hope that insult was just tongue-in-cheek."

Star just rolled her eyes. She didn't mean to be hurtful. But she was also willing to try any method she could think of to keep Steve from going on the mission.

"Okay, let's be serious. I'm planning to be with you for the rest of my life. So you're going to go off and get killed. Think of us," Star said.

"I understand your point," Steve said. "Please understand mine. Lisa's almost a daughter to me. I've been like an uncle to Lisa since her birth."

Star got up and walked away. Nothing was resolved. She was a soft-spoken woman but filled with great resolve. Who better to ask for help than Chengua? Chengua, being her father, was as influential a person as there was. She explained the situation to him.

Star said, "Do you really need him to go with the rest of you?"

"I'm afraid it's his decision. I haven't the authority," Chengua said.

"We were going to ask you about marriage. He's not a good fighter. You won't miss him."

"It sounds like you want to ask me something else."

"You're as perceptive as ever. Don't you want any grandchildren?" Star asked.

Chengua didn't know what to say. He knew speaking to Steve would be useless. But he still wanted to do something to try to help his daughter. He opted to try his luck with Bret. He hugged Star and said he would try something.

Chengua asked Bret if he could speak to him privately. He figured Bret was ultimately running the show and had some juice in the matter. "I just spoke to my daughter. You've seen her with Steve."

"I know. They don't call them the crowbar couple for nothing."

"Then you understand I have a problem. We have enough practiced executioners without him. I wouldn't ordinarily make this request. He might be more in the way than useful."

Bret understood what Chengua was driving at. He didn't want to get into a confrontation with Steve, but Chengua's remarks made sense.

"I'll try. You do know that I can't force him to stay," Bret said.

"I know that. I also know if you give him a good pep talk, he'll see things your way," Chengua said.

Bret sought out Steve. Steve was sitting by the wagons and was looking somewhat disheartened after his conversation with Star. Bret sat down, trying to think of the best way to say what he had to say without offending Steve.

"Is something bothering you?" Bret said.

"Star and I had words. I don't want her to leave me."

"I'm sure she won't. Do you want to discuss it? We need to resolve things quickly. Time is against us."

"I bet you don't know she asked me to stay behind like a scared wimp," Steve said.

"Yeah, Chengua just spoke to me."

"She put him up to that? I don't know if I can forgive her."

"Hold the phone," Bret said. "Let's talk about this. I've actually been thinking this over for some time, and certainly before Chengua approached me."

"You don't want me there either? I'm definitely not a coward."

"Stay with me on this. There will be lots of communications with the hub here at the ranch. They'll come from other sources besides us. It will probably include governments, both friendly and unfriendly. Niz is a very capable man. At his age though, I'm not sure he can keep up with this grueling job. If he falters, we're all in serious trouble. Please try to understand."

Steve was a little confused. It wasn't as if Bret was giving a lame excuse. Everything Bret said made perfect sense. Steve sighed. After a moment of silence, he agreed to stay behind.

Jim was left with other issues. The chiefs already had a problem with the timing. They felt the horses needed some sleep at night. Riding the entire night was out of the question. The entire group would also need brief periods where they could lie down.

Jim said, "We really need to cross the border under cover of darkness. We don't know who could be monitoring it."

"Maybe there's a solution," Red Hawk said. "We can cross the border at night and take a break after several miles. We'll be deep in the heavily wooded area, away from prying eyes."

"Okay, that's acceptable," Jim said.

There wasn't much loading left. The staging area where they would be starting out was looking like an old western wagon train. As always, there was an unexpected talk from the chiefs. Red Hawk approached Bret and said George needed to consult with him and Jim about something. It sounded serious.

"I don't see any means for taking prisoners," George said.

Jim said, "There aren't any provisions for that. It will be too difficult a task to get back alive and also carry prisoners."

George said, "I'm not sure we're clear on the total purpose of this journey."

Jim said, "I thought the entire idea was to get the young girl back to safety."

Red Hawk said, "It's a lot more complicated than that. Listen to George for a sec."

George said, "When I started the Indian Economic

Cooperative, it was the toughest coalition to hold together in history. The people on the different reservations were as different as you are to Asians and Africans."

Jim said, "What has that got to do with—"

George said, "Stay with me. A business coalition is a lot different than changing one's sovereignty. The idea of statehood and forming a new singular nation was completely foreign to most Indians."

"And?"

"Have you forgotten the original crime was committed on NASA territory? We have sovereignty over the wanted criminals."

"Does it matter that much? I'm pretty sure some of them won't live through this rescue attempt."

George said, "At least for the moment, I'm the president. I've been contacted by many of my constituents since the news of this abduction spread like wildfire."

"What do they want?"

"Frankly, they want the perpetrators on trial by our system of justice. It's quite different than yours."

Jim said, "And if we bring back no one?"

"I'm afraid the secession would revert back to ground zero. They don't want rumors of neutralizing a criminal. They want a trial they can see. I'm not asking. I am insisting we have a wagon for prisoners. One of those wagons can hold a dozen of them."

"What about the supplies ticketed for your wagon?"

George said, "My people will forfeit our wagon. We can carry all the food and supplies we need on our horses."

Jim had to agree. He also had to figure a way to separate any surrendering Purps from the others.

His scheme was actually pretty simple. He would ask the troops to allow any Purps who run away to let them go. The troops could defend themselves against anyone who refused to drop his weapon. Except for the known higherups, they could take up to a dozen prisoners at random and bring them back across the border.

That left a clear cart, but the Africans asked if they could use it temporarily. They wanted to bring a couple of old, worn car tires and two five-gallon gas cans along as well as some fire extinguishers.

"That's a hazard in a wooded area," Jim said.

Nkuma said, "They know how to use it in a very localized area. They have experience and will douse the flames immediately after use."

"May I ask the purpose of this?"

"That's not important now. In the unlikely event it's needed, you'll find out," Nkuma said.

Jim had his own secret equipment. He loaded a sealed box onto his wagon. It measured about two-by-two feet square and one foot in height. The contents would stay with him, and nobody needed to know what they were at present.

Jim loaded another box of similar size. The difference was the second had a tripod taped to it.

The rescue team departed on their long journey ahead.

Chapter 27

With the rescue team gone, Niz and Steve thought they could get a few nights of normal sleep. They decided to cut off communications with the team at present since they didn't know the Purps' capabilities to intercept voice and text messages. The only exception would be for emergency purposes.

Shortly after dawn, those left at the ranch were awakened by a rumbling sound. It wasn't horses or a cattle stampede. The earth was actually shaking.

Steve and Niz thought it was an earthquake. Though it seemed implausible because there were no fault lines in the area and no written history of quakes. But when it didn't stop, they knew it wasn't a quake.

Both of them grabbed their binoculars and ran outside, as did the other residents of the ranch. They looked in all directions, and one of the hands pointed toward the airport. There was a lot of thick dust and dirt flying in the air. With no funnel cloud above the fog-like density, it was clear it wasn't a tornado.

Things got a little clearer, and everyone was astounded as they saw heavy military vehicles, including a mass of tanks.

"Those are a lot of tanks," Steve said.

"I would say battalion strength at least. It's weird. I don't see any support infantry," Niz said.

It didn't end there. They observed large howitzers along with smaller cannons. They also saw several oversized flatbed trucks. Each piece of cargo was covered with an opaque tarp.

They heard a thunder overhead. The roar was a group of jets coming in for a landing. These were not transports. They were stealth fighters.

Niz said, "This is serious business. I wonder which military this is. NASA has no heavy equipment. It could be the USA, the CSA, the PRSSA, or even Canada. The uniforms are all similar."

It appeared the formation had ceased, and the military were taking positions near the airport. The artillery was put in a position facing the border. That made them wonder: Was a war imminent?

Those at the ranch had their weapons drawn. They saw a small motor vehicle driving toward the ranch. Niz immediately gave the order to lower all weapons.

Alex came running up to Niz and Steve. He seemed to be in a panic, waving his arms. "We have to evacuate the women ASAP."

"That's useless. They could squash us in a minute if they wanted to," Steve said.

"Spread the word to lower all weapons. I especially mean those lunatic Russians," Niz said.

As the vehicle got closer, they saw it was a jeep.

Steve was shaking his head in disbelief. "I thought they stopped using jeeps years ago."

Niz said, "It doesn't surprise me. After the secession, I heard the divided militaries were all short of equipment. They took everything out of the mothballs, including jeeps."

The vehicle got closer, and they noticed two stars on the front.

Now it was Niz's turn to shake his head. "That's a major general in the passenger seat. It just gets stranger. They usually don't command anything as small as a battalion."

The vehicle arrived, and there was a captain driving. He exited the vehicle and walked toward Steve and Niz. He didn't mince words.

"Are you two men in charge here?"

"There really is nobody with that authority here. I suppose you can talk with us, since we can make some decisions," Niz said.

"The general would like a word with you. I think he can answer at least most of your questions."

As the captain walked back to the jeep, Niz noticed the tarps coming off the trucks, revealing some kind of aircraft with the shell looking much like the other stealth fighters. The general approached Niz and Steve, smiled, and shook their hands.

He said, "I see you've noticed my cargo. I'll explain. Why don't you ask your questions first?"

Steve said, "Which country do you represent?"

"CSA."

Niz said, "You're trespassing on the territory of a sovereign nation. Is this an invasion?"

"Not at all. I can't give you political details. Let's just say we were invited."

As they were speaking, the roar of more engines sounded overhead. Nothing could be seen because the sky had become overcast. It sounded like the aircrafts were flying at a low altitude. Just as quickly, the sound of the engines faded away.

The general looked back toward the airport. He pointed in that direction. It seemed like the clouds were giving birth. Parachutists began appearing out of nowhere.

The general said, "Impressive, isn't it?"

"I don't understand the relationship between the two units," Steve said.

"It's nothing so dramatic. This was a sudden assignment. There were no infantry bases nearby to provide support. We just cannibalized some of our airborne. Questions?"

Niz said, "Are you aware of our situation at this ranch?"

"Yes, and that's part of the complication. Things are going very badly between the fragmented pieces of this once great nation."

"Are you allowed to give us any details?"

The general was offered a seat at a picnic table. His pleasant attitude disappeared. He spoke about all his years in the military and how he had never seen such complexities.

"Every nation in the Western Hemisphere is involved. Many of those overseas are also. Beyond all the mistrust are violations of the various fragments of the secession agreements."

"Yes, I never thought it would get this far," Niz said.

The general said, "I'm aware of you. You're no longer a phantom presidential advisor. You should have known the players involved can't be trusted."

"Examples?" Steve said.

"That land we acquired from Mexico. The PRSSA went nuts. The agreement of no foreign troops here. We went nuts along with the USA and Canada."

Niz said, "Which countries are involved?"

"We don't know yet," the general said. "It blindsided us. Intelligence doesn't have a read yet. We just know unmarked aircraft, submarines, and ships have been delivering troops to the West Coast. So far, we only know they're coming from the direction of Asia."

"It sounds like the CSA is innocent in all this," Steve said.

"We're not. You saw that cargo out there? Spread the word that there's twenty-four-hour guards and they have orders to shoot to kill."

"And?"

"Part of the secession agreements was to share any military technological advancements. This is an important one, and we refused."

This technology was part of a complete change in modern warfare. Wars in the Middle East and Asia had accentuated the weaknesses of tanks on the battlefield. Some had suggested they were becoming obsolete.

There was increasing belief the future of modern warfare would lie with the use of drones because they were cheap and effective. One of the advantages the old USA had was that while secrets were always stolen by enemies, the USA was always one step ahead.

"Secrets were stolen, but it took years for the enemies to catch up. We're not budging until the other violations are resolved," the general said.

Niz said, "This is turning into a mess."

The general said, "I'm afraid the secession agreements are turning into toilet paper. Those jets you see on the trucks are the new generation of drones. We figured out ways to make them cheap, stealthy, and capable of Mach one or two. Pilots are the ones becoming obsolete."

Steve said, "Aren't the old drones still dangerous?"

"Not anymore. The new technology will pluck them out of the skies like clay pigeons. The new generation of perfected lasers work against anything, including hypersonic missiles.

Nothing is faster than a laser."

Niz said, "Do you think there will be a war since we're trying to rescue the girl?"

"I hope not," the general said. "I'm sorry my president couldn't help more. That's why we're here. We're supposed to protect the ranch and warn the PRSSA off of any invasion they might be planning."

"If they find out," Steve said.

"They already know we're here. I'm betting they don't have the belly to start shooting."

Niz said, "We'd be happy if you and the captain could join us for dinner. Our cook is pretty good, and it has to be better than field rations."

"It would be a pleasure. The captain would also like to have a word with you before we go back to our bivouac."

The general walked back to the jeep. He had a few words with the captain. He climbed back into the jeep as the captain walked toward Niz and Steve.

"We have one soldier who went AWOL. Have you seen any strangers?" the captain said as he approached the two men.

Niz and Steve looked at each other. They both shrugged.

Steve said, "We have the identity of everyone who crossed the border with our rescue team. I haven't seen anyone. Do you think he's around here?"

"He's from this general area. He told his friends he was going, and it was personal. He also said he would be back but didn't show up."

"Is he dangerous?"

"No. He's in dangerous territory, though. He's reaching the AWOL limit. Any longer, and he will be charged with desertion.

That means a court martial and probably a long prison sentence."

Niz said, "Is he that bad?"

"Actually, he is a good soldier," the captain said. "He is so good that he's on the promotion list to become a noncom. He goes by his first name, which is Danny. If you see him, tell him he has to come back. The general will try to keep his punishment light. We'll be waiting when we go back after dinner."

The captain said goodbye and walked back to the Jeep. After the officers left, Niz and Steve thought it would be good to look around. There were few places a deserter could hide on the ranch.

"When Danny returns, I guess he will get the courts going with appeals. Eventually, another Supreme Court case," Steve said.

"He can't," Niz said.

Niz was going to teach Steve something he never knew. There was no appeal for military personnel to a civilian court. Contrary to popular opinion, the SCOTUS was not the final legal word. There were other courts that worked independently such as in the military. The US Tax Court was another example.

"I see," Steve said. "Let's go see if anyone has seen this guy."

They went to Ramón first. He was standing in his usual place next to Rosa.

"Okay, where is he?" Steve asked.

Ramón and Rosa looked at each other. They acted like they didn't understand.

Steve said, "You know . . . the runaway soldier."

"I swear. I know nothing about this," Ramón said.

"How about your hands?"

"I don't know. Their quarters are different than mine. They

bunk together. I'll speak to them. If they pull a stunt like that, they'll get shipped right back to Mexico."

Niz walked away, but Steve was watching Ramón as he gathered his workers. It didn't take long before he was gesturing wildly. He was waving his arms in all directions. Ramón walked with one of the hands over to their bunkhouse. Steve waited for him to come out.

Ramón called out to Danny, and he came out from a closet. It was time for Danny to tell his side of the story. It was nothing against him, but the army wasn't allowing leave due to the secret cargo they had.

The timing couldn't have been worse. Danny's mother was dying from cancer. She only had a few days left. He told Ramón he was willing to sacrifice his future to see his mom one last time.

Ramón convinced Danny to speak to Steve. He brought him out of the bunkhouse. Danny was thin to begin with and had lost weight after days of starvation.

After hearing the story, Steve was livid. He couldn't believe the army wouldn't have made an accommodation had they known the truth.

Danny said, "I didn't want to tell them my personal business."

Steve said, "Did you join the army to get stupid? Now you're in the soup."

"It doesn't matter. I lost my mom. It was worth it to hug her one last time and say goodbye. She was the only family I had left. Now she's gone."

Now Steve was getting upset for Danny. He remembered how Niz told him the story of his own mother dying during childbirth with him.

"I tell you what," Steve said. "If you agree to go back, I'll run some interference for you. Your chances are through the general's good graces. I can't promise anything, but he has a lot of leeway."

"Why would you help me?" Danny asked Steve.

"Because I lost the mom I never knew."

Danny allowed Steve to set things up, and he agreed to take whatever consequences were to come. Steve would speak to the officers at dinner.

Niz agreed this would be the best course of action. They needed to resolve this quickly so they could get back to doing whatever they could for Lisa.

The foursome met for dinner. Steve was not in the mood to wait. He held the small talk to a minimum.

Steve said, "I found Danny. What both of you have to understand is I would've gone AWOL in the same predicament."

Steve explained Danny's situation, and the general just raised his hands with his palms up. He sucked his teeth in disgust.

The general said, "I'm not an ogre. I would have granted it as long as he agreed to have a couple of MPs accompany him because of the sensitive nature of our project."

The general looked at the captain. He asked for his opinion. The general was weakening while thinking of the severity of the penalty. The captain was always levelheaded.

"We can't let it go unpunished. If the men see that, discipline will be shot. On the other hand, Danny's a good soldier. Locking him up for too long won't make him a better soldier," the captain said.

The general said, "That's why I rely on you. I think I'll give him thirty days in the slammer. Let the men hear about it. They'll think I was mean. Then I'll let him go after a couple of days."

Niz said, "What about his service record vis-à-vis an honorable discharge?"

The general smiled and said, "I'll amend his record and expunge the AWOL charge. It'll be as if nothing happened."

Dinner was ready to be served. Of course, the waiter was Danny. He immediately apologized to the two officers. He asked what they would do in his situation.

The captain said, "I would have told the truth first. If I was turned down, I likely would have done the same thing you did."

The general surprisingly said about the same thing. He invited Danny to sit and have dinner with them. He explained Danny would have to receive some punishment. Then he put his arm around Danny.

"Welcome back to the military, son."

Chapter 28

While Bret, Ani, and Jim led the expedition, George rode at or near the front. He was looking for telltale signs or trail markers that Sam would have been sure to leave.

They followed the instructions the Purp prisoners gave them. It was gratifying to discern they were on the correct track as both the Purp instructions matched the markers left by Sam.

Many of his markers were easy to miss. That was why George was up front. He knew his son well. Everything was very small and intentionally easy to miss. Some were tiny bits of material tied to overhead branches. People rarely looked up when following a trail. Others were light tree carvings. Sam even moved horse manure in a symbol only George could interpret.

They reached a clearing. The Purp instructions continued, but Sam's markers stopped all at once.

The ground was messy, indicating signs of a struggle. There were enough hoofprints to indicate multiple horses had been present. George could even see some garbage strewn about.

It upset George when he saw what looked like dried blood on some of the rocks. They kept looking for any clues that would help. Bret then pointed over to the side. It appeared to be an animal carcass.

Bret and George approached it. George looked at it intently trying to see if there might be any significance.

Bret said, "It's a mountain lion. Do you think it attacked Sam?"

George said, "That can't be it. It has at least two bullet holes. Sam had no guns with him."

George looked closer. His thought processes were coming together. He started to realize Sam's final sentences, which were dismissed as incoherent, were actually quite lucid.

What he thought was Sam's allusion to his childhood pet actually referred to this animal. When Sam referred to Shmaska, this one had the same name, except this was Shmaska the Second.

What sealed it for George was even more upsetting. Shmaska had two large pieces of purple cloth, one in her mouth and one in her claws. Now George was able to piece together what had happened.

Shmaska had died while trying to defend Sam. She'd forfeited her life, trying to save and protect the human she loved.

George immediately asked for a shovel and a contractor-sized garbage bag.

"I'll bury her in that soft ground over there. Someone can help me move a large boulder on top of her grave. I don't want the scavengers to eat her little body."

He also asked for a tool kit they had brought. He took out a hammer and chisel. After the boulder was moved into place, George began to chisel out an identifying note:

Here lies Shmaska, the cougar, puma, mountain lion. She was murdered while selflessly trying to save her beloved human's life.

George's final words over her grave were, "Sam, I hope you can see and hear this. I hope you approve. When we meet again, I hope she's walking next to you and your mother."

They were still a few days away from where the Purp prisoners had said Lisa was most likely being held. The group had to get moving with stops only to rest the horses and mules.

Jim had devised a thorough scouting system. The wagons themselves would be like the hub of a wheel. He had scouts extending in all directions, just like spokes.

Each day, the scouts reported back at the end of their shift. Jim wanted to avoid electronic contact as much as possible. The only exceptions were for an emergency or information that required immediate action that could alter their mission.

They had been moving west, then north. This day, every scout reported back with no new sightings or discoveries. That was all except one scout who had been moving due north.

The scout heard someone walking ahead of him. He didn't think it was an animal. He thought it sounded more like a person. The sound was getting closer, so he hid in the bushes.

The figure became visible. It was a woman. Her clothes were tattered, and her hair was uncombed. She looked somewhat emaciated.

He hid while she passed but then jumped out from behind and grabbed her tightly with one arm around her midsection and one hand over her mouth. Even while struggling fiercely, she appeared reluctant to scream.

"I won't hurt you. I can help. Promise you won't scream if I remove my hand. Don't try for any weapon," he said.

She nodded. Not trusting her, he removed his hand and arm very slowly. She didn't yell. She didn't try to run. She looked exhausted.

She said, "You're no Purp."

"Nor do I wish to be one. You look hungry. When's the last time you ate?"

"Couple of days."

He took out a piece of jerky from his pocket. He apologized and said that was all he had. She chewed away.

"Are you British?" he asked her after hearing her speak.

"Wrongo. I'm Australian. You can call me Debbie."

She willingly spoke about running away from the Purps.

The scout decided to bring her back where the group was camped for the day for debriefing

Back at the stopping point for the day, Jim was getting concerned. The scout was well past due. So he went to the three chiefs. He wanted their opinion on whether to send out a search party.

The scout was one of Red Hawk's men. Red Hawk suggested they give him some more time. "He served a lot of time in the army. He knows what he's doing."

Chengua wasn't so sure. He said the man could be in trouble. He wanted to move after only a brief rest.

George was the most antsy. He was in a hurry. He felt he had an appointment with those who murdered his son. He told them he would go on alone if necessary.

"I will be allowed to fulfill my destiny," he said eloquently.

When the scout returned and the group saw the woman he had with him, they had questions. They asked where she came from.

Debbie told them she had been cooking for and cleaning the Purp residences.

Bret said, "Please don't be insulted. You don't speak like a maid."

"That's because I'm not. I was kidnapped along with some others from a university. I was a visiting professor of astrophysics. They used me for domestic duties."

They wanted to ensure she was fed and rested before she continued on her journey. Debbie thanked everyone for helping her. Ani asked about Lisa. Debbie confirmed they were keeping her in the two-room shed the Purps had mentioned.

"Have they hurt her?" Ani asked.

"I don't think much. I saw Josey hit her a couple of times. You would be proud. I never saw her cry once," Debbie said.

Ani groaned and muttered, "My baby."

Jim reviewed everything Debbie could tell him about the Purps' operation. She did say they had a network of cameras monitored twenty-four hours a day.

That's when Jim looked at Bret. "This is why I told you sneaking in and rescuing her wasn't realistic." He asked Debbie if she had anything else they could use.

"Beware of the Nokors," she said.

"I'm sorry. I'm not familiar with the term. Who or what are they? Are they humans or animals?" Jim said.

"I don't really know. I heard the Purps talking about them. All I know is the Purps are deathly afraid of them . . . even that animal Frank."

George overheard the conversation. He immediately wanted to hear what she knew about Frank.

"He is scum. I know I'm not attractive, so the Purps left me alone for the most part. Not Frank. He raped me twice and used a broom handle on me," she said.

Ani said, "Say no more. Men don't understand these things. I'll be with you until you leave."

Jim said, "There's nobody behind us and the trail is well marked. We'll give you enough food for plenty of days. You should have no trouble making it back across the border—"

"No, if you're going to get those bastards, I'm going with you," Debbie said.

"Jim said, "You can see we're heavily armed. Any attempt for a rescue is going to be gory."

"I don't care. I'm going. Just give me a gun. If I get the chance, I'm going to put a bullet right between Frank's eyes."

The next day, a scout was late. He was looking east, back toward the border. Once again, the chiefs were consulted and told Jim about the same thing, except for George.

"Let's wait a bit," George said. It was the opposite direction of where they were headed. He wanted to go and be done with it.

Jim got a text message from the scout saying he was following two soldiers. Deciding it would be worth the risk, Jim called him.

"What's going on?" Jim said, breaking the silence.

"I see these two guys in camos. They seem to be alone," the scout said.

"Are they scouting?"

"I don't think so. They're in a jolly mood and not whispering. One stopped to take a leak. I'm guessing they're just off duty."

"Can you see where they're based?"

"Not yet. I'm going to follow them. They haven't seen me."

"Okay, be careful," Jim said.

The scout followed the soldiers a longer distance than he expected. They were farther away from their base than he originally thought. He saw what looked like a large clearing. He sent Jim a message that he was climbing a tree to get a better look. Once again, they spoke.

"Are you hidden well enough?" Jim asked.

"Lots of branches and leaves between us. They haven't got any idea I'm lurking."

"What do you see?"

"They cut down a lot of trees to clear this area. There's a lot of tents and some major artillery."

Jim and the scout agreed that the large canons were probably brought in by helicopter. It was concerning that the canons were all pointed toward the border.

Bret approached Jim.

Jim said to Bret, "This is concerning. War is a real possibility, and we're caught square in the middle."

Bret said, "What can we do?"

Jim was blunt about it. He was worried about contingencies when the time came.

"You can't plan for everything. I still have a few tricks up my sleeve," Jim said.

The scout said, "By the number of tents, I'd say they're at company strength."

"Well, that's more than enough to wipe us out. Just bang this up and get back."

"Wait a minute. There's one tent that's a lot larger than the other. Maybe it's some kind of headquarters."

"If there's nothing else—"

"Hang on," the scout said. "There's two officers leaving that tent. They are walking over to a howitzer. They look like they're inspecting it."

"Is there anything else unusual? We have to get going," Jim said.

"Yes. It's the hats the officers are wearing. There's something familiar about their puffy style hats. I think . . . Hey! Those are

North Korean regulars."

"Okay, get back here on the double. We're moving out. You can catch up."

Bret said, "How does this affect us?"

"Now we know who the Nokors are. We have to get away. They don't take prisoners. Speed and stealth are the watch words now," Jim said.

"But, Jim, how about the VP's promise? How do you know their ways?" Bret asked.

"I know because I know. That's how I know. The VP can't stop them, even if she wanted to."

Ani said, "Don't doubt Jim, babe."

Chapter 29

There was a heavy mist just after dawn at the Purp location. Their neighborhood consisted of one cul-de-sac. Both sides were lined with houses, and there was a large center in the middle of the street. Multiple trees were randomly planted.

There were no other homes anywhere near this location. The closest inhabited area was a small town, and that was miles away. The Purps drew all but one of their utilities from that town. They never paid for anything as the town was always alarmed the Purps would mount a reprisal for any bad event.

The exception was water. While they had running water, John didn't trust the source. He felt the town could poison their supply. That's why he had a well with a pump installed for drinking water only.

He had a rule regarding this. He deemed dehydration would occur overnight. He therefore insisted everyone grab a bottle of water by the pump each night before bed. John made a mistake though. Since the pump was located behind the cul-se-sac, it was in a blind spot for the cameras.

When the neighborhood was being built and the homes were almost completed, the Purps had forced the contractor to sign them over to the Purps at no cost. All previous sales were voided. The contractor certainly didn't want to be killed, so he complied and took the loss. No government agency or law authority would help him.

There was only one paved road leading to and from the

only street. It led to the small town. John's paranoia led him to believe any attack with heavy equipment would come along that road. He had it sabotaged using dynamite and jackhammers. The result was that access to the neighborhood was limited to horseback.

John secretly brought in some normal-width wagons. There was a wide trail heading north of the cul-de-sac. When he first discovered it, he explored it and found that the trail ran all the way to Canada.

The early morning mist hadn't burned off yet. The forest was practically invisible. Most of the Purps were still sleeping.

Josey woke and saw the space next to her was empty. John usually slept a little later. She decided to look for him. He wasn't in the master bath. She checked the kitchen, and he wasn't there either.

A few moments later, he came from the bathroom, kissed her good morning, and went to the back lanai. He had a large sketching pad with him.

"Where are you going, my husband?" Josey asked.

"I'll be working in the back for a time," John said.

Josey was curious but didn't want to disturb him. She opted to make him coffee. She watched him through the slider doors sketching.

She thought she would surprise him with bacon and eggs. This was out of character for her. While living with her parents, she never cooked a meal, made a bed, or washed her clothes. She bragged that she would never clean a toilet. All of this continued here as the Purps kidnapped people like Debbie to do domestic chores.

When the food was ready, she brought the breakfast out to

the lanai and laid it on the table. She took a seat next to John.

She said, "I don't want to disturb you. Is it okay if I sit here?"

"It's fine. I'll give you a rundown of what I've been doing this morning."

John told her he had gone out to inspect his sentries. They were posted a quarter mile from their little hamlet. There were very few, but they pretty much surrounded the homes.

"I don't feel so great," John said.

Josey said, "Are you sick?"

"I'm okay. I can just feel in my bones there's danger lurking out there."

"You mean the girl's parents?"

"Her captivity is causing problems. It's too quiet. I'm not sure they want to negotiate after Frank screwed things up."

"I don't want her to cause you problems. Do you want me to slap her around some more?"

"Don't hurt her yet. She may be useful. I'm letting Gary watch her from now on."

Gary was one of Frank's henchmen. He was almost as mean as Frank. He was under orders to kill Lisa if a rescue was mounted and might be successful. He had the same sadistic character flaw as John, Josey, and Frank.

"I called all the scouts in," John said.

"Do you think that's wise?" Josey asked.

"If anyone is out there, they can pick our scouts off like cherries. They will serve us better by defending this area. The sentries can give us enough warning."

This was a huge mistake on John's part. He was never in the military. He underestimated the importance of advanced reconnaissance. This answered the question of Jim being befuddled about not encountering any Purp scouts.

John had been drawing a general picture of his fiefdom. He showed Josey the sentry location. They couldn't be in a tree because the heavily wooded area would block their sightline. They would all be on the ground.

"We should be okay. I don't think the parents and a few ranch hands can give us too much trouble," John said.

"They may have gotten more," Josey said.

"How many can they have? Too many and the army will spot them. We have a lot of fighters. They may be inexperienced, but they believe in my cause."

"And if those pigs attack?"

"Then I will annihilate them . . . before they do the same to me."

Josey was a little confused when John mentioned the cause. They never talked about it. She was under the impression they would just live in this house forever.

She said, "It's so beautiful here. I wish we could stay. After we resolve the matter with the girl, nobody will bother us."

John smirked. He had no intention of being there permanently. He had much bigger plans. "Don't get too settled in. I have something fantastic in mind for our future."

Now Josey was all ears. John had drawn sketches on other pages. It showed routes, town names, and roads. He pulled out a map from the back of the pad.

"Once I crush those idiots, we'll start moving," he said.

"Where?" she asked.

"We'll start with this nearby town."

John's grandiose plan was even greater than Josey could have imagined. He would invade and secure the town close by.

The Purps already had enough sympathizers to keep the town under control. He would recruit more members from there.

The Purps would start marching west. They would take small towns in a similar fashion while impressing more guerillas. He was turning this cell of Purps into an army.

Josey said, "What about the Nokors?"

"I've already talked to them," John said. "I'll give them access to our products, and in turn, they'll let us advance to the end."

"The end?"

"I mean the capital. We'll take over."

"Don't you think the PRSSA will balk? The East Coast will have a baby."

"The pimp of a president will do absolutely nothing."

"Certainly the VP isn't going to step down quietly."

John had been doing a lot of research. He saw the Capitol building was lightly guarded. There were a handful of police in the front and very few inside the building.

"Can't they see an invasion coming?" Josey asked.

This was where John was meticulous. Nobody would be in uniform. They would be using standard automobiles and coming from all directions on all streets.

John said, "We can secure that building and the whole downtown area in minutes. They won't know what hit them. They wouldn't dare send in any force and go against the Nokors."

"What happens then?"

"Once we have the northwest under control, we'll turn south. By then, I'll have an army of thousands."

John's plan was to eventually take the entire West Coast. He was acting like the megalomaniac he was called when he was in the corporate world. His thirst for power and his short stature had some people refer to his behavior as little man syndrome.

Josey was listening with her eyes glistening, like she was in a trance. John's grandiose plans were mesmerizing.

"I'll show those fools how to run a country," John said.

"You sound like you want to be king," Josey said.

"I already am. I am King Juan the First, and you will be my queen."

"I like the idea. So you're translating your name back?"

"I think it's fitting."

"Sometimes you sound like Frank. It worries me."

"You know the difference between me and Frank? I like it out here. It doesn't matter to him whether he's inside or outside the clink. All his buddies are in there. He gets three hots and a cot. That's free food, free bed, free internet, free TV, free gym, basketball time, free everything."

"It makes sense."

They had to leave the dream world and get back to the task at hand. John wanted to have a talk with Lisa. He brought Josey with him.

They entered the hut and told Gary to wait outside. When she saw Josey, Lisa immediately stiffened and backed up against a wall, petrified from her previous beatings.

"You better tell us what we want to know, you little brat," Josey said.

John put his hand in front of Josey, indicating she should stop threatening and let him speak.

"Don't be afraid. I don't want to hurt you. I need to know more about your parents," he said to Lisa.

Lisa was breathing heavily. She refused to cry. She couldn't imagine any of her knowledge would be helpful.

"Are they good with guns?" John asked her.

"I've never seen my dad with a gun. He's a peaceful man," Lisa said. "My mom taught me how to shoot. If something bad happens to me, she'll come after you with everything she has."

"And if you don't get hurt?"

"I don't know what my parents will do."

"Do they have a lot of friends?"

"I don't think so. There's just the old men back at the ranch and a few on the island where we live."

"Where is that?"

"In the South Sea."

"How about that Indian who died?"

"Someone died?" Lisa asked.

John forgot for a moment that Sam's demise came after Lisa was taken. It seemed like she was being honest. She couldn't predict what her parents would do.

"Do you think they'll come for you?" John asked.

"I hope so. My mom always says if I'm in trouble, nothing will stop her from getting to me. If I'm ever sick, she said she would fight to the end."

John and Josey saw they had gotten as much as they could. They went outside. John told Josey he didn't want Lisa hurt for now. He also told Gary the kill order still stood.

"Did you gain anything with this little interview?" Josey asked.

"I'm convinced more than ever that they're coming," John said. "I'll post extra sentries and tell them to be especially vigilant."

Chapter 30

The rescue caravan was nearing its end location. Jim was still befuddled as to why they hadn't encountered any Purp scouts. At this point, it didn't matter. The leaders all agreed with him. It was time for total commitment.

Jim was following every bit of trail marking closely. He saw they were just out of range of the sentries. This was in step with what Debbie and their prisoners said.

Debbie said, "You might want to take those sentries at night. They're usually sleeping on the job."

Jim said, "That's exactly what I had in mind. It's getting near dusk. I just want to run a confirmation."

Bret and Ani didn't exactly know what Jim was talking about. Their question was answered when he removed one of his boxes. It contained a screen and a small drone.

Jim said, "This isn't what you buy on the internet. It has a special powerful camera. The night vision is crystal clear. It also has a heat sensor to identify a warm body."

Bret said, "What if it's an animal? Is this thing reliable?"

"It can distinguish. There shouldn't be many animals. Perhaps it might see a few squirrels and such. Either way, I'll send it in to get a better look when it senses heat."

Ani said, "That'll be a tall order with all those thick branches."

"It has a special deflector. It can wind its way around anything ahead of it. It's so quiet, the Purps won't know it's there,"

Jim said.

Jim would look at the perimeter first. He wanted to make sure where the guards were stationed. He would then circle the hamlet at a low altitude. He was pretty sure nobody would be looking up. Even so, the tiny drone would be near impossible to spot.

The drone took off almost silently. Ani blew a kiss to it. It spotted the hamlet, showing that their force was still almost a mile away.

It started circling the edges of the property. It picked up nothing. Jim kept expanding the search until it reached approximately a quarter mile from the hamlet.

The drone finally picked up heat sources. Jim brought it closer for a better look. One after another, the drone performed beautifully. It correctly identified a Purp at a mini-campsite.

Jim said, "Now I know what happened to their scouts."

He discovered there were more sentries than either Debbie or the prisoners had said. He quickly summoned George's archers as well as Carlos and the Shuar. They needed to see how much of the silent, lethal material they had. Jim had snapped pictures of the guard locations and showed it to this unit. Even with the added sentries, they had more than enough deadly material.

He continued to look at the buildings and their surroundings. Because of the island and trees in the middle of the cul-de-sac, they would spread word that the Purps had barriers if they were shooting.

Jim saw the shed where Debbie said they were keeping Lisa. It looked like there were two rooms with one window in each. She previously said the Purps were complaining because the windows were only a thin pane of glass and leaked.

The drone confirmed there were too many cameras around the shed. All that could be done was to be in a dominant position and request surrender.

Now they knew exactly where the guards were. Jim brought the drone back and had the initial units fan out to a location close to the sentries. Radio silence was over. When they were in position, a text would come to neutralize the guards.

Once word was sent, Jim would wait for confirmation. Every few minutes, he would receive a text that a shot was successful as each Purp fell.

The well was behind the houses. Jim gave the word for a few men to spike the water. They approached the well and put in a noxious dose. It was getting near bedtime, so they had to hurry. They performed flawlessly and got back without being detected.

Jim verified the drone count, and there were no guards left. He gave the word to surround the hamlet. They all crept closer. This would take a bit of time. Each unit had assigned positions. Once they were in place, it was time to get some sleep.

Jim awakened all those who weren't already up slightly before any light was visible. He quickly unboxed his other piece of equipment. It looked similar to a large house fan. With Bret's help, he mounted it on the tripod. Although a distance away, it had a clear view of the neighborhood island.

Jim said, "It's a sonic gun. It won't do permanent damage, but it will make them nauseous and weak. Hopefully, it will reduce their desire to fight." He turned it on. It had a slight whine, but it was only audible for several feet. No one in the town would hear it.

The bathroom lights were predictably on in many houses. The laxative had been effective.

The Shuar next snuck up to several houses carrying their basket of snakes. The Purps never locked their windows. The Shuar released the snakes, and Jim waited with his megaphone for the inevitable screaming. He knew anyone leaving their house would have a rifle, as that was John's standing order.

"Snakes!"

The Purps were running from their houses. They were confused and looking around. That was when Jim made his announcement.

"You're all surrounded. Drop your weapons and surrender."

Jim's fear that a peaceful resolution was unlikely was borne out. The Purps panicked and started firing wildly in all directions. Well protected behind trees, the rescue force returned the fire.

Each unit was set up in pods, allowing space for the Purps to drop their weapons and run away into the forest. For the pods to be strong enough and due to the size of the cul-de-sac, several individual battles would have to be fought.

While Jim was manning the sonic gun, Ani took Micah and the two other canids and was trying to creep closer to the shed. While she was still a distance away and out of sight, Micah started barking and pulling. Ani had difficulty restraining him. He kept going and finally broke loose.

Bret was trying to creep closer. He was alone, and that worked against him. He heard two clicks—the sound of a magazine bullet being chambered.

"Don't turn around. I'm guessing you're the father of that brat."

"Please, I just want to take my daughter home," Bret said.

"You ain't never gonna see her alive again. The king has spoken." John raised his gun to the back of Bret's head.

There was a loud crack, and boom of a gunshot. Bret cringed, but he wasn't shot. Instead, John crumpled to the ground. He was dead.

Jim appeared from behind a tree. He unexplainably had a thought that Bret needed him.

Bret said, "You show up at the best times."

"I'm just returning a favor," Jim said.

"You mean your wife and kid?"

"I mean the day we met by the mountain. I was so thirsty, and you brought me a lemonade."

They both laughed and continued the assault. Bret barely noticed the flash of the figure behind him that had been appearing to him for some time now. It was only a second, but the figure seemed to be nodding its head.

In the hut where Lisa was being held, things were getting tense. Seeing things weren't going so well outside, Gary grabbed Lisa by the hair and forced her into the back room. "I thought my Purps would take them down. I guess not. You're not going back either. Sorry, kid."

Gary raised his gun and pointed it at Lisa. She backed against the wall and just looked at the floor.

There was a sudden sound of broken glass, and something flew through the window. It was Micah. He charged and hit Gary with force. The gun dropped out of reach. The fight was on.

Somehow, Micah knew Lisa's life depended on his defeat of the Purp. But Micah had a problem. The long sprint along with the trauma of breaking through the window and associated lacerations was taking its toll. Exhaustion was setting in, and Micah was losing his battle. He was giving every last ounce of his strength to save Lisa, and she was screaming.

"Please don't kill Micah. Please don't kill Micah."

Another blur bolted through the window. It was the warrah. Her wolf-like genetics took over as she joined the fight. She already had a litter with Micah. She wasn't about to lose her mate.

A third figure jumped through the window. It was the thylacine. It used its unique ability to open its mouth eighty degrees and put a death grip on Gary's throat. The fight was quickly over.

Micah collapsed to his side and closed his eyes with the other canids guarding him. Lisa ran through the door and shut it behind her. She was hoping to protect Micah, even though she thought he had died.

Lisa made a mistake. Now in the main part of the hut, the front door flew open. Josey was standing there with a pistol. Josey closed the door behind her and leaned her back against the door. She turned the pistol backward with the butt sticking out.

"You think I'm going to shoot you? You're not that lucky. I'm going to fix it so you'll never be pretty again."

Lisa couldn't get help from the surviving canids with the door closed. Suddenly, there was a slam at the front door, and Josey went tumbling to the floor, losing her gun. Ani was standing there with her own pistol. She looked at Josey.

"Go for it . . . please," Ani said.

Then she noticed Lisa and the bruises on her face. Ani immediately put the knuckle of her index finger in her mouth and bit hard, drawing blood. Bags had taught Ani this was a Sicilian way of inflicting self-pain to calm oneself down during a stressful moment.

Josey stayed frozen as Lisa ran and hugged her mom. Ani was seething. She had Lisa get Josey's gun. Josey was now defenseless.

"I taught you how to shoot. I don't want to be a sore loser, but after I'm finished with her, if I lose, you put a bullet where she breathes," Ani said to Lisa.

"But, Mom."

"Just do what I say."

There was a workbench next to Ani. She picked up two hammers and threw one toward Josey.

"You better pick it up. This will be a fight to the death," Ani said.

Josey got up from the floor. She wasn't obliging.

Ani took a few steps toward Josey and flung her hammer to the other side of the room. She gave a full swing of her fist and caught Josey in the jaw. As Josey fell, Ani jumped on her and straddled her stomach while slinging punches. There was one word in between each punch.

"This . . . is . . . what . . . you . . . get . . . for . . . hurting . . . my. . . baby."

Jim and Bret arrived. Jim held a gun to Josey. She was dazed and in no condition to run. Bret grabbed Ani to pull her off. She was still yelling at Josey.

"If you ever touch my baby again, I'll crawl up your ass and come out of your eyeballs, you filthy strumpet."

Lisa directed Bret to the back room and started crying. "I think Micah's dead."

Bret opened the door. He saw Micah lying there motionless among the blood and glass. He was flanked by the two other canids, and Gary's body was face down.

A tear ran down Bret's his cheek as he walked over to his canine son. "Oh, Micah."

He started to brush the broken glass off Micah's side. He was startled as Micah opened one of his eyes.

"You're alive!"

Bret gently lifted Micah and brought him outside and laid him on the grass. One of the men summoned the vet. It was dangerous because the shooting was still going on. The vet came and examined Micah.

"He's just dehydrated and exhausted. I'll give him a bag of fluid. Don't worry if his stomach bulges. He'll use it up."

The battle of attrition was winding down. Little by little, Purps were fleeing into the forest. Some were still on the island behind trees, unwilling to surrender. The group couldn't just leave because there was some shooting in the woods.

One Purp came running back from the woods. He went to the closest other Purp.

"There's some crazy Black guys out there howling with weird paint on their faces. Another thing. You know how John keeps saying the kid's parents don't have all those fighters? Well, they have them!" The Purp then ran away in another direction.

The Africans approached. They didn't know John had given orders to feign surrender and then try to kill an attacker. One African approached and took the Purp's weapon. The Purp drew a knife and stabbed the African. The other Africans grabbed the Purp.

Another Purp was in the area where the Gurkhas were at

the edge of the forest. He ran out of ammunition. A Gurkha approached. He was the young man Pramesh had saved and the son of Pramesh's friend.

The Purp had a glass bottle of gasoline with a rag stuffed in the top hidden behind a rock. It was a crude fire bomb.

As the Gurkha approached, the Purp hurled the bottle, and it broke at the Gurkha's feet, sending flames up to his face. The other Gurkhas jumped out and dragged him to safety while extinguishing the fire.

Seeing his son burned badly, the father Gurkha rose to his feet. He walked slowly toward the Purp. He dropped his gun along the way. The Purp just stared at him as he stood a few feet away. He didn't see the Gurkha had his kukri sheathed behind his back.

He then spoke. "So, you want to throw a bomb, do you?"

The Gurkha drew his kukri and skewered the Purp in the heart. He withdrew his weapon and ran back to his son.

The fighting was nearly over. The group of Purps on the island surrendered. It was time to take inventory of casualties.

Some of the Purps came running back, yelling about a time warp.

"There's some guys wearing medieval armor chasing us with their swords."

The Chinese emerged unharmed. The Gurkhas were fine except the one had bad burns. The examining doctor said he would recover nicely.

Things were wrapping up well until the Africans emerged holding one of the Purps. Another was holding a tire, and a third was holding a gas can. Nkuma went to Bret and said they would give him a necklace—they were going to put gas in the tire, hang it on the Purp's neck, and light it up.

"This isn't civilized," Bret said.

Nkuma said, "He faked surrender and killed one of mine. Don't interfere."

They sat the Purp down and were about to get started when Nkuma yelled, "Stop!"

They all turned and saw the wounded African being carried from the forest by his two friends. He was alive and would survive.

Ani was beginning to worry. None of Bags's men appeared. If they perished, how would she explain that to Bags? No sooner had she thought that than they all came out. She was relieved.

Kid said, "We got sidetracked. Some of them wanted to rock and roll, so we had to learn 'em a lesson."

Bret said, "Where are they?"

"Oh, you won't see them jokers no more," Kid said.

"But—"

"Babe, don't ask questions," Ani said.

Chengua was nearby, watching Lisa. He cringed when he saw her face. He asked Ani if that woman did this. Ani told him yes. He then called Cho over.

Chengua said, "I'm going to revert to my old comedy act. Tell the men not to laugh. She needs to be tortured a little." Chengua walked to Ani and winked. "Squaw did this to the girl?"

Ani said, "Yes, she did."

Chengua said, "Bring rope. We hang now."

"No," Josey said.

Bret interjected. He wanted no more violence. Chengua turned his back and stuck his tongue out at his men. They did all they could to stifle a laugh.

"You no like hanging? Okay, bring sticks. We burn her."

Josey dropped to her knees, begging for them not to. Chengua had her convinced he was serious.

Bret said, "You can't do that. She can face trial when we get back."

"I think a few minutes," Chengua said. He looked up at the sky. He came up with a response. "Aw, squaw no good. We hang now."

Cho grabbed Bret and told him it was just a ruse. They wanted to make her feel mental anguish the way Lisa had felt.

Almost everyone had been accounted for. George was concerned. Jack and a few of his men emerged from the woods with a prisoner. He was bald, heavily tattooed, and wearing an eye patch.

Jack approached George. Everyone knew it was Frank.

"Give me your knife," George said.

"Don't do this. It would be best if I fight him in your stead. I insist," Jack said.

"He was my son. I must."

"That beast is bigger than you and half your age. It's not an even match."

"You forget I'm an old infantry man. I know hand-to-hand combat. I'll bet he never had a fair fight in his life."

"Your stamina?"

"I see fear in his eye," Bret said. "Besides, with one eye, he has no depth perception. I'll try to make it quick."

Jack said, "I've never argued with you. This time I must—"

"Sam is watching. You know that. If willed, I'll join him. What would you do if you were in my place? Now give me your knife."

Jack couldn't look George in the eyes. His eyes welled up. He looked the other way and handed over his knife.

George's men made the crowd back away, giving a large open area. Bret was standing next to Red Hawk. He was in disbelief.

Bret said, "This is crazy. Can't you stop it?"

Red Hawk said, "You've been my friend for many years. I'm afraid you're not capable of understanding the old ways."

"This isn't centuries ago."

"If you do anything, it will be very bad for you. Please believe that."

George faced Frank at a distance. He threw the knife to Frank. Frank just looked at it.

George said, "I can see you're frightened."

Frank spit on the ground. He was trying to upset George.

George then spoke in a loud and clear voice. "I'm now going to fight this man. If I lose, I'm ordering my men to set him free."

Maybe that would give Frank the incentive to pick up the knife.

Chengua watched and whispered to Cho, "Listen to me carefully. I made no such promise of freedom. If George dies, you allow that man to go no more than one quarter mile into the woods then kill him. Also, do it the traditional way . . . slow and painful."

Cho said, "It will be my pleasure."

When George mentioned his son's memory, Frank spit on the ground again.

That got to George, and he responded. "I've always said every man makes a contribution before leaving this earth. Yours will be leaving this earth."

With renewed confidence, Frank picked up the knife. He suddenly ran at George with the knife overhead so he could thrust in a downward motion. George easily blocked it by hitting his arm to the outside. He simultaneously moved to the side with his leg out, tripping Frank while chopping the back of Frank's neck with his fist. Frank fell with his knife next to him.

He looked up, and George was wiggling his wrist in an up and down motion. He was indicating Frank should take his knife and get up. Frank was stunned. He still grabbed his knife, and while getting up, he thrust his knife in an upward motion. George again blocked it and kicked Frank in the testicles.

He gave Frank a minute to recover. Jack was beginning to worry about the fatigue factor since George was not a young man. They suddenly heard a loud voice from the audience. It was Debbie.

"Stick him!"

Jack knew he had to think of something fast, so he yelled out, hoping to get George's attention. "Come on, chief. We have to get out of here. Get it over with."

As usual, George didn't react. He waited for Frank to get up. This time, Frank surprised George by making a side-to-side slashing move. While George jumped back, the knife caught his chest. It was only superficial, but the blood was visible. Everyone groaned.

Frank tried it again, but George was ready. He hit Frank's wrist upward and at the same time drove his knife deep into Frank's chest.

Frank's legs gave out, and George held him up with a few words.

"That was for killing my son."

He withdrew his knife and stabbed it deeply in the side of Frank's neck, killing him. Frank dropped to the ground. Then George bent down and took his knife.

"And that was for butchering his body."

George took the weapon Sam had gifted him and began to walk away. He quickly turned around and stood over Frank's body.

"Hear me, you evil soul of this wicked man. I curse you to burn and rot in the flames of hell until the crack of doom."

Jack rushed to George and started cleaning his wound. Jack had wanted to say something to him for a long time. "I know I can't replace Sam. Nobody can. I lived with you as a child. My greatest desire in life would be your calling me your son. I don't ask for much. I'm asking now."

George didn't smile much. He put his arm around Jack. "We'll see."

Chapter 31

The aftermath of the battle and rescue had an eerie quietness. The smell of burned shell casings filled the air. After everyone was accounted for, the wounded were treated. Fortunately, nobody on the rescue team suffered life-threatening injuries.

The only deaths were Purp members. Bret felt they should be given a proper burial. Ani vehemently disagreed.

"Whatever the animals don't scavenge, let them lay there and rot," Ani said.

Jim was less emotional. He had a more practical impression of the situation. He knew George would have the same reaction as Ani.

Jim said, "Everyone is exhausted. We still have to stock the wagons. I suggest we get back to the ranch and inform the VP. She can make arrangements for a burial or cremation. She already has Steve's money."

Jim wasn't aware of the VP's resignation and ensuing flight. He was hoping for the team to take a day or so to rest before the long trek back. Things would change quickly.

Bret and Ani wanted to call the ranch and give them the good news. They let Lisa make the call. Niz answered.

"Hi, Grandpa," Lisa said.

"Lisa, my sweet. You're safe?"

"You know nobody can keep this kid down."

"I'm so happy. I'll call Grandma and let her know. For now, please put your parents on the phone."

There was a sense of urgency in Niz's voice. He wanted the phone on speaker so both parents and Jim could listen. His immediate concern was their well-being.

Bret said, "We're all in one piece. Jim's directing the restocking. Maybe we can leave tomorrow. We'll follow that trail back. We left a lot of markings."

Niz said, "You can't do that."

He told them how the army shared some satellite photos of the traveled area. The artillery was now turned and facing in the direction of the Purp hamlet. The troops were fanning out. They were ready to move.

"They have just stopped. They're not moving, or at least not yet. Sooner or later, they'll be headed in your direction," Niz said.

Bret said, "What does it all mean?"

"It means we've been double-crossed. I bet the VP is allowing enough time for one side or the other to be destroyed. Then they'll pick up the pieces and finish the job on the survivors," Jim said.

"That's probably why we haven't seen any aerial surveillance. That sneak didn't want to tip us off," Ani said.

Jim said, "We have to get ready to leave in a hurry. Forget about the rest. Now you know why an alternate route was planned."

The alternate route was a trail heading due north to Canada. The prisoners at the ranch described it as wide enough for normal wagons. The party wondered why the Purps had the wider wagons. Now they knew.

There was plenty of food and supplies in the houses. There would be enough room in one of the large wagons for the new prisoners. Jim felt he had enough people to handle twenty-four-hour guard duty. This was important as the Purps couldn't be trusted.

Nkuma and Carlos were watching as the Purps were loaded. They had an uneasy feeling. The Purps were looking all around as if they were planning something.

Nkuma said, "Are you thinking what I'm thinking?"

"All I can say is if a knife is missing, the first place I'm going to look is in Bret's back," Carlos said.

Nkuma and Carlos wondered how they could help. They both felt a fear factor could at least temporarily stop the Purps before they started. What if they tried the same ploy that was done to the Purps on the ranch?

Carlos said, "It might work."

Nkuma said, "It just might."

The Africans were already in their fearsome paint. The Shuar had their shrunken heads. Carlos, Bret, and Nkuma approached the prisoner wagon with an African and a Shuar. They appeared to be arguing in their native languages. The Purps were all ears, as the voices were purposely loud.

Bret said, "Why is that guy pointing to his mouth and stomach and the other holding one of those heads?"

"My men feel we may run short of food. They want permission to eat these Purps first," Nkuma said.

Carlos said, "The Shuar don't want any new bodies disturbed. Since they weren't allowed to take the heads of the dead ones here, they want to take the heads along the way."

"That's not going to happen for now. They all agreed to let me have the final word," Bret said.

He could see some of the Purp's legs quivering. They bought

the story. As Nkuma and Carlos walked away, Bret turned to address his prisoners.

"As you can see, they're serious. I don't want any monkey business. If you try to escape, I won't be able to control them. Remember, your survival is dependent on my good graces."

The wagons were fully loaded. All the unused horses would be brought with the rescuers. There was a fear they wouldn't otherwise survive.

They set out. The following days had nothing eventful. For the time being, the Purps were behaving themselves. The only negative was the remoteness made reception blank, and it was impossible to communicate with the ranch.

Eventually, they were lucky enough to find a signal. Bret made the call, and Steve answered.

Steve said, "Where in the heck are you, man?"

Bret said, "Sorry, we had no signal. We're the wilderness . . . no street signs. The best I can guess is we're at or near the Canadian border."

"You better keep going," Steve said. "The photos show those troops are on the move. You have a day or two before they see what's left of the town. There's no indication they're going north . . . yet."

Bret underestimated the caravan's progress. Out of the woods stepped a soldier with a rifle and wearing a maple leaf insignia. It was a good thing because they came to a fork and didn't know which way to go. The soldier pointed to the right, and he led the way.

They made it to a clearing and were met by an officer. In front of them was a train with several cars.

"Welcome to Canada. Arrangements have been made for

you," the officer said.

Jim was surprised there weren't many soldiers. He counted a platoon, which explained why only a lieutenant was commanding. The officer related the train setup to the three leaders.

There were several boxcars. The lieutenant explained the first contained a small truck in case of emergency. All of their ammo and supplies were there. The next set of cars was for the horses. The following cars were for passengers. The last car was for the prisoners.

Jim wanted to know about the security. The prison car had metal mesh in front of the windows. There was only one side entrance. The rear was welded shut. The front had a small area separating the door and a metal partition with a slot. This would house an armed guard. The train would stop once to give the prisoners food. There was no bathroom break, as it had its own lavatory.

The officer said, "Returning the horses is impractical. We can always use them. The government will pay you a fair price."

Chengua was sad to see one of the horses try to follow him. It was the same horse Cho rode to the ranch.

"Cho rode him to the ranch, but he is my pet horse. I don't ride him much. We just like spending time together," Chengua said.

The lieutenant said, "We'll tag him and make arrangements for his return."

Word spread to everyone pertaining to these conversations. The group however was very casual about it all. The Purps also heard everything. Nobody paid any attention to the Purps' whispering conversation.

"This may be our last chance. I have an idea," Josey said.

The Purps were apprehensive. They were worried about the constant threats.

Josey continued, "Do you still have that hidden belt knife?"

She was speaking about a knife that was sheathed inside where the belt leather was split. It would be essential for her plan to work.

The military was in the car right in front of the secure car. They created a buffer between the passengers and the prisoners. The train departed.

Josey decided to try her luck with the guard. Although they were separated by the metal grating, she wanted to keep him distracted with some provocative movements and statements. He held his rifle by the slot as she approached. She unbuttoned the top two buttons of her top, exposing some cleavage.

Josey said, "Hey, baby, do you like the way I look?

"You're an attractive woman, ma'am," he said.

"If you help us get out of here, I'll be real nice to you."

The soldier put his gun down, reached in his pants, and pulled out his wallet. He removed a photograph containing his wife and young child. He showed it to her.

"I'm sorry, ma'am. You may be an attractive woman, but for me, my wife and child are all that exists outside of the army."

Josey's smile quickly turned to a frown as she sauntered back to her seat. She wasn't used to being turned down. She assumed all men had their hormones working day and night.

Josey still had a trick up her sleeve, and it would be a big one. She still had some resistance from some of the Purps. She reminded them of what was waiting back at the ranch.

"There are no bleeding hearts there. It might as well still be a reservation. Do you guys know about their system of justice?

They'll fry us. You question whether those maniacs connected with the attack on us will do anything? Why worry? We have the Canadian army protecting us."

Josey made her point. Now the Purps waited. Sooner or later, the train would have to stop so they could bring them a meal through the only door on their train car.

Josey had learned some strategy from John in these situations. She had the Purps sit strategically. Hours later, the train began to slow. The Purp removed the hidden knife from his belt and stowed it between his legs. It was small, being no more than four inches. That was enough to do the trick.

The train stopped, and two armed soldiers stood outside on either end of the door. A soldier stepped out of another car. He was carrying a case of water bottles. On top of the water bottles were two large bags containing sandwiches.

The door was opened, and the soldier entered the prisoner car. He was about to put the items toward the back. The Canadians deemed it safe, as there were multiple riflemen.

He walked out of sight of the two outside guards. One of the Purps stuck his leg out and tripped the soldier, who fell clumsily forward on to the floor. The Purps immediately jumped him and held him down. The knife wielder held his weapon to the soldier's throat.

The inside guard held his rifle through the slot and took aim.

Josey presently yelled. "Drop your guns, or your man has no jugular left."

The outside door was quickly closed and locked. The inside guard couldn't fire for fear of hitting his own man. He lowered his gun and put it on the side.

The outside guards summoned help, and the platoon

surrounded the car.

The inside guard tried to calm Josey down. "I did as you asked. Please tell me what you want."

Josey said, "First of all, I want you out of here. Send that guy who's running this outfit."

The guard left through the front door. The sergeant replaced him.

One of the Purps called out, "He's a noncom. Don't deal with him."

"You heard him. Get that officer, and I mean now," Josey said.

With all the commotion, the passengers knew something was up. Bret jumped out and walked to the front of the prison car. He was stopped by the corporal.

Bret said, "What's going on?"

"We have a little problem. They're giving us some trouble."

"We can stop them."

"You can't. You have no jurisdiction. A deal was made. Let the Canadian army take care of this."

The lieutenant came to the back car. He held up his arm, indicating to everyone to calm down. "Okay. Take it easy on my man. I assume you want to go free."

Josey said, "You've got to be kidding. You release us and you shoot holes in us. You're not getting off that easy."

Josey caught the lieutenant off-guard. He wasn't prepared for her knowledge of the contents of the car behind the locomotive.

"We want that truck, and its gas tank better be full."

"I think I can arrange that. I need authorization."

"Well, get it and don't take too long."

The officer left and discussed his next steps with his sergeant.

He wanted to initially buy time until reinforcements could arrive. He went back to the last car.

"I have limited authority, if that's all you want," he said.

"Are you on drugs? I want food, guns, and ammo. Another thing . . . I better not see any helicopters," Josey said.

"You have to know I can't get authorization to turn over weapons. I suppose I could try if you release the soldier."

"You're a funny man. We'll release him at a time of our choosing. Remember, we better not be followed, or he's finished."

Josey had the idea of taking the soldier with them back to the point of entry to the forest. They would execute him and get back to the PRSSA side.

"We'll be home free," she said.

The officer knew he couldn't get authorization for the weapons. He also knew it wasn't worth the soldier's life. He didn't want to make his wife a widow. It was a dicey situation. He summoned the sergeant.

"I'm going back to talk to them again. I'll try to reason with that woman. Wait exactly ten minutes. Then throw the switch," the lieutenant said.

"But you'll be in the car—"

"That's an order, sergeant. Just leave a bottle of aspirin by my bed."

He made his way back to the prison car. The officer's presence would help to mitigate any suspicion of a rescue plan.

He said, "This is going to take time. Any transfer of weapons' approval has to come from the highest echelon."

"You think I'm waiting forever? You don't have a choice. I couldn't care less if you're court-martialed. Let's get started," Josey said.

"You have to give something in return. How about you let us stay in contact via radio with the soldier? That way, we know he's safe."

"And the minute we release him, you blow up the truck? I congratulate you on your stupid plan."

The officer was running out of stalling tactics when something promptly changed. Some of the Purps were getting dizzy. The knife holder fainted. Even the officer sat on the floor as his eyes started drooping. It was a knockout gas being released through the vents.

Josey said, "What did you do, you son of a . . ."

The soldiers waited long enough to make sure the gas did its job. They opened the front and side doors to ventilate the room. Even at that, they entered the car wearing gas masks.

They removed the two army men and the knife. They lifted the Purps onto their seats and reclined their seats back. They also left a bottle of aspirin on the floor.

One of the soldiers went to the passenger cars and said everything was secure and under control. He assured the passengers they could rest easy. The rest of the trip would be quiet.

Chapter 32

The train was progressing at a fairly high speed. Now that the Purps were behaving, the rumbling of the cars was quite soothing.

Along their route were magnificent vistas of the Canadian wilderness. Unfortunately, most of the passengers were so fatigued, they slept through the entire trip and missed the views.

The locomotive started lowering its power after a couple of days. The cars were slowing. That didn't disturb the sleepers. What did was a deafening blow from the whistle. One of the soldiers walked through and informed the passengers to gather their belongings. They would be stopping soon.

The soldier drew some laughs as he smiled and imitated a conductor. He was good at making people feel welcome.

"Last stop, all must exit."

As the train approached the stopping point, all on one side were looking out of the window. There were several military trucks and a barren dirt area where some buses were parked.

A group of familiar faces were waving wildly. Someone was holding up a crude sign reading Welcome back, Lisa.

The waiting group wasn't large in numbers. They were comprised of drivers, along with some others from the ranch.

The passengers could see a total of four buses. Three of them were newer models and looked like fancy tour coaches. The fourth was an older bus painted in a drab gray color. Except for the color, it looked like a school bus. It curiously had darkened windows.

As people exited the train, they were met with hugs, kisses, and handshakes. Several people separated into smaller groups. Most wanted to walk a bit to stretch their legs. The army told them to stay nearby as they would be leaving soon.

Steve drove one of the buses. Star had ridden with him. When the rescue group arrived, she immediately walked around, looking for her father. But she couldn't find Chengua anywhere.

When the train had stopped, the first thing Chengua did was go directly to the boxcar containing his pet horse. He didn't want others to see his emotional reunion with his beloved pet. He wanted people to envision him as a warrior from centuries ago. He never even gave the animal a name. He just called him Horse.

A few moments later, Star found Chengua. He couldn't fool her. She knew his tender side. She didn't announce herself immediately. Star wanted to give him a moment. The horse was nibbling at Chengua's face, and he was hugging the horse's neck. Then she quietly climbed into the car.

"Hi, Dad."

Chengua was startled. He walked over to her and squeezed her tight. There was no holding back of emotions now. She was grateful he appeared in good health.

He was still a bit forlorn. "I don't want to leave my pet. They promised to send him back, but I know better."

"Maybe you should take a look outside. Look behind the military truck."

There was a small horse trailer attached to an automobile. The lieutenant had radioed ahead. Steve and Star had even brought a ranch hand to drive it. Chengua's cherished pet was going home with him. Star never saw her father shed a tear before. He did this time.

"You're the best daughter a man could ever hope for. Now, what's this on your hand?"

Star was wearing a diamond engagement ring. She and Steve agreed if everyone returned safely, she would wear it. It was a big rock. Steve had it sent from a famous diamond importer who just happened to be his client.

"You were supposed to get my permission first. This isn't our way of doing things."

"Aw come on, Dad. This isn't centuries ago. We don't live in tepees anymore. If you don't approve, I'll give the ring back to Steve. It'll break my heart, but I'll do it."

It was a moment of tradition verses reality. What could he say? She had her father cornered.

"You're playing unfair," Chengua said. "You know it would break my own heart to hurt you. Let's just say your thought waves asked my permission and my thought waves gave my consent before the ring was on your finger."

Star was ecstatic. They both left the boxcar to talk to the others.

Chengua saw the other two chiefs speaking near one of the buses. There was a man sitting on the bus steps. He was slumped over with his hands covering his face.

It was Hans. Due to his advanced age, driving the many hours was exhausting. He insisted on driving because he drove a bus many years ago to help pay for medical school. He wanted to be a driver because he had special skills from his experience.

As Chengua joined the conversation, Red Hawk spoke of his friendship with Hans from the old mountain days. He referred to Hans as a stubborn German.

"You know I warned him he would be too tired to drive. This bus will end up in a ditch before we reach the border. But I know Hans. He'll fight us tooth and nail," Red Hawk said.

George said, "Maybe Bret could convince him."

"I don't think so. He has to be forced, and I can't in good conscience do that," Red Hawk said.

"Is that all you want? Leave it to me. Just turn around because I know you two old fossils might start laughing," Chengua said.

Chengua was going into his act again. He could be very convincing. People like Hans only understood movies about the old Indian wars. They didn't know reality.

Hans hadn't seen the war paint and garb before they left the ranch. The paint hadn't worn off. Chengua still looked like a killer.

Chengua approached Hans, who still had his face in his hands. He stood a few inches away. Hans didn't realize he was standing there. Chengua then gently kicked Hans in the shin.

Hans looked up and shook for a second. He was certainly spooked. He didn't know what to make of Chengua's cold stare. If there wasn't a crowd of friends, Hans would have called for help.

"Me big chief Chengua. You get away from my horseless carriage."

Hans said, "But—"

"Me great war hero. Me great war captain."

"But—"

"You go now, or I take a knife and hang your scalp in my tepee."

Chengua was right about one thing. George and Red Hawk couldn't contain themselves. They turned around and were holding their hands over their mouths to stifle their laughs. They weren't very successful, but Hans was oblivious.

Red Hawk saw Hans was legitimately frightened. He collected himself and approached the pair. He did his best to play along.

"Hans, you've been my friend for many years. You really need to listen this time. He's a good man. Even though we fought alongside one another, he's crazy. I don't trust him."

Hans finally relented and walked toward another bus. Chengua ran around the other side of the bus where nobody could see him and started laughing uncontrollably.

Bret saw Steve standing alone by the bus. He had some questions.

"Okay, how did you do all this?" Bret asked.

"The CSA army came after you left. That's how we got the satellite photos. They weren't allowed to get directly involved, especially at the Canadian border."

Any contact between the two militaries would have been considered a provocation by the PRSSA. They requisitioned the four buses.

"What about that horse trailer?" Bret asked.

"That was Star's idea. She asked the Canadians because she thought it would be a nice surprise," Steve said.

"What about that gray bus?"

"That's a bus designed for transporting convicts. I asked Jim if he could take care of that for now."

"What about my mom?"

"We flew her back home with a doc and nurse. She's doing

really well."

"Anything I can do? I feel like a fifth wheel."

"The only thing you can do is get your butt in one of the buses and rest," Steve said.

While everyone was happy, the most excited were the three canids. It certainly didn't hurt with all the fuss everyone was making over them. Especially noticeable was Micah's energy level. He was completely healed and ready for playtime again.

Rosa had been looking for Ani. When their eyes met, she ran and hugged Ani tightly. They released, and Rosa held her hand out. It was shaking.

Ani beamed when she saw a diamond ring. "Rosa, you're engaged!"

Both crowbar couples got engaged at the same time. Steve ordered both diamonds at the same time. Ramón didn't have much money, but Steve paid and said it was a wedding gift.

Rosa finally met Lisa. While hugging her, Rosa noticed the bruises that weren't healed yet. Her eyes had that usual bulge. "Who did this to you?"

Lisa looked at the prison bus. She saw Josey standing there, and they made eye contact. Lisa immediately looked at the ground, traumatized from her experience.

Rosa said, "That woman did this? I give her a low haircut."

Ani said, "Take it easy. I already gave her a beating. She'll now have to face justice. In my opinion, her future isn't very bright."

Rosa said, "Okay, I want five minutos in bus alone with that woman. Rosa teach her about Mexican rage."

Lisa suddenly jumped at Rosa and clung tightly. It affected her that a stranger would care about her so much.

Rosa said, "Your mama be your best friend. Rosa be your best friend in a different way."

Rosa then licked the tip of her index finger and drew a cross on Lisa's forehead. Everyone was startled and wondering what Rosa was doing.

She looked at Lisa and smiled. "Listen, child. That is a mark of protection. As long as Rosa is alive, I never allow anyone to hurt you again. I protect you and your mom always."

Lisa took Ani's arm and dragged her aside. She wanted to whisper. "Mom, can she come home with us?"

"You know Grandpa Niz has complete say over immigration matters. Let's not get ahead of ourselves."

Lisa wasn't prone to wielding her power over Niz. She knew she could twist her grandpa around her finger.

Jim was standing by the prison bus as the prisoners boarded. Steve had a perfect transport solution—the two young Russians. Being armed, they wouldn't hesitate to shoot.

The bus itself was similar to the train, with bars on the windows. The guard's cage was in the back. There was also a cage around the driver, so his only exit was the driver's side door.

Even with all the security, Jim was still a bit concerned. The Purps had proven resourceful in the past.

Kid walked over to him. "I was in one of those seats in the past. It looks secure, but . . ."

"You think there's danger?"

"I've seen a big buck rip down those cages."

"Maybe I should ride with the Russians. Their life is sort of my responsibility," Jim said.

"Not necessary. My boys and me will shack out with them."

It was a good idea. Kid's men got along well with the

Russians, since they were in a similar business. The one thing the Purps reacted to was scare tactics. Kid and his men were just what was needed.

Jim said, "Unless you're in danger, please, no rough stuff."

"Nah. Maybe I grab one by the coglioni and turn him into a soprano. Don't worry. My pezzonovante said no dice."

Kid and his men boarded and walked past the Purps while giving dirty looks. That seemed to be enough to get them back on their heels.

When he reached the back, one of the Russians asked Kid what they should do if there was trouble. He didn't seem to be concerned. He thought it best to lay down the rules of the road.

"I'm gonna have a chitchat with these clowns."

Kid walked in front of the Purps. His heavy eyebrows were enough to stop a clock.

"I hear youse guys acted like a bunch of Wyatt Earps back on the train."

Kid sighed. He looked at the ceiling and shook his head. The Purps didn't know where he was headed.

"That's why I hate the army. There are too many rules."

Josey started muttering under her breath. "Bull—"

"What's that? Like I always say, you can put lipstick on a pig and it's still a pig," Kid said. He saw some smirking. He knew he would have to ratchet it up a bit. "I can see by the look on your mugs, we gotta do this the hard way."

Kid removed a black plastic square from his pocket and unfolded it. After several times, he showed it to be a fifty-five-gallon contractor garbage bag. He then took out a meat cleaver and mimicked sharpening it on his pants.

"Any of youse stronzetti get outta line, you get chopped and in the bag. Believe me, ain't nobody gonna find the pieces."

Now he could see some of them quivering. Kid knew he'd said what was needed. He walked to the back again.

The Russian asked if his speech worked.

Kid pointed to a leg sticking in the aisle. The guy was wearing light tan pants. "You see that? That guy's gonna have a fun time trying to get the yellow stains out of his pants."

Chapter 33

Everyone was cheering and clapping as the buses drove onto the ranch. This was the first time since the rescue team departed that they could truly relax.

The CSA army would take possession of both the buses and the prisoners. After a brief overnight rest, most of the team could barely wait to leave for home.

As people were leaving the following morning, there were some notable exceptions. The three chiefs had to stay and complete their meetings regarding the completion of the casino and other entertainment projects.

Life with the animals was getting back to normal for the foreman and his ranch hands. There were several others staying temporarily behind. Niz requested Bret's friends who'd lived with him in the mountain to stay a couple of days. He had something specific in mind.

Niz had a dream when he started Nizland. He wanted half the island with ultraluxury homes where only the most important people in the world were allowed. The wealthiest and top politicos weren't necessarily welcome.

This was separated from the other half, which would be a vacation paradise. What made it different was it was an invitation-only island. This policy limited the number and types of visitors. He didn't feel the need for large government offices or a police force.

Nizland was protected by an international military force.

It was made up of many countries, including those that were traditional enemies.

Things had changed since Essi's stroke. Not only had Niz retired, but he now had more time to spend with his wife and Bret's mother. She was still recovering from her stroke. Steve had to spend much of his time traveling for the business his father had built. Bret was overwhelmed with special projects.

It was impossible for the infrastructure of the island to support the growth. Niz realized he couldn't keep the island stagnant. Too many external factors prevented this. He had no alternative but to bring in skilled help in many areas.

He was having trouble finding the right pieces for his paradise. Niz was very particular. Some called him too fussy. Just about every qualified person with the right attitude didn't want to live permanently on the island. Many who were anxious to be employed at Nizland had either questionable character or were hiding a sordid background.

Bret suggested Niz speak to his old friends. They had the needed specialties and were morally without vices. If any were interested, Bret thought it would be a perfect marriage. In addition, there were some others who would possibly work out.

Bret had already gotten approval and sent his French friend, Vera, to run Niz's art gallery on the island. Her expertise was almost unmatched. Niz soon received reports that she was running the business beautifully. Her pricing structure was already turning a sizeable profit.

Bret, Ani, Steve, and Niz would interview each person who wanted to go to Nizland. Bret thought it best to save his friends for last. They first called over the three chiefs. It was decided they could be spoken to all at once.

"I understand you men built a powerful economic cooperative as well as a new country," Niz said.

Red Hawk said, "Bret has already given us a heads-up as to why we're speaking."

"We could sure use people like you on the island. You'd be living in a paradise," Niz said.

"I am extremely flattered," George said. "However, I must say no. I gave my blood, sweat, and tears, accomplishing my lifelong desire to bring as many Indian nations together as an economic force and bring everyone out of poverty. I lost my son in the process. I was elected president. I can't abandon the trust and confidence, the honor that was bestowed upon me."

Red Hawk said, "Let me be even more blunt. Bret understands me well. Much of what we did together on my reservation years ago was for my people. I couldn't in good conscience abandon them now. However, if I'm welcome, an occasional vacation . . ."

"Do you need to ask? I would be insulted if you didn't show up," Bret said.

Now it was Chengua's turn. As usual, he was a man of surprises. He couldn't help reverting to his comedy act. He first looked at Steve. "I understand you're coming to my area for one wedding and then a second wedding on your island. Do you have a reservation?"

Steve thought he meant a hotel for both Star and him. Chengua twisted the meaning of the old definition.

Steve said, "I have two reservations."

"You own two reservations? Must be a lot of land. Okay, I'll be nice to you because you're loaded," Chengua said.

After the laughing ceased, Chengua got serious again. He

was in a quandary of having a southwestern wedding for Steve and Star along with a South Sea one.

"As my friends said, I'm grateful, but I won't leave my people. I will even come to the wedding even though I have acrophobia and never been on a plane. By the way, I'll drag along those two old fossils standing next to me."

Bret, Ani, Steve, and Niz next wanted to speak with Ramón. Although they barely knew him, he was running the ranch, which was no small deed. His loyalty to Lisa's cause put his standing over the top.

When they approached, Ramón wasn't alone. Rosa was with him.

"I understand you're losing your job. Weren't you running this entire operation?" Niz said.

Ramón said, "A casino doesn't need smelly and noisy cows and horses. I handled the training, kept the books, the inventory, cost figures, et cetera."

Niz said, "What qualifications did you have?"

"I ran my father's ranch in Mexico. I went to college at night. I have dual degrees in management and accounting."

"Where will you go now?" Ani asked.

"I'm not sure. I think I can get something where they need a bilingual guy. I'll survive."

Niz said, "We live on an island paradise in the Pacific. I need someone to run a small town on a day-to-day basis. He'd be sort of a mayor or town supervisor and report to me. The other part would be running an animal sanctuary I have . . . Interested?"

"Sure I am, but Rosa and I are to be married. I only go with her."

"No, you must go. It's great for you. I try to live okay

without you," Rosa said.

Ramón said, "If you think I'm leaving you, I have a bridge in Brooklyn to sell you—"

"We have something for her. Remember we were having a problem with domestic help reliability. Maybe she could supervise them," Ani said.

Rosa was ecstatic. She also had a couple of suggestions. "If you no have Mexican restaurant, I know very honest man. He had restaurant before gangs forced him out. I also know woman who can run your new police. She US customs agent. Also, very honest."

When everything was a yes, Ani looked at Lisa who was watching in the distance. She gave Lisa a thumbs-up.

Lisa gave the biggest smile and came running. She jumped into Rosa's arms. "Will you still protect me?"

"Rosa give my life for you."

It was time to speak with Bret's friends. Niz could no longer do without formal medical care on the island. He had built a hospital but was having problems staffing it with trustworthy medical professionals. The common thread for Bret's friends was they were all doctors.

Bret, Ani, Steve, and Niz first spoke to Wang. Niz told him about their island. Wang was apprehensive because of its proximity to China. His fears were allayed when he heard the makeup of the international protection force. He was shocked the island had a nuclear bomb. He was even more shocked that Chinese, Russians, and North Americans were part of the protective force.

Wang said, "I never would have believed it. I don't want to become nomadic like my friends. They ran from China. They ran from San Francisco. I'm too old for that."

Wang was always the philosopher. He gave the proposition some thought.

Bret said, "You'd be with friends."

"I suppose my ancestors would be pleased if I took this opportunity," Wang said.

Pramesh had different thoughts. He first wanted to know if there were any Indian or Pakistani people on the island.

Bret said, "To be frank, there are some but not many. Does it bother you?"

"There are some problems coming from India since this country is fragmented. Most Indians have settled in their own neighborhoods," Pramesh said.

Steve said, "You mean ghettos?"

"'Ghetto' has a poor ring to it. Most Indians in North America have money. Don't believe the media. The caste system in India still exists. Poor people can't leave."

Steve said, "How does it affect you?"

"With the political mess here now, old prejudices are starting to resurface. We always lived peacefully in our neighborhoods with Pakistanis. That's disappearing."

Bret said, "How so?"

"Nothing too overt. It's somewhat subtle," Pramesh said. "Street gangs are shaking down merchants. Both nationalities are suffering broken windows. I think you know what I mean."

"I know you're easy to get along with. Maybe there aren't many Indians in Nizland, but there are many nationalities. Nobody wants any nonsense. I think you would be happy with us."

"I'd like to try. There's really nothing here or back in India for me."

Hans was next up. Niz and Steve assured Hans he wouldn't have the stress like when he drove the bus. He looked tired and drawn but was still a talented physician.

Hans said, "I defected here because I had nothing overseas. The East Germans, Soviets, and Russians destroyed my friends and family. The government fools here gave me a new ID and settled me in a southern neighborhood where they speak with southern drawls. Can you imagine how much distaste they had for a German accent?"

Niz said, "On my island, we have people from many countries with many accents. Our commerce is conducted in English. Otherwise, I don't care what language is spoken as long as it's the language of love."

Bret said, "We need a friend and talented doctor like you."

Pramesh said, "I want to get as far away from the Germans as possible."

Niz said, "There are a few. One owns a restaurant. He makes some of the best Wiener schnitzel and sauerbraten that you'll ever taste. Not to mention, it's only a block away from the hospital . . . perfect lunch. We have some very nice German people on the island."

"Okay, okay, I'm in."

Nkuma came over to them. On the trip back, he had been speaking to Bret about joining the fight to regain some of the African countries. The look on Nkuma's face showed he was interested in their proposition.

Bret said, "Were you serious about going back there to fight?"

"Yes. It's a tribal thing," Nkuma said.

"At your age?"

"Maybe they can use me as a doc. To be honest, I would fight and likely get killed in the first skirmish."

"You told me you weren't happy with the goings-on over by the East Coast here," Bret said.

"I was contacted by my old girlfriend. She wanted to get back together. She's the one you met."

Niz said, "Bret told me about her. She's a privileged model and partially turned revolutionary. That concerns me. We have an African herbalist as well as a couple of other families. They're sort of old-fashioned. I'm not sure she would be a good fit on my island."

"I took care of it," Nkuma said.

"How so?"

"I borrowed an expression from Ani's La Cosa Nostra friends."

"What did you say?" Bret asked.

"I mimicked a Brooklyn accent and told her to take it on the arches, suction," Nkuma said.

Ani laughed loudly. She couldn't believe a man with such a refined and refreshing accent would say that.

They would call Carlos after Nkuma left.

When Bret, Ani, Steve, and Niz called, they were surprised Carlos was still at the ranch because the Shuar had already left.

"How will they get back home after landing?" Ani asked.

Carlos said, "I have an anthropologist friend who knows them. He's meeting them at the airport and will get them home."

Bret asked Carlos what he thought of the offer to be a doctor in Nizland. Like the others, Carlos had a surprising answer.

"I look at what happened in North America, and I see South America coming. The garbage that's eating up those countries will soon be coming here . . . with or without shooting."

"So you're coming with us?" Bret asked.

"I'll go anywhere that's not engaged with revolutionaries. Enough is enough."

The last two would be the toughest for Niz to convince. Alex and Lana were not only married, but they were also Bret's closest friends and administrators when they lived in the mountain. There was a dicey problem here.

"How are your sons doing in college? You previously said they were doing well," Bret said.

Alex said, "They're still doing well."

Bret said, "I know you both aren't happy living under the PRSSA rule. You know we've been offering the others positions. Even more than the others, I want to take you along but—"

"Bret's beating around the bush," Niz interrupted. "Here it is. Your son is engaged to a gang family woman. I'm sorry to say people like that are the worst of the worst. They will never be welcome in Nizland."

Lana said, "You're quite blunt. I will be even more blunt. He broke up with her yesterday. It's over."

"Wow, what happened?" Bret asked.

Alex said, "She made it clear her first loyalty was to her family. My son gave her an ultimatum. It's over. Nobody feels bad. The only feelings are ours . . . feelings of joy."

"We had something special in mind for you two on the island. You could both administer the hospital and run the research lab like you previously did with Bret. Of course, you would also be on call for medical duties," Niz said.

Lana's eyes were filled with happiness. Although their one-time indiscretion was in the past, she and Alex were ready to go.

With all their talks done, Bret gathered everyone together for a final word.

Bret said, "One of my special projects on the island was getting a new section of really nice homes built in walking distance from the town. While the floor plans are similar, they're all a little different. I think you'll all love them. You're all reasonable people. Since they're almost done, let's cooperate with the choosing. You can't go wrong with any of them."

Wang said, "To live in a paradise with all my friends, I would live in a tent."

Bret turned because he thought he saw that flash again. He was getting better at trying to intercept it. All he could see was maybe a nodding head. But it was still too fast.

"Did anyone else see that?" Bret asked.

He was met with a bunch of shrugging shoulders.

Chapter 34

It was finally time for Bret, Ani, and Lisa to go home. Ani and Lisa decided to take a nice long walk together through the fields while Bret finished up at the hotel.

They spoke about benign subjects. Ani was careful to try to steer the conversation away from Lisa's catastrophic time. She knew Lisa was obviously troubled. It was understandable that there was some psychological damage.

Lisa was distracted. She kept looking toward the mountain range. Her thirst for knowledge kept bringing her back to that horrific kidnapping. Ani decided it wasn't going to help if she denied Lisa the opportunity to speak openly.

"I see you looking toward that bad place you were held. Tell me what you're thinking," Ani said.

"I'm having trouble expressing myself. I guess I should want to get as far away as possible. Something keeps drawing me in. I'm so confused."

"Were you actually thinking of asking to stay?"

"I don't know."

Ani was taken by surprise. Lisa wasn't often confused. She was a remarkably clear thinker. She didn't know what to say. It wasn't often that Lisa's precocious abilities bewildered her.

"Your dad and I have always tried to give you good advice. We've always tried to allow your input regarding your personal decisions," Ani said.

"I know I'm loved," Lisa said.

"I know you're feeling bad right now. I want to help so badly. Maybe I'm not a good enough mother."

"You're not only a good mother, you're the best mom a girl ever had. I'm just sorry I was in so much trouble."

"Listen to me and try to understand. You're almost grown now. I feel we can talk about anything. I carried you for nine months. Every part of your life's essence, including your soul, is part of me. That's why it's physically and mentally impossible for you to ever be trouble for me."

"That's why I trust and love you and Dad, Mom. I can't imagine ever being without both of you."

"If you want my advice, I'd say we need to get far away from here," Ani said. "If you'd rather be here, I'll speak to your dad. Maybe we could work something out where you can continue your education in North America . . . just away from here."

"You would really do that for me?" Lisa asked.

"It's against my better judgement but I just want you to be happy. At the same time, I have fears because of what happened. I would insist on being with you. I'm afraid to leave you alone ever again."

"So what should we do?"

"I tell you what. I'll stay here, and you can walk alone for a few minutes. Think about our discussion. Maybe you can clear your head a bit. I'll try not to force a decision on you."

It hurt Ani to even allow Lisa to think about coming back. Ani went against her better judgement. Even though it was against her better judgement, she was concerned any argument now could sever their bond.

Lisa stayed in Ani's sight. Sometimes Lisa walked straight. Sometimes she walked in a circle. She even walked in a square pattern, stopping at each joint.

Lisa came back. She wore a smile on her face. She grabbed her mom and kissed her cheek. Ani was worried.

Ani said, "Have you decided what you want to do?"

"I think so," Lisa said. "I hope you and Dad are okay with it."

"Does that mean you want to stay?"

"Nah. Let's go home."

Ani didn't often cry, but her eyes welled up and she squeezed her baby tightly.

"Let's not tell Dad about this? He gets so worried," Lisa said.

Ani put her thumb and index finger to her lips and made a turning motion as if she were closing a lock. She winked at Lisa. "What he doesn't know won't hurt him."

They left for the airport.

At the hotel, Bret was doing a final check in the general area and their room to make sure they hadn't forgotten anything. While in his room, Bret saw the flash again. But it was different this time. It was first transparent, then translucent, then almost opaque. It was the first time he was able to get a clearer view of it.

There was an image with the face of an older woman. Belying her apparent age, she had dark hair. The image was still fuzzy below her next, but he could make out that she was wearing some sort of white gown.

She was wearing a scarf around her neck. He could see a kind of monogram on the end of it. It looked like a fancy, capitalized English letter *A* in cursive.

Bret had never heard her speak before. He never saw a facial expression. He never saw any motion other than her head shaking or nodding. It was time.

"Do you have a name?" Bret asked the image.

She smiled, then pointed to the monogram. “I am Anna.”

“Are you human? I mean, are you alive?”

“I was. In your frame of reference, that was centuries ago.”

“I don’t understand.”

“For me, there is no such thing as time. There is only eternal infinity.”

“If you’re not alive, what are you now?”

“On your planet and in your culture, I might be called a guardian angel or a guiding light,” Anna said. “I am not a being. You could describe me as a focal point between this and the other world.”

Bret said, “It seems you’ve come for me. Does everyone have something like you?”

“I don’t have that knowledge. I believe there are very few points of reference like me.”

“Have you been involved directly with my life?”

“I can implant suggestions in your mind. I can sometimes do it to others if it benefits you.”

“You seem all powerful. Why did you let Lisa’s terrible experience happen?”

“That was an event. I have no such control. Only the creator of all things has control over events.”

“I thought I saw you nodding and shaking your head at times. Why?” Bret said.

“I planted a suggestion. I nodded when you listened, shook my head when you didn’t.”

“What suggestions did you plant?”

“They were a subliminal stimulus,” Anna said.

“Examples? I mean, if you can.”

“Both stealing a painting and your tiny affair with Vera were met with my head shaking. You returning the painting was met with a nod."

"You said you can plant suggestions to others if it affects me?"

"When Jim saved your life, I suggested to him you needed his help immediately. There was a nod after that."

"What happens after you die? I mean like, do we go to heaven or hell?" Bret asked.

"I can tell you a little. I gained universal knowledge. You can have a spiritual connection with others. I don't know about all other humans."

"Can I find people who have crossed to the other world like you?"

"I am in contact with those I loved the most," Anna said.

"That sounds sound. But would an evil person like Frank have this too?"

"I don't have that knowledge. We have rumors just like you. It has been my understanding people like him suffer from severe eternal loneliness. Try to imagine your existence while being locked in a room with absolute silence. Living humans will usually go mad."

"It sounds like he couldn't even take his own life because he's already dead," Bret said.

"There is no death after death," Anna said.

"Are you here because I will die soon?"

"I don't have that information. I don't think my appearance is relevant for a person's mortal lifespan."

Bret had so many questions. He never heard of someone being in contact with a guardian angel. He sensed his time was limited. "I wish you would stay visible to me my whole life."

Anna said, "You would refer to it as bad news. I must

leave now."

Bret went to his knees and clasped his hands as if he were praying. For a man who wasn't often emotional, he was losing it. He started begging. "Please don't leave me, Anna. I need you so!"

"Perhaps another world, or in your sense of time, in the future. Most likely not."

Anna's image started fading.

Bret was desperate. "No! No! No! Please, Anna!"

As she disappeared completely, Anna left Bret while voicing one word.

"Goodbye."

About the Author

Robert Miranda

Bob Miranda was born in Queens, New York. He started working after school at age twelve. It taught him discipline and respect for hardworking people, men and women, citizens and refugees, healthy and challenged individuals. He has three degrees: BS–meteorology, MBA–accounting, and PhD–natural health.

Bob has worked with thousands of people from all walks of life. Bob's writing shares his life impressions of the way real people are and the real human emotions of people in a fictional manner.

www.ingramcontent.com/pod-product-compliance
Lightning Source LLC
Chambersburg PA
CBHW070539310726
48982CB00010B/1413/J

* 9 7 8 1 7 3 5 6 5 6 7 6 2 *